BAE Novellas
THE COLLECTION

Christa Tillman

Heart Ink Press

Copyright

Dedication

First and always, I must thank **God – My Heavenly Father** and **Jesus Christ – My Lord and Savior.**

I appreciate all the beautiful people that God has placed in my life. I must thank a few people, Adrienne Horn (Editor), my king—Damian Ross, Tonya Gordon, Angela Griffin, Kimberly Armstrong, Karen Hooker, Jasmine Ross, Lesly Louis, Tatiana Nunley, Chrylene Williams, James Williams, my entire Vista Sand family, and the best damn book club in the world (On Another Level).

I can always count on these people. I cannot say thank you enough for all your support.

God Bless you and continue to weave your story!

Summer Paradise

Chapter 01

Leveraging the sturdy wall in front of him, RB admired the skills of the woman kneeling before him. In shift motion, she magically made his lengthy penis disappear. He stroked her silky black hair while guiding her mouth up and down his shaft. Her muffled moans and his jovial grunts filled the space.

His only plan was to connect with his lawyer before their business meeting, but she'd lured him to her office with lies concerning paperwork he neglected to sign. The second her office door closed, she was on her knees, freeing his manhood. He could have protested, but he needed to release his pent-up anxiety.

RB could hear his lawyer questioning his assistant on his whereabouts. He tapped the beauty on the top of her head. She wrapped her ivory arms around the back of RB's knees, forcing his penis farther down her throat. A knock on her door compelled his body to flood her mouth with watermelon seeds. He groaned in relief as she polished his penis clean with her tongue.

RB strolled out of her office, greeting his lawyer. First, he smiled at RB, then disdain for his co-worker's actions etched his face.

RB's manager cut the silent tension by reminding the group they were running late and needed to get going.

Romello "RB" Brooks strolled into the private business event at Tongue and Groove nightclub with his lawyer and manager in tow. A flood of rainbow lights strobed throughout the club, providing visibility of all the beautiful ladies.

"Business first, and maybe a little pleasure later," RB mumbled to himself.

Tonight was about him handling business for his new alcohol beverage line; if it ended with a beautiful woman pleasuring him even better, he thought, spotting a caramel beauty eyeing him from the bar.

They all shook hands after the deal. The entire table agreed RB and Malik would be the face of his new Mello Champagne, although he suggested his friend and teammate, Malik, be the brand's only face. He launched Mello Cognac six months ago, and it was flying off the shelves.

Waitresses dressed in skimpy shorts and tight shirts waved bottles of Mello Champagne in the air. Some waitresses balanced glowing trays of Mello Cognac mixed drinks. He watched a group of women lined along the bar with Mello Cognac shots. The clubgoers laughed and downed the smooth alcohol. Watching the clubbers enjoy the free drinks of Mello Champagne and purchasing the Mello Cognac pride rocketed in his chest.

RB's business manager was congratulating him on his success and talking about the next moves. Instead, his attention was zoned on a group of gorgeous exotic beauties. RB nodded his head, slowly fading his manager out.

The women nodded their heads in RB's direction. He knew they had recognized him and were waiting all night for him to acknowledge their presence. One of the exotic beauties stared at him, then seductively twirled a maraschino cherry with the tip of her tongue. His rod flexed. He hoped she could work his manhood over as well as she was working the maraschino cherry.

She hunched her shoulders at RB, pointed to the VIP entrance, gave him a slight wink, and approached the VIP section. RB's manager went to retrieve the exotic beauty.

She strolled over to RB, swaying her hips from wall to wall. Her yellow bodycon dress accentuated her voluptuous curves, and the deep V halter top was struggling to keep her voluptuous breast covered.

Atlanta women stayed gossiping about RB's massive third leg, stating you only get one taste. No woman has a story about him doubling back. He is famously known for providing women with one unapologetic night of multi-orgasmic pleasure.

The exotic beauty swore that if she ever had a chance to ride his massive pole, she would ride it all night long. But, unlike the other women, her story would not end with a one-night stand. Instead, it would continue throughout a lifetime.

The exotic beauty traced her lips with the tip of her tongue then moaned. "You're handsome. Tell me something about yourself."

RB chuckled before taking a puff off his cigar. "I'm confident, handsome, and hella rich. What else do you need to know about me?"

She loved the arrogance oozing off him. She eyed his large hands, then skimmed his size thirteen shoes. "Please tell me your hands are not the only thing massive on your body," she said through a purr. "I pray your third leg is as long as your feet."

She twirled her hair and pressed her ample breast against his side.

"I can guarantee you my third leg will put my hands and feet to shame. So don't go wasting a good prayer on me."

She giggled.

"My pole and I are willing to give you the best orgasmic experience of your life tonight."

The exotic beauty batted her eyes. "What if I want more than tonight?"

RB sat up straight and looked deep into her eyes. "Then I am not the man for you. All I can offer you is one evening."

"OK!" She turned her head, then mumbled, "You will be singing a different tune by morning."

The exotic beauty was like most women who overestimated the power of their yoni. She believed one night with the infamous Romello Brooks was all she needed to have him craving her pussycat. It wasn't her fault the other women lacked her acrobatic bedroom skills. She had already told her girls if he allowed her to go home with him, she would ride and suck him until his head exploded.

"If I only get one night, I am ready to go. Don't waste my time sitting here."

RB took out his phone and texted his driver, Lou. He responded quickly, advising that he was on the road and would arrive in fifteen minutes.

RB held up his glass to his manager. He knew he must have hit up Lou. RB never took a woman home unless Lou walked her through the protocol and the paperwork.

The exotic beauty eyed the buckets of chilled Mello Champagne on the table. "How many drinks have you had tonight?"

The moment she spotted RB strolling into the club, she stopped drinking. Everyone knew RB did not take drunk women home. She cleared her throat. "One."

RB's left eyebrow rose. He did not utter a word. He realized his silence would force her to talk, and she would spill her guts.

"All bullshit aside." He nodded, and she continued. "I spotted you when you walked into the club. I told my girls I was going to ride your dick tonight. They all laughed. My girlfriend took my tequila shot and drank it, informing me you do not allow drunk women to go home with you."

He smiled.

"I ordered a sweet mixed drink and nursed it all night long while trying to get your attention. I figured if you noticed me, I would go home with you and experience incredible sober sex. If you did not take me home, then I missed getting drunk this Friday night. I can get turnt up tomorrow."

Starting at her feet, RB scanned her body. Over the years, he had run into a couple of cover girls. They looked nice and smelled lovely until their panties came off. If her feet were dirty or toenails were chipped, the conversation was over. He smiled as his eyes reached her calves and thick thighs.

If her and Uncle Lou's process went well, he was ready to make her pull her hair out while screaming his name.

Chapter 02

Romello "RB" Brooks was an alpha male. He didn't have to chase women; they plotted their pursuit for one evening with him. Sometimes RB missed the thrill of the hunt. The last time he pursued a woman, he was in junior high school.

The exotic beauty sitting before him cleared her throat, attempting to gain his attention.

"I know you said one evening. Does that include breakfast?"

"No."

"I bet I can turn that no into a yes," she replied, drawing her bottom lip into her mouth seductively. "Unless you want me all weekend."

RB smiled.

Women had become predictable over the years. He didn't know if it was his money, status, or good looks that made women hurl their beliefs out the window and toss their panties at him without knowing his deepest fears, hopes, and dreams.

It amazed him how people read tabloids, watched him catch a football or hit a baseball, and assumed they knew everything about him.

Some women confessed they expected him to propose after one evening. Good sex didn't mean they were compatible. As far as RB was concerned, he would be like Jay-Z. He would never give his heart to a woman and would forever be a respectable player. He had never lied to a woman concerning his true intentions. He promised all women one evening of earth-shattering sex. It wasn't his fault women thought their pussy was extraordinary to the point it would make him change his mind about their agreement or wife them.

He desired a woman that could bring more than a scrumptious body to the table. Yonis are good to eat, but they do not stop starvation nor pay the damn bills.

RB was a brand, and as much as he loved yonis in all shapes and shades, he was not willing to throw away everything he had built for a warm cookie.

Uncle Lou had a set of rules RB had to follow because he would not sit by and watch RB lose everything over tail and head.

RB's cell phone buzzed. It was Unk. "Let's go, beautiful."

Taking his hand, she smiled at her friends as she and RB headed towards the entrance.

Uncle Lou was already holding the rear SUV truck door open when they exited the club. Lou closed the door behind RB then hopped behind the steering wheel.

Unk turned around and eyed the exotic beauty in her face. "Before we leave, we need to handle some business."

The exotic beauty gawked at RB then back at the tall driver with dark smoky eyes and a pinch of salt in his beard.

Lou waved the paper in her line of sight. She smacked her lips then snatched the paper from his hands. Unk passed her a pen, retrieved his phone off the passenger seat, then hit the recording button. "The document in your hand is an NDA (non-disclosure agreement). Before you sign the agreement, I need you to read it over."

"Is Mr. Clean serious," she questioned RB.

Lou ran his hand over his bald head. "My tall Black ass is dead serious – if you're trying to go home with the man sitting next to you."

She pulled her bottom lip between her teeth as RB poured himself a glass of cognac. He knew better than to interfere while Uncle Lou did his spiel.

RB paid Lou handsomely to act as his driver, his notary, and witness. Lou taking on the role of his uncle was a bonus. Lou had been looking out for RB and his baby sister, Raven, since they were kids running around Oakland. When Lou got out of jail, RB went to Oakland to retrieve him. He tried to make Lou the manager over his properties. Lou insisted he would be his driver and always have his six.

The girl's gaze floated towards RB. She smacked her lips to get his attention. He refused to intervene.

Lou cleared his throat. "The NDA is non-negotiable. If you disagree with anything, I can make sure you can get back into the club and give you a little something for your troubles."

Lou, an old-school player and gangster, created this one-night stand NDA. He figured it was his job to protect RB from gold-diggers, knuckleheaded haters, untrue allegations, and himself. But he stressed a long time ago, no matter how much RB desired a woman, if she wasn't willing to follow the rules, she had to find another baller's bed to fall in.

She glanced at RB again. He still didn't utter a word.

RB had seen many celebrities accused of taking the cookie, and he never wanted the stamp of rape on his brand.

The beauty waved the papers into the camera phone. "I read the entire document and signed it, Mr. Clean."

"Did anyone pressure you into signing this paper?" She shook her head. "Lovely lady, I need you to use your words."

"No, shit! I signed on my own free will, and I am not drunk. I only nursed one drink because I want to ride his dick tonight. RB already asked me these questions. I asked RB to take me home and fuck my brains out. Any more questions, Unk?" She bucked her eyes at Lou.

"Mm's! Mm's! Mm's," Lou growled, "you fast tail ass girls. I swear you are getting bolder and bolder and more desperate every day."

"And you are getting balder and balder every day," she retorted, "with your pitch-black ass."

Lou stamped the paper and logged it in his notary book, then tossed it in the seat. RB could tell this girl was getting on Lou's nerves. RB patted him on the shoulder, and Lou's shoulders deflated. "Unk, I think we are ready to roll out."

Lou smirked at RB, then pulled out into traffic, cruising towards Midtown.

Lou tried to stay focused on the road as the girl started undressing in the back seat. He chuckled as RB kept redressing the fast-tailed girl.

Lou silently prayed RB would find him a lovely wife and stop with all these meaningless wham-bam-thank-you-ma'ams.

Chapter 03

RB laid on the massage table in the dimly lit room. Soft jazz played in the background, and the smell of mint and eucalyptus oil filled the air. He loved his weekly masseuse visits because she had transformed his guest bedroom into a spa haven.

He admired the artwork Raven had purchased for the room. Each week the masseuse bought colorful bowls of crystals and flower petals. Incense burners and lit candles decorated the entire room.

A small table with a water pitcher with lemons and cucumber slices sat to his right. He smiled when he noticed a bottle of Mello Champagne chilling on ice.

RB's body contorted as the masseuse worked a lump in the middle of his back. "Right there. Shit, this feels good." She massaged her fist deep into his tangled muscles, never uttering a word.

His eyes fluttered, then slammed shut. He moaned and growled while the masseuse moved down to his thick muscular thighs.

RB's cellular phone rang the second he drifted off to sleep. He attempted to ignore the interruption when his phone rang again.

He turned his head and spotted his phone on the small table next to the oversized manicure chair, which was custom made to match the room's décor. He had hoped nobody would call him until he finished getting a manicure and pedicure. RB huffed at his wishful thinking.

"Tenderoni, can you pass me the phone?"

RB needed to ensure it wasn't his baby sister, Raven, calling. She was the only woman who could interrupt his world and cause it to stop spinning on its axle.

RB strolled through his call log. He had one missed call from his boy, Malik, and the other four calls were from his maid, Auntie Hill.

Malik had made him miss his self-love Sunday, and he was not about to ruin his make-up Monday. Malik was always whining over some woman. RB wished Malik would be more of a player and stop falling in love with every damn woman he kissed.

RB chuckled, pondering if he should return Auntie Hill's call. He wondered if somebody had broken into his condominium. His relaxed demeanor was slowly diminishing.

He started to text Raven to see if she had forgotten to pay Auntie Hill, then he paused. He knew Raven had paid her because his baby sister never missed a beat.

RB stopped speculating and dialed Auntie Hill.

"Slow down." RB could not understand Auntie Hill through her rage and thick Nigerian accent.

The last time Auntie screamed at him like this, one of his guests had become pissed when she woke up alone; therefore, she took a piss on all his furniture.

RB shot straight up, hoping he would understand Auntie Hill better. Instead, his swift movement caused the masseuse to jump.

"Your Saturday guest is crazy. She is refusing to leave. I would have called Lou, but he would have the poor girl arrested."

RB had a low tolerance for women who did not follow the rules on the damn card. "Auntie Hill, please call me from the house phone and put me on speaker."

Auntie followed RB's instructions. RB scrambled his brain for his guest's name as the phone connected. Unfortunately, RB was horrible with names; therefore, he called all women "Tenderoni."

"What do you want, RB?"

RB cleared his throat. "First, take all that damn bass out of your voice. When we met at the club, I told you it was a one-night thing, and you agreed."

"Ohmigod, my girlfriends told me not to sleep with you. We did not meet at a club; we met at a restaurant on Saturday night. This situation is all fucked up. First, you made me sign an NDA and do a consent video, and then you dipped out in the middle of the night. Second, the other bedroom had make-up on the pillows, so you smashed another bitch this weekend besides me. Ugg!" She huffed as if reminiscing was hurting her heart. "When I woke up on Sunday, you still hadn't returned. I laid in bed and watched television, hoping you would return soon."

RB shook his head. RB never placed televisions in any of the rooms at his playhouse because it was for playtime, not movie time. However, there was one screen in the cinema room, which he used when he hosted a game night.

The young beauties screaming interrupted RB's thoughts. "I was comfortable waiting on you until that damn laminated card assaulted me under the covers."

RB ran his hand over his wavy mane — damn, a second lie. The card was in the bathroom and by the front door sitting on a table with her parting gift.

"Why didn't you follow the instructions on the card? I left you a lovely goodie bag and money for transportation by the front door."

She chuckled. "You left me a hangover bag, a bottle of your Mello Champagne and Cognac, and two hundred dollars. My yoni is worth way more than two hundred dollars."

Now it was RB's time to laugh. "Tenderoni, I do not pay to lay. Those few bills were for transportation. I have no idea where you live, but I wanted you to have enough for a cab or a black car."

The young beauties' voice cracked, "RB, when you kissed me...."

it shook me to the core. The fire and desire between us were magical. There is no way you were faking those emotions of love."

RB slid his feet into his bamboo house shoes. "I kiss every woman with the same lust. It was lust, not love, Tenderoni."

RB held the fluffy white towel around his waist as he paced the floor. He looked at the masseuse drumming her right fingers on her left forearm. "You can go, Tenderoni, thank you. I will see you next Sunday."

RB pulled the phone from his ear and gawked at the screen. His Saturday night beauty was screaming at the top of her lungs. RB shook his head as Auntie Hill warned the young lady to be quiet. "RB, I cannot believe you left our bed to go smash another girl."

RB retrieved his business cell phone and texted Raven.

RB // 9:00 AM: Auntie has a problem. She needs your help.

Raven // 9:01 AM: Call Unk!

RB // 9:01 AM: No! I called you. You know how Lou gets.

Raven // 9:06 AM: Fine! I am on my way. If she starts tripping, I will drag her out.

RB // 9:06 AM: I got bail money ... LOL!

Raven // 9:06 AM: Shut up and go sit down.

RB // 9:07 AM: Luv ya

RB placed the phone back to his ear, and the young lady was still yelling something inaudible. "Auntie, Raven will be there soon."

RB laughed as Auntie Hill attempted to warn the young beauty. "My friend, my friend, you better leave now. If I were you, I would leave before they get here, my friend."

RB chuckled because he and Auntie knew Raven and her crew did not play.

Chapter 04

A career as a pediatric oncologist was not for the faint at heart, Naja thought, listening to her father's tirade about her specialty choice. After starting oncology research with Dr. Luna Lee, a urologic oncologist, Naja chose her career field.

Naja gained firsthand knowledge of oncology care at a major cancer center, which included observing initial consultations, chemotherapy infusions, and face-to-face with patients' tumors as she observed in the operating room. She enjoyed the hopeful spirits of the pediatric patients. Amid death, they found the strength to appreciate every moment God granted them.

Midway through her sophomore year, Naja was hospitalized for postoperative infection after an orthopedic procedure. During that brief hospital stay, she was overwhelmed by the compassionate care she received in the emergency room from the nurses, residents, and doctors. She reasoned she had always had dual passions. Why should her career choice be different?

"Naja…Naja. I know you don't have me talking to myself, gyal."

"No, Tata."

"The fuckery with Dakari going abroad without marrying you as planned by your muma and his upset me. Therefore, I have four men lined-up to marry you."

"You have what?" She queried, gawking at her father in disbelief.

"Four suitable 'usbands," he announced unapologetically. "I know dem fathers personally."

The muscles in her face twitched, and she fought to keep from frowning. The last thing she wanted to do was give her father an attitude. However, in this case, it would be justified, being this was the 21st century, and arranged marriages were outdated.

Naja pressed her index finger against her temple.

"One young man is a doctor; the other is witty and shares your confidence; another is a professor of economics, and he shares your polit ical views; the last man has your father's work ethic and understands the role of 'usband. He will effortlessly provide for you and your future family."

This time Naja slapped the back of her hand to her forehead as if she were fainting.

"Daadi!"

"No dramatics. I know you like dem tall like your old man." He paused, thinking of something else he could say to persuade his daughter. "The boys are all handsome. You guys will make beautiful grandbabies."

Instead of responding, she rolled strains of hair between her thumb and pointer finger. Her father noticed her annoyance, but all he desired was his only daughter's happiness.

Naja was the baby. She had four older brothers. Just when her mother and father had accepted they only created boys, Naja was born. Ecstatic does not describe the joy her father felt gazing into her nutmeg eyes.

"Daadi wants you to be happy and have an 'usband that will take care of his princess. You understand that, right?" Naja opened her mouth to speak, but her father halted her words by continuing to speak. "Don't you want to be happy and shop endlessly like your mother?"

Naja expelled a long stream of air.

"They all come from wealthy families. I can't have my only daughter with a poor man."

He rocked and chuckled at his comment.

"Daadi, I make my own money. I will make sure I always eat."

"You are my only daughter, and I worry about you. You are gently removing all traces of your legacy. You speak like the rest of these fools. I'm losing my princess."

Growing up, Naja despised constantly repeating herself. To avoid the continuous request to repeat herself, she took speech classes in high school and college — the type of classes news anchors took. Like a faucet, she could tap into her Jamaican accent at will. To her father, that meant denying one's heritage.

"Yuh nuh haffi worry about dat," she said, smiling affectionately.

"Ok, my baby still in there; watch the slang. I spend too much money for yo' education."

She raised a skeptical brow then smiled.

He winked. "How yuh fren' duh?" I chuckle at his attempt to use slang again.

"My BAEs are good, Tata."

Miya, the youngest member of the Black and Educated social group, launched the group in high school. Naja became a member when she met Miya in college. Their clique is composed of five members -- Imani, Miya, Naja, Tamia, and Lexi.

Naja nuzzled into her father's arms, contemplating if she should tell him that she and Dakari broke up. According to him, she decided what would be the purpose when her father was already attempting to arrange marriages with suitable "'usbands."

"Before I start my combined residency in pediatric oncologist and emergency medicine, I need a vacation. Can I take the jet and go to Hawaii?"

"Are you taking the BAE's?"

"No," she rapidly replied. "I am going alone."

"You should go to Turks and Caicos. You haven't been there since you were a child. You used to love that place. I will pay for everything if you go there."

Naja tapped her lips with her index finger as she considered her father's offer. She could feel her father was up to something, but she could never turn down a free trip. Five beautiful days on a majestic island would cure her soul because she was done crying and eating ice cream with her BAE's.

"Deal!" She sang, wrapping her arms around her father's neck.

"Then when you come back, you can start dating your potential 'usbands."

Naja nodded her head in agreement. By the time she returned, getting board-certified in her two fields would consume all her time, leaving no room to grieve over Dakari or the energy to date anyone else.

Chapter 05

RB heard the elevator door ding, then the hard clacking of Raven's stilettos against his hardwood floors echoing throughout the house. He rummaged over his white shoe rack, searching for his white Louis Vuitton loafers. The seventeen rotating shoe shelves were organized by color, and he wished they were by color and designer. He scanned the other nine racks of shoes, wondering if they had a service that would arrange his shoe racks.

Frustrated, he snatched a pair of white Alexander McQueen sneakers from the shelf and changed into a pair of Armani chino linen shorts and a fitted tee. He despised mixing designers, but his tolerance was short today.

RB lurked in the hallway listening to Kris and Raven bicker while raiding his pantry.

"I hope this crazy plan of yours works for once," Kris voiced, playing with the two pom-pom ponytails in her hair.

Raven smacked her lips. "Can you support your future wife for once and have my back?"

Kris slammed the glass jar lid closed then straightened out her button-up shirt.

Raven spun around to Kris with fury in her eyes. Visions of her handprint across Kris's peanut butter skin invaded her mind.

"What the hell," she yelled, staring Kris in her dark round eyes. "Do not break his damn candy jar. I need him to be happy, not pissed off."

Kris lifted the lid, slammed it closed, and then waited for her girlfriend's reaction as she peered into Raven's hazel brown eyes.

Kris gripped Raven by the belt buckle, attempting to slide her hands down Raven's jeans.

Raven slapped her hands away.

"Fuck. I have your back. RB is my boss, and I handle his business affairs, not his personal life. You have assumed the role of his mother, not me. RB is a twenty-eight-year-old man. Your mother raised him once, so you cannot raise him twice."

The girls had their attention locked on each other. Therefore, they overlooked RB until he cleared his throat.

He knew any mention of his mother struck instant rage in Raven.

He did not know if Kris and Raven ever fought, and he wasn't going to find out while they were in his house. If they wanted to battle it out, they needed to go home and destroy their condo, not his penthouse.

RB stepped into the pantry, pulled Raven out of Kris's face, and then wrapped his stable arms around her. "Ladies, what's good?"

Raven turned her wrath towards him. She pulled away from his embrace and punched him in the chest.

"I am sick and tired of you and all these tramps."

RB clenched Raven's cleft chin and kissed her on the cheek.

Raven yanked away and shoved RB. "RB, do you truly love me?"

RB anchored his attention at Kris, hoping she would explain what was going on. The mention of his mother always sent Raven into one of two moods. It was clear she had chosen anger instead of anguish.

RB decided to use the silent technique he used with his one-night stand hoping Raven would spill her guts.

An irate gaze cut across Raven's face. "Daddy-Brother, did you hear my damn question?"

RB blinked with feigned innocence and smiled. "I love you more than breathing, baby sis! You are the only thing in this world that truly matters to me." He leaned down and rested his forehead against his sister's head.

Kris oohed and ahhed.

Raven whipped her head around, firing daggers in Kris's direction.

Kris twisted her lips unphased by Raven's behavior.

"Brother, I need you to do me a huge favor, and if you love me, you will agree."

RB filled his lungs with air and held his breath.

Raven's lashes swept up, and she blinked back a tear.

RB's heart crumbled, and he knew he would lasso the moon if she requested. But he could never stand to see a tear form in Raven's hazel brown eyes.

His eyes rolled skyward, then back to Raven. He swiped the tear from her cheek and gently caressed her face in his large hands. "If it will help you know how much I love you, then the answer is yes, I agree!"

Raven did not utter a word. Tears rolled down her silky latte skin. RB continued to wipe them away. "I am sorry about this morning. I should have gone to handle my Saturday night guest."

Kris stepped closer to RB and Raven. "Homegirl was mad crazy. Raven and I hauled her out, kicking and screaming. She ranted about having nude pictures of you as you slept. Her face cracked when Raven revealed you never sleep next to random chicks. I was shocked; she did not claim to be pregnant. The girl was delusional as hell."

RB nodded.

Kris gave RB a fist bump. "Drop-dead gorgeous but crazy as fuck."

"Kris, you know I was out of bed the second I heard purring escape her body."

RB always waited for his guest to go to sleep before he slipped out. Seeing a woman on her knees pleading for him to stay and willing to do whatever it took to convince him to remain pulled at his heartstrings.

Kris chuckled.

Raven did not smile. RB gawked at Kris and contorted his lips.

He gripped Raven by her hand and led her to the kitchen bar stool. She sat down and locked her fingers together on the top of the bar. RB caressed her bawled fist. "What do you need me to do, baby girl?"

Raven twirled the tip of her deep brown hair. "I want you to go on vacation with me, Kris, and Uncle Lou. However, no one-night stands. This vacation is about you and me developing a closer bond."

RB did not want to seem petty, but Raven was allowed to smash her girl, and he had to go cookie-less.

He glanced over at Kris. "Can we have the room?" Kris nodded, then headed for the elevator.

Raven rolled her eyes at Kris. She hoped Kris would have demanded to stay and support her because the comment she made about their mother opened a door of pain she thought was bolted shut, and Kris once again was not there to ease the pain.

RB gawked at Raven. One heavy brow slanted in solid disapproval. "I don't mind going on vacation with you for a weekend with no sex. But, Sis, why do you get to bring your girl?"

Raven buried her head in the palm of her hand. "Fine! Kris can stay here. Also, we are staying in Turks and Caicos for a week."

"A whole week?"

Raven twisted her lips. "Three days without Uncle Lou and Kris. You can have your meaningless one-night stands after Uncle Lou arrives."

RB reluctantly agreed. "We are leaving tomorrow. I have the jet and a private villa reserved."

RB chuckled, then disheveled his sister's hair. "You played me. Nice one. You killed me with the silence and the tears."

Raven brightly smiled, although RB could still sense a hint of pain in her eyes. He walked around the bar and pulled Raven into his arms. The tighter he held her, the more she wept. "You know Mom is proud of you."

Raven buried her face in his elbow, strengthening her grip around her brother's waist. "I know."

RB asked who would tell Kris and Lou they couldn't come until Saturday night to ease the tension between them.

Raven stood on the tip of her toes, depositing a kiss on RB's cheek.

"You," she asserted through laughter, beelining towards the elevator.

RB roared in laughter. He was happy to see his baby sister leaving with a smile gracing her adorable face.

Chapter 06

Naja took the private path from her rental down to the secluded beach. Her eyes trailed the uneven shoreline as she buried her manicured toes in the warm sand. She watched the waves roll inland, dissolving into foam on the beach, then roll out, pulling her feet with it. Rocky bits and seashells strewed the sand.

This view was all the therapy she needed to heal her fractured heart. The sun glowed across the horizon, reminding her she hadn't called her mother or father informing them of her safe arrival.

Before the phone could ring twice, Naja's mother answered.

"Hello, Princess."

"Hi, Muma. How are you?"

"I was wondering how long it was going to take you to call me."

"Not an entire week. I needed to clear my head. My concentration must be centered around my career, not my heart."

Her mother nervously chuckled. Whenever her father added a new lover to his circle, her terrible habit surfaced — rendering her mother with one option, acceptance.

"What did Tata do, Muma?"

Her mother inhaled so profoundly that she extracted the breath from Naja's body through the receiver. "He sent a suitable 'usband to the island to sweep you off your feet."

Naja closed her eyes tightly. She couldn't believe her tata invaded her space even though she promised to go out with his candidates upon her return. But, damn, he couldn't wait for me to return, she thought.

Through clenched teeth, she spoke, "Muma, do you know what he looks like?"

"Like money."

A rumbling belly laugh escaped Naja's lips.

"Is he tall? What color is his complexion?"

"I heard your faada on the phone with him. He was thanking him for staying next door to you and looking after his baby gyal. 'Usband, please. He sounds like my gyal personal bodyguard," her mother jokes.

"Do you know his name?"

"Princess, I know he is not Dakari, and his name starts with an R."

She knew it bothered her mother that her father was attempting to marry her off to someone who wasn't Dakari. Her mother and Dakari's mother were best friends. She could recall her mother telling her that Dakari was her prince at four years old, and she was his princess.

"Be careful, Princess. You know your faada always gets what he wants. He admires this young man. He says the boy reminds him of himself."

"I wonder if he has tata's immoral characteristics?"

The line went silent, and instantly she regretted her comment.

Her mother tried to keep her father's immoral conduct from her. However, Naja's blinders slowly rose the older she became, and she witnessed her father's philandering behavior firsthand.

A few weeks back, Naja's friend, Tamia, joked about her father having a baby due soon by a woman in California. Tamia alleged that she spotted the woman and her father out shopping. Naja asked Tamia for pictures because she always had receipts. However, this time she had no proof, which left Naja torn. Tamia is a Zelig, not a liar. She's an opportunist — the type of friend that would sell Naja's father the pictures of his indiscretion to make him believe it was for his benefit.

Naja contemplated telling her mother what Tamia said and encouraged her to investigate. But the more she thought about it, she decided to keep quiet until she had proof. Since they were kids, her parents had been together, and an outside child would break her mother's spirit and heart.

"Have you heard from your prince?" Naja knew her mother was referring to Dakari.

"He has called a couple of times. But I am not ready to speak to him."

Naja didn't tell her parents about Dakari's ultimatum or snide remark about him fighting off other women plotting to take her place. She believed if another woman took her spot, Dakari had invited her to take a seat, and that's precisely what he had done.

Three weeks before he was scheduled to leave, Naja's friends convinced her to go with Dakari. They all promised they would visit and assured her that crossing a continent would never sever her bond with the BAEs.

Naja fasted and prayed for two days. On the third day, she felt something yanking her towards Dakari's apartment. When she arrived at his apartment, she found him entertaining a girl. According to him, the young lady was also going abroad to do her medical internship, and his academic advisor had connected them.

Naja is the type of person who asks plenty of questions to gain knowledge while shelving her ego. Unfortunately, when she attempted to ask questions, the female presented her with a negative mindset, and Dakari was upset that she questioned his loyalty.

He went as far as noting he was not a cheater like her daadi, and unlike Naja, he didn't observe his father cheating and disrespecting his mother. But, until that day, nobody could convince her that Dakari would wash her face in her family's business to establish superiority in front of a stranger.

She refused to reveal their fight to her parents because she was still digesting the situation. Dakari had hit her below the belt numerous times. Telling her mother would tarnish her vision of him.

"Princess, did you hear me?"

"Muma, if I run into Tata's friend, I will be nice. However, I am not making any promises to you or Tata on whom I am going to date or marry."

Chapter 07

On the jet, Raven continued to remind RB he could not have one sexual encounter. They were both going to be on vacation. To ensure he complied, Raven flashed RB her endearing hazel brown eyes. Raven had been melting RB's demeanor with those eyes since the day she was born.

She wondered if she should have had Uncle Lou compose an official contract. Raven blinked with feigned innocence. RB shook his head as he fixed his eyes on Raven. She blinked her eyes rapidly at him, then made a silly face curling the edges of her mouth before playfully slapping his leg.

After a long flight, RB was exhausted and ready to see the villa Raven bragged about during the flight; however, Raven was rushing to eat lunch. He started to protest but had promised himself he would do whatever it took to make Raven understand how much he loved her.

After Raven checked them in, they went straight to a restaurant while their bags went to the villa. RB inventoried his surroundings and noticed an ivory beauty three tables to the right of him, staring him down.

Raven cleared her throat, and RB nervously chuckled. "You could not hold out for two hours?"

RB gave Raven a devilish smile. "She is staring at me."

"And you were looking at her as well," Raven countered.

"I have no plans on sleeping with that woman." RB smiled, revealing his million-dollar smile. "I gave you my word. A man is only as good as his word, right?"

Although RB's force was solely on Raven, he could feel eyes undressing him. He purposely dropped his table linen. While retrieving the napkin, he noticed the ivory beauty was checking him out.

RB admired the ivory beauty every chance he could. She had a slender build and looked to be about 5 foot 1 inches tall. RB had to admit he loved the way he towered over short women. She smiled at him hungrily as their eyes locked. He wondered if she was a lonely tourist looking to reclaim her groove like Stella. He knew exactly what her body desired. However, she would have to wait a couple of days before he could give her body the strokes it craved.

"RB, I see you are looking at that woman," Raven noted. She kicked him under the table. "You aren't slick."

Raven rose from the table. Delight zinged through RB as Raven approached the ivory beauty's table. His eyes were greedily drinking in the view of the ivory beauty as her and Raven spoke. When they glanced in his direction, he displayed his million-dollar smile. His grin slowly dissipated as the realization of Raven's actions squeezed his heart like a vise grip. RB composed himself in the chair as Raven approached the table.

He cleared his throat. "I am more than capable of going a couple of days without the company of a woman," he declared with authority before Raven could sit down.

Raven's crumpled face spoke volumes.

"I love you enough to entertain you and only you." Raven gave RB a skeptical glance. "Raven, all bullshit aside, you know how much I love you, don't you?'

She hunched, and a tightening sensation sieged his chest. He had provided for his sister for the past decade. How could she not see the love in his actions? Could he have done a better job? Yes, but he was a child thrust into a parental role at an immature age struggling to balance the responsibilities of fatherhood and be a professional athlete.

Over the years, he had gotten better as a parental figure, he thought until this very moment.

"I saw you were eyeing her, so I invited her to dinner."

RB frowned, and Raven started singing while flinging her arms in the air. "You know me. I'm your sister. Your main girl, thick and thin. I'm your pusherman." Raven roared with laughter, but RB's face remained somber.

"I don't need a woman to help me spend a couple of days with you, Sis!"

After eleven years, he was still blaming himself for every family secret. Indulging in the pleasure of a woman nightly brought him a temporary escape from reality. He didn't know how to explain this to his sister without sounding egotistical.

Through it all, he was proud of the woman before him. She and Kris owned a personal management company. Who knew you could make money managing people's daily lives? His baby sister.

Raven patted RB's hand. "When she comes to dinner tonight, prove it."

RB huffed. "Prove what, baby sis?"

"That you can entertain a woman and allow her to leave without bedding her."

"Bet!"

Chapter 08

RB walked around the Sanctuary's three-bedroom house. The rental exuded a peaceful spiritual vibe which caused his body to uncoil. Antique fixtures and teak furniture decorated the interior resembling a Hallmark greeting card from Mother Africa. Warm walnut wood floors and cool limestone bathrooms added to the ambiance. RB instantly felt tranquility when he stepped onto the polished ipe wood terraces. When he turned around, he bumped into the butler.

"Afternoon, Mr. Brooks. I am Sir Forbes, your private butler."

"What type of wood is this?" RB asked, pointing to the pathways.

"European walnut. The walls are cedar and coral stone. This path will lead you to your private powder-white sand beach."

RB spun around again, admiring the ample space. He wished his boy, Malik, had accompanied him. He would have enjoyed the villa. Plus, Malik would make sure he stayed away from women. However, these days Malik cannot go five minutes without Sabrina. RB never trusted his baseball and football groupies, but Malik had fallen in love with one. Groupies are for pleasure, not marriage. Nonetheless, RB tried to like Sabrina for Malik's sake, but something about her rubbed him the wrong way.

RB inhaled the crisp Atlantic air. He wished he hadn't given Raven a tough time because he needed the renewal of wellness.

"Sir, I have unpacked your bags and set you up in one of the ocean-facing suites. If you want me to move you to another suite, please let me know." RB nodded. "Would you like me to get you something for dinner?"

"No, Mr. Forbes. I will be going to the guest villa for dinner with my sister."

Mr. Forbes nodded.

"The guest house is 140 yards from the main house. Would you like me to take you in the buggy, or will you drive yourself?"

RB gazed across the pavilion that separated the properties. "I will walk."

"Sis, you are a football field away from me. How are we supposed to bond if you are over here?" RB asked, walking into the guest house?

Raven emerged from the kitchen. "Why are you yelling, bighead?"

"Where is your butler?"

Raven spun around the room. "I am all alone. No, butler!" RB scratched his head. He wasn't too happy having Raven in a four-bedroom house all by herself. Anything could happen to her, and he was 140 yards away.

RB deepened his voice. "I think you should move to the main house with me. I do not know why you rented both houses."

Raven rolled her eyes at her brother. She was twenty years old and did not need him to protect her from the boogeyman anymore.

"If you recall, Uncle Lou and Kris were supposed to be here with us. The top floor was for Uncle Lou. Kris and I were going to take the lower level. You have the entire main house to yourself. I know you are not scared of staying here. Your penthouse occupies two floors. Hell, you didn't need to buy two penthouses and make one, but you did."

"Raven!" The base in RB's voice caused Raven to jump and revert into a teenage girl.

"I am sorry, Dad. I figured you would appreciate the extra space." RB realized he had scared Raven.

He softened his tone. "I do appreciate the extra space, but I do not want you to stay alone."

"Can we eat dinner then talk about this later. Our guest is out on the deck, enjoying a cocktail," Raven announced.

She had more pressing matters besides her living arrangements.

RB nodded and joined the ivory beauty outside. "Hi, my name is Romello, but everyone calls me RB."

She smiled. "My name is Karan Norwalk."

"Dinner is ready," Raven announced.

Karan and RB followed Raven around the deck to the side of the villa. A long natural wood table accented with flowers and lined with seafood, fresh fruit, and beverages caused RB to soften his demeanor.

RB blessed the table. Karan started talking before pulling the crab meat from the shell; RB tried to zone her out.

He preferred his tenderoni to be admired, not heard. The purpose of a conversation is to connect, and the only connection he enjoyed was two naked bodies in bed. Women desiring a relationship needed to find another man because RB was strictly for pleasure.

RB glanced at Raven. He was still pissed she wanted to stay in the guest villa by herself. He failed to protect her once, and he would never let that happen again.

"I can see how much you love your sister," Karan noted. "I can also see the overprotective lion in you." RB nodded and continued to eat. "Have you always been overprotective?" Before RB could answer Karan, she plowed him with more questions.

Karan was rubbing RB the wrong way. She was conducting an interrogation, and he was not in the mood. RB lowered his fork and stared Karan in her eyes.

"Who are you, Karan? Was this a random meeting, or did you arrange our accidental meeting?"

Karan intensified her scrutiny. Instead of answering RB's question, she launched another round of inquiries.

RB cast his eyes on Raven. Usually, Raven would be livid if a person asked all these questions. She hated people attempting to pry into their personal lives. Raven stared at RB's lips as if she were anticipating his answers as much as Karan.

"No, I am not suspicious of everyone. However, my gut is telling me I should be suspicious of you."

Karan placed her drink down and leaned an inch forward before she spoke. "I am Karan Norwalk, a psychologist. Your sister brought me here because she did not think you would agree to come to see me in California."

Before Karan could finish her well-rehearsed speech, RB pushed back from the table. His nostrils flared. "Raven, what the fuck!"

Instead of responding, Raven leaped from the table and dashed down the walkway to the beach.

Chapter 09

Dr. Norwalk expected this outcome. However, Raven assured her this was the best tactic. Dr. Norwalk watched RB's nostrils flare, and his light brown eyes turned dark as coal. She braced herself for his outburst.

"Fuck! Look what you've done, Karan!

After scolding Dr. Norwalk, RB raced after Raven. It ripped him apart to see his sister in turmoil. When did their relationship deteriorate, he thought to himself as he ogled to the right and left, searching for Raven?

He was pissed. Raven lied about her true intentions of the trip but was dismayed that she felt it necessary to deceive him.

He was more than her brother. He was her dad and her friend. Raven was the world to him; without her, life would be meaningless.

Raven slowed down, and RB called out to her. She picked up her pace. RB hated treating her like a child, but she was behaving immaturely right now.

Growing up, RB rarely had to spank Raven. She was afraid of his deep voice and the thought of a whipping. He tried the whole punishment tactic and took what she loved away from her. None of those worked because Raven preferred to be alone, and she quickly adapted to uncomfortable situations. He recalled giving Raven one spanking a year to keep her on track. Chastising her ripped his heart apart.

RB stopped and roared from the depth of his gut. The thunderous rumble made Raven stop instantaneously. "Now come here, young lady. I will not chase after you. I didn't do it when you were a kid, and I am not going to do it now."

Raven slung sand in the air with her feet as she stomped over to RB. She lowered her head. "I'm sorry, Daddy-brother."

RB gently placed his index finger under Raven's chin and lifted her head. His heart dropped when he saw her teary face.

"I am disappointed in your behavior." Raven nodded. "I know your heart was in the right place, but you could have told me what you wanted. I love you! The Y-shaped dimple in your chin and mine means you and me for life, kid."

A tear slipped down her cheek, and RB swiped it away. "I don't know what to do to show I care about your feelings and your heart, Rave." RB could feel his voice cracking as he became overwhelmed with emotions.

Tears streamed down Raven's face. RB pulled her into his arms, and she snuggled her face under his armpit, wrapping her arms around him tightly.

RB failed to understand that Raven was no longer a child, and he could not camouflage his emotions. Raven could feel the pain trapped inside of him. He was all she had in this world, and she could not lose him.

"Daddy-brother, it is not your fault."

RB kissed Raven on the top of her head. He wanted to explain why everything was his fault, but Raven was already upset, and he did not want to add to her anguish.

"Why did you bring Dr. Norwalk here?"

Raven's gaze gently caressed RB's physique. "She is here to help you understand that none of this is your fault. RB, you never allow any woman to get close to you. That is not normal. I am afraid to leave you because you would not have anybody in your life. I was happy when you allowed Uncle Lou and Malik inside of our bubble."

She slammed her eyes to push back the tears. Once she had recomposed herself, she continued speaking, "You are my brother and the only Dad I acknowledge. I worry night and day about you. But, Daddy-brother, something inside you is damaged, and it keeps you from loving and trusting people. Please let Dr. Norwalk help you. Please!"

RB engulfed his sister. He had no idea his pain had mutilated his sister. He laid his head on top of hers, struggling to keep his tears at bay.

Raven shivered in his arm as she wailed. "If talking to Dr. Norwalk will help you, then I will."

Deep inside, RB hoped it would help him as well. He yearned to snuggle in the bed next to a beautiful woman. He even tried a couple of times. Nonetheless, the night always ended with him creeping out of bed, going to his penthouse to sleep alone.

Raven and RB walked into the guest house. Raven had her left arm wrapped around RB's waist and his right arm draped over her shoulders. Dr. Norwalk smiled at the sight of them.

"Did you two manage to work everything out?"

Raven nodded. "RB, Dr. Norwalk will be staying upstairs. There is an office up there. You can meet her here or in your villa. The first session is tomorrow morning."

Mentally exhausted, RB agreed.

He kissed Raven and said goodnight to the ladies.

"Did you have a wonderful dinner?" Sir asked RB when he climbed into the buggy.

"It was interesting."

Sir could see the stress dangling from RB's brow.

"I'll make you a drink," Sir announced the minute they walked into the house.

RB paced the deck as Sir poured a glass of cognac. The idea of his session with Dr. Norwalk was already stressing him out. How could he allow this stranger to peel back every layer of his personality? He swallowed the lump in his throat. She represented his secret fear of vulnerability.

He wasn't ready to have anyone probing through his thoughts, but he understood he had to endure this process for Raven. Their bond was the only factor his heart could consider.

Without sex to ease his tension, he knew he would have to watch movies. He retreated to the screen room, deciding he would be sleeping there tonight, praying he would doze off soon.

Chapter 10

Raven rested her back against the wall adjacent to the front door. She was worried that RB would not show up for therapy. A knock at the door eased her fears. The sight of Sir Forbes, RB's butler, caused her to smile.

"Morning, I told RB I would come to tell you he is running a couple of minutes behind. No worries, Lil Miss, Sir will make sure he comes to talk to Dr. Norwalk."

Instead of being pissed that he was inserting himself into their family business, she was grateful. Something about Sir screamed regal elegance, and Raven knew he meant every word. Raven finally understood why Dr. Norwalk personally picked the butler.

Last night when Raven's insomnia kicked in, Dr. Norwalk entertained her. During their conversation, Dr. Norwalk revealed that Sir Forbes was a good honest man who she thoroughly trusted and vowed he would never repeat anything he heard to a tabloid.

The confidence she placed in Dr. Norwalk shocked her. Raven's trust in people died in her teenage years.

Sir smiled at Raven when RB approached the door. "I was coming back to get you," Sir addressed RB.

"You had everything laid out for me. It took me no time to get dressed. Walking and running will keep me fit."

RB kissed his baby sister's cheek, then went upstairs for his first session. Once he reached the office upstairs, he lingered at the door admiring Dr. Norwalk's skin shimmering like white silk. He had two more days, and then he could bed the doctor. He understood why Raven brought her here, but he also saw how she undressed him with her eyes.

Karan eased from the desk and walked over to the window admiring the beautiful island. Last night reminded her of her college years. She and Raven devoured junk food and watched television until two in the morning. Karan slowly turned around because she sensed another presence.

RB flashed his award-winning smile at Dr. Norwalk.

"Should I sit or lay down?"

Dr. Norwalk smiled. "Which do you prefer?"

Speaking through his firm body language, RB hovered over Dr. Norwalk before taking a seat on a long-cushioned turquoise bench that resided to the right of Dr. Norwalk. He figured he would insert his power early. If anyone were going to compromise during these sessions, it would be her, not him. She had no control. The sooner she accepted that one fact, RB figured the sessions would benefit him and her.

Dr. Norwalk pulled the oversized chair from the table in front of RB. She locked eyes with him. "How are you doing today?"

"Great and yourself?" Karan adjusted herself in the seat, and a ray of light poured across her body. "You have beautiful blue eyes; it is the same hue as the ocean outside your window."

"Thank you, Mr. Brooks. What are your expectations for these sessions?"

RB ran his tongue across his top lip than the bottom, applying his heartbreaker charm. "Besides sexing you, none."

"Do you always use sex to express yourself?"

RB regretted the words already. He was embarrassed to admit he wished these sessions helped him sleep throughout the night without having meaningless sex. He also hoped Raven would recognize how much he loved her and that he'd raised her the best he could.

Staring at Dr. Norwalk was like examining his soul in a mirror. Her reflection reverberated all the pain, secrets, and insecurities that RB had buried within himself. He feared people would use his inadequacies against him or cast bitter judgments.

Malik's parents once told him, "we all have a past, but we learn and grow from them. Society tends to believe that celebrities don't have a history or you guys don't stumble and fall. They miss the growth because they are always focused on the bad". He agreed because gossip and scandal attract people's goodwill, and charity repels them.

RB's statement did not phase Dr. Norwalk because her patient's roster was composed of arrogant celebrities.

"Mr. Brooks, you are my patient, and there will be no relations between us."

Normally RB would have let the matter go, but the scowling look upon her face rubbed him the wrong way. "Do you think you are too good for me?"

Dr. Norwalk jotted something on her pad, then stared at RB before speaking, "Do you think I am too good for you?"

A mischievous smile skipped across his face. Dr. Norwalk was trying to shrink him, he thought. He hadn't met a woman who didn't desire a roll in the sheets with him and his money.

"Do you think I am a handsome man?"

"Should I?"

He hunched his shoulders. They both sat there in silence. RB was analyzing the textured walls attempting to find animals in the patterns. It's something he did as a kid with his father and mother. He could feel a stinging feeling building in his nose. He covered up his face with his hands.

Dr. Norwalk stared at him. "RB, are you ok today."

He looked at the doctor and wondered if he should lie or tell her the truth. "I'm a bit exhausted," he honestly replied, "I haven't been sleeping well."

The truth was he hadn't slept for eight hours since he was a teenager.

After he finished all his business emails, he refused to give in to his body's desire for an erotic connection, so he went running. His energized body and mind still demanded climactic relief in exchange for rest. He contemplated stroking his penis, but he was ten years old the last time he did that. Shit, he didn't even think he knew how to do it anymore.

"Are you getting your standard eight hours?"

"I rarely sleep. I sleep for two or almost three hours if I am lucky."

RB slid to the edge of the chair and rested his elbows on the small wooden desk. "Dr. Karan, did you know Donna Karan designed the house interior? Her last name is your first name," he noted, then chuckled.

When the doctor did not laugh or crack a smile, he was done with therapy for today.

"I am sure Raven is not paying you to stare at me. Hence my exit."

He paused at the door waiting for Dr. Norwalk to tell him to stay. She did not utter a word.

She noticed his attempt to assert his power. After counseling some of society's top elite, she was well diverse in this game. The most challenging part of her job was getting her clients to understand that their therapy success resided in their willingness to share.

Tomorrow Dr. Norwalk planned to join RB and Raven at the island's fish fry. She hoped he would open up to her over a couple of drinks in a communal environment.

Chapter 11

Sitting across from Dr. Norwalk, RB found it hard to breathe. This session was nothing but pure torture for him. He was ready to go to the island fish fry tonight. He needed a change of atmosphere. He was doing an excellent job at keeping his promise to Raven. Yet, she was still monitoring his every move.

Raven called him every morning and evening to make sure he was not late for therapy. He was supposed to have treatment once a day, but Raven bumped it to twice a day.

Last night RB called Uncle Lou and told him and Kris to come two days early. Lou declined until RB lied about Raven being depressed over Kris's absence. Lou agreed they would come a day earlier.

Raven had made Uncle Lou aware of the rules, which stated RB could not entertain a woman until Kris and Uncle Lou arrived. Raven would be ecstatic to see Kris and forget about him and Dr. Norwalk if his plan worked.

RB patiently waited for Dr. Norwalk to finish jotting notes on her pad. He knew she would have three or four follow-up questions. RB sliced the silence between them. "When I am on the road, I don't need to have sex every night. I am not a sex addict. I know a guy who is an addict, and I am nothing like that guy. I only need sex two to three times a week or whenever I am extremely stressed out."

Dr. Norwalk wrote something else on her pad. RB tried to look at the notepad. She knew if she remained silent, RB would speak to ease the awkwardness. After three sessions together, she realized RB hated to be pressured and dismissed by pushy women.

Based on the conversations Dr. Norwalk had with Raven, she knew it would take her some time to break down RB's walls to address the roots of his issues. "Do you feel all you have to offer a woman is your looks, sex, and money?"

RB cleared his throat and leaned forward. The sweet scent of Dr. Norwalk's perfume tickled his nose, and he chuckled. "Most women's goals are to bed me and spend my money. They think I am a handsome and charismatic man. What do you think?"

"Did you seek your mothers' approval when you were growing up?"

RB twisted his lips. Doesn't every child seek the approval of their parents? What kid did not want to hear well done, fantastic job, or I am proud of you from their parents? "I think I sought approval as much as any other child would from their parents," he replied, feeling as if he had won this round of questioning.

Dr. Norwalk leaned back in her seat. "Did your mother shower you with praise?"

RB closed his eyes and pictured his mother, Robin Brooks. She was the hardest working woman he knew, working two jobs to take care of him and Raven. He outwardly smiled as he heard his mother's voice whisper in his head. No matter how busy his mother was, she always took the time to tell him and Raven how much she loved them. When RB was upset, you could hear his mother's Jamaica accent slide off his tongue.

"My mother was the best woman in the world. God doesn't make them like her anymore. I gave up on trying to find a woman who resembles a pinch of my mother. She was strong and confident. You could not place labels on my mother because she knew who she was. Her parents moved from Jamaica to New York when she was ten years old. At sixteen, she became pregnant with me. Livid, my grandparents kicked my mother out. My father was still living with his parents as he was only seventeen. My grandparents begged my mother to come home, but she moved to Oakland, California, with her cousin. Pregnant with me, my mother worked two jobs to move out of her cousin's house because her cousin was married. My mother was a fearless woman."

He opened his eyes and noticed Dr. Norwalk's eyes glued to his lips.

"My father, Owen Lewis, joined my mother in Oakland when he turned eighteen. When my father arrived, my mother had already found an apartment. She stopped working to take care of me. She even started a daycare in our house with some other kids. My mother always pulled her weight. She never expected anybody to give her anything for free, unlike these women today. These women keep their hands out. What happened to the independent woman?"

"Are you searching for a mate that reminds you of your mother?"

RB chuckled until he rolled halfway off the bench. "God stopped making women like my mother. When I started school, she enrolled in a vocational school. No matter how exhausted, my mother made sure my father and I had a hot meal, and she showered us with love and attention. We did something different every weekend. We were the three musketeers until Raven came along."

"Were you upset that Raven destroyed the three musketeers?"

RB skeptically eyeballed Dr. Norwalk. He could not tell where she was going with this line of questioning. Nor did he know what answer she expected to hear.

"By the time Raven came along, my mother was a certified nursing assistant. My father went from working at night to working in the day. My mother's two days off rarely fell on the weekend. My parent's schedule never matched. My father was lonely. Somehow, he found himself cheating on my mother. My mother always told her friends that if my father cheated, he did not deserve her. He cheated, and my mother walked away without a second thought."

RB was waiting for Dr. Norwalk to finish writing on her notepad. "How old were you when your father moved out of the house?"

"I was twelve when I became the man of the house."

"How did it feel being the man of the house?"

"Raven was my baby from the time she was born. She stayed at the daycare until I picked her up after baseball or football practice. I was determined to become a professional athlete, so my mother would never have to wipe another person's ass again." A tear trickled down his cheek, and he quickly swiped it away. "If God would have left her here a little while longer, she would have had a great life. I would have given her and Raven every planet in the galaxy. I was the man of the house."

RB slammed his hand on the bench. "God took her away from Raven and me. I tried to raise Raven, right, but– I am tired of this session. Are we done?" Before Dr. Norwalk could respond, RB rose off the bench and headed for the door.

Halting RB's steps, Dr. Norwalk asked him, "Is there anyone special in your life?"

"Yes, Raven!"

RB gripped the rail of the door, hoping Dr. Norwalk would stop talking. He didn't want to be rude, but he could not answer any more questions today. "Tomorrow, can we discuss your relationships with women?"

"Do one-night stands count? If not, I don't have any relationships to discuss," he boasted. Before she could reply or ask another question, he exited the room.

Chapter 12

Naja's body moved to a rhythm that ears could not hear, but eyes could see. Her orange and pink silk swimsuit cover wafted in the breeze flowing through the villa as she slowly approached the front door.

RB's eyes traced every inch of her frame. Instantly he became overwhelmed by her presence. RB fondled with the chain dangling around his neck. He'd rehearse his speech a couple of times before coming over.

She flipped her hair off her shoulder, and the aching need for her rushed over him like a tidal wave.

Since the island fish fry, RB had sent his neighbor several offers for brunch. He sent her flowers and fruit baskets and purchased her a spa day.

He questioned Dr. Norwalk about his neighbor; she pretended she never spoke to a woman at the island fish fry. He watched for over twenty minutes as the women engaged in conversation and laughed. Their body language was relaxed and familiar. RB couldn't understand why everyone around him was so deceitful, but they wanted him to be receptive.

Last night he couldn't shake the throbbing desire to be lying next to the ebony goddess. To ease his mind, he ran up and down the beach until the sun tipped over the horizon.

Tonight, he was going to force her to reveal her plans with an indecent proposal. He wondered how far his neighboring doctor, Raven, and Dr. Norwalk were willing to take this charade.

With Dr. Norwalk and Raven residing to his left and Eboni to the right, he felt a bit boxed in.

She cleared her throat, and he smiled at her hungrily.

"Will you join me in a nightcap, Ms. Eboni Dream?" RB asked.

Naja frowned when he called her Eboni Dream. She recalled telling her mother she was booking her trip under that name to avoid her potential 'usband.

Her mother's only response was, "Don't allow Eboni to come out and play. Your twin is irresponsible. Do not allow her to get you in trouble."

Naja nodded at the phone as if her mother could see her.

RB waved his hand in front of Naja's face. She smirked at RB; his smile widened.

She was sneering at the vision in her head. She could imagine her father evoking her alias from her mother with gifts and romantic gestures. She could hear her mother cooing as she swooned, not realizing she had betrayed her daughter.

So much for throwing her father and his suitor off her trail, she thought.

Her butler was already calling her Eboni, so one more person calling her by her pseudonym shouldn't matter, she reasoned with herself.

RB was confident he was saying the name Dumais provided correctly. "Eboni Dream, did you hear me?" he repeated, pronouncing every syllable of her presumed name.

She swayed her head from side to side, admiring his smugness. The arrogance of using her pseudonym when he knew her government name invoked a playful banter inside of her.

Game on, I will pretend not to know who you are nor your true intentions, she thought.

She hunched her shoulders.

"Well, if you can hunch, you heard me."

She snickered playfully, and his tight-fisted muscles recoiled.

RB attempted to dazzle Eboni with his million-dollar smile. When she didn't seem receptive to his charm, he continued with his question. "Will you join me in a nightcap?" he repeated in his deep husky voice.

The sparkle of hope she caught in his golden-brown eyes matched the glint of the five-carat diamond earrings shimmering in his ears.

"I am already having dinner," Eboni replied. "Besides, I never drink and eat with strangers."

His body tilted a bit in disappointment. When a slight smile caressed Eboni's full lips, he realized she was playing with him again. He chuckled. She wasn't dismissing him; she was making him do something he hadn't done in years -- earn the privilege of taking her out on a date.

He paused. He knew Dr. Norwalk had shared his file with her. He was also confident that Raven had given them a play-by-play of his antics when she signed up for this week of therapy.

"Luckily, I'm not a stranger," he replied, matching her sly smirk. "Strangers don't send flowers. I'm your neighbor from across the way." He gestured to the darkness on the left side of him. "Plus, our butlers are homies. Sir can vouch for me. He knows me better than I know myself."

Tuesday, Sir received a call from his old friend requesting he watch over his baby girl.

"I'm pretending to be a butler this week, and I've already started watching the young man," Sir told his old friend.

Titus chuckled. He never understood why a man as rich as Sir went around pretending to be a butler for Dr. Karan Norwalk.

Karan had called Sir two weeks prior requesting his help with Romello Brooks. She asked Sir to keep RB away from the island girls because he was a Casanova. Sir believed men had the right to indulge in as many women as they could handle, but he would do anything for Karan, so he agreed.

Sir called up another close friend of his, demanding he emulate a butler. Dumais was hesitant; he wasn't sure he could pretend to be a poor man. Once Sir revealed who her father was, Dumais agreed.

Dumais recalled Titus and his family visiting when Naja was a little gyal because they always stayed at Sir's compound. Many people would be surprised to know that Sir Forbes accumulated his riches by facilitating the North American ganja supply before moving to Turks and Caicos.

Titus also informed Sir he was sending an 'usband to court their little doctor. Since Naja was using the alias Eboni Dream, Sir would have to assist the wooer. Sir knew he would have his hands full; therefore, he had the resort place Naja in the Tamarac suite by RB's villa. He instantly regretted his decision when RB requested that he find out his neighbor's name.

Sir tried to persuade RB to find another woman to court. Sir knew the only way to convince RB to leave his neighbor alone was to reveal her identity or reveal what Karan shared in confidence; therefore, Sir pretended he couldn't obtain her information.

Titus called Sir back, informing him Naja's future 'usband might not come. Sir, in turn, told Titus about Romello Brooks, an NFL player who had eyes for their lil doc.

"He should have a good portfolio," Titus' replied. "He could provide for our gyal. I recalled the young man originally played baseball, then both. I also read an article stating his mother was from Jamaica but died when he was in high school. I think he would be a good match, old friend."

Sir agreed. He honestly thought RB was a great guy who loved the ladies like him, but he could sense RB had some past demons hunting him.

The only problem her father could foresee was Naja's hatred for sports and him knowing she would never date an athlete due to some statistical studies suggesting most athletes cheat while on the road. Sometimes Titus wished Naja didn't read so much. Everything out of her mouth was studies prove this, statistical data reveal that, or statistics support this. She would allow life to pass her by while analyzing the data instead of doing some field research.

He despised how his strong, confident daughter wasted her time with Dakari. He knew Naja followed him to the college of his choosing. Titus adored all his sons, but Naja was his twin. She was more like Titus than she realized, and she needed to unleash the boss trapped inside her and stop following a man. He preferred her to lead and bend men to her will. His father always told him, "The key to a happy life was finding a wife that loves you more than you love her." He needed Naja to flip the script and find a man who loved her more than she loved him, and Dakari was not that man. He wondered if RB could be that man, but if RB broke his daughter's heart, he would break his legs ending his impressive career.

Later that day, RB caught Sir and Dumais talking and smoking outside of his villa. RB instantly pressured Dumais for his neighbor's name. And Dumais replied, "Eboni Dream."

Sir eyed Dumais sternly when he gave Naja's alias instead of her real name.

Dumais hunched his shoulders at Sir. He didn't understand why a handsome guy like RB was going through so much trouble for one woman when the island was full of beautiful goddesses that would love to be showered with gifts.

"You are painfully aware that our butlers barely know us. Unless you frequently come to the island to court women."

RB released a wholehearted chuckle; he hadn't heard the word courting since it flew from his mother's lips. The first time he told his mother, he was going to marry his junior high school sweetheart. She laughed then replied, 'Romello, do you know the proper way to court a woman?'

He would never forget his reply. He stood tall, bubbling over with confidence, and responded, 'with respectable actions to reinforce his words.' He recalled his mother's astonishment. She kissed him on the top of the head and beamed with pride.

He rubbed his head as he admired the stellar actress before him. "You know if this doctor stuff doesn't work out, you can always be an actress." He flashed her a smile, crescent moons formed on both sides of his cheeks and a Y-shaped dimple in his chin.

"I prefer to help people, not entertain them." His smile widened, and his dimples winked at her.

"He is a tall glass of chocolate milk," she mumbled slightly above a whisper to her twin. She couldn't see his muscles, but she knew some resided under his tracksuit.

Eboni examined RB's smooth cocoa skin. She envisioned her hand riding the waves on his head. She wasn't looking for RB to become her exclusive lover.

He could be our summer paradise fling, her naughty twin echoed in her head.

His warm smile and mischievous laugh evoked an unexpected response from her body. She crossed her ankles to calm the stimulation growing between her thighs.

RB brushed back a few strands of hair that had floated in her face. "Can I expect you around five o'clock tomorrow?"

"No."

His face contorted.

"You asked for a nightcap, not dinner," she replied, obliging her grin to remain undercover.

"But-"

"No, buts. You only get one chance to ask for what you genuinely want. You can't keep changing the rules."

The wounded look on his face made her want to change her mind. Something inside of her refused to bend to his demand. Naja figured she had done enough of that with Dakari. This trip would be about men bending to her wants and desires.

"I understand," he grumbled.

"I will see you tomorrow around seven o'clock after I finish my dinner."

Chapter 13

Sir observed RB pacing in front of his quarters. He would open the front door then close it right back. After the numerous invitations, flowers, and fruit baskets, she finally agreed to a nightcap. He had other plans besides a nightcap.

"I can answer the door when she comes," Sir informed RB.

"I think she might stand me up."

Sir was confident that lil doc would not stand RB up. She was her father and mother's child. Therefore, he knew she would honor her promise. He started to reveal he had spoken to Dumais earlier and lil doc was excited and nervous about tonight. From what Dumais could gather from listening to her calls, she had only been with one man, and he broke her heart by leaving her behind.

"Can you retrieve her in the buggy for me? I don't want all of your arduous work to go to waste."

"Son. My son, I am confident she will come."

Naja could hear Sir and RB talking as she stood on the other side of the door. She reasoned RB was Sir's son, and her father was behind all their chance run-ins. She desired to go back to her villa, but she promised her friend Lexi she would give RB a chance.

A knock on the door halted the conversation, and Sir retreated upstairs to the pool deck to get everything ready.

The moment Naja walked past RB, he pulled her back against his bare chest, wrapping his arm tightly around her waist. A sexy whimper escaped her throat. Her eyes closed, body tingling at the anticipation of his soft lips brushing across her smooth skin and landing on her lips.

Her frame tensed when his lips grazed her earlobe. Her stiff nipples pressed against the thin fabric of her swimsuit. He fought the urge to nibble on the fleshy tip of her earlobe. He sniffed her hair, and his manhood reacted to the crisp aroma of honeysuckle and coconut with a hint of seaside lily.

"Thank you for coming over." She arched her butt and leaned her shoulder back, hoping he would place warm kisses on the blade. Her body deflated when he said, "Give me five minutes, then join me upstairs."

Naja couldn't stop glancing at Sir Forbes as he entertained her until RB was ready for her to come upstairs. Her mind kept sending flashes from her childhood. The vision was of her on a swing. A tall, handsome man with a cleft chin and jet-black curly hair was pushing her.

The man standing before her could be the same person. He stood at five feet eleven inches like her. However, his jet-black hair had curly gray strands sprinkled throughout his head.

She remembered him calling her lil doc. As a child, she knew her purpose was to become a doctor. She was merely unsure of her field of study. Before her thoughts could journey deeper, a vision of a compound set off from the main island flooded her thoughts.

He couldn't be the same man; that man had servants; he wasn't a butler.

Naja snapped her fingers. It all made sense. She heard Sir call him, son. Her mind journeyed back to what RB said about their butlers. He must be RB's dad and her father's close friend, she rationalized.

She chuckled at how her tata had wrapped her in a ring of deception full of people he trusted.

If a show is what they wanted, then that's precisely what we will give them, her inner twin exclaimed. Sit back, Naja, and allow Eboni to drive.

"Well, if everyone else is pretending to be someone else, so will I. Tag you're it, Eboni," Naja mouthed at the reflection in the hallway mirror.

Eboni sauntered onto the deck and paused midway to admire the romantic ambiance which had stolen her breath away. RB had decorated the pavilion with balloons and colorful bags. Some of the bags glowed like lanterns.

"Gifts are not just for kids," RB announced, handing her three bags.

"Are these for me?"

"All the bags on the deck and by the pool are for you." Eboni could count at least thirty bags on the deck and terrace.

RB settled into a seat on the veranda.

Sir Forbes had bought all the gifts RB provided him pictures of when he trailed behind Eboni in the marketplace. He could tell her money was long; however, he admired how she haggled with the merchants. Brains, beauty, and frugal, what more could a man ask for, he wondered.

Sir was not impressed by RB's jewelry selection, so he took it upon himself to buy his lil doc a pair of black diamond earrings with a matching anklet, chain, and bracelet. Halfway out the door, he spotted a diamond moonstone bracelet with matching earrings he had to get her. Sir figured with all the gifts RB had purchased, and he wouldn't notice a couple more bags.

Eboni turned around and shook some gifts in RB's face. She was surprised he purchased all the trinkets she eyed in the marketplace. She didn't know if she should be impressed or call him a stalker.

She smiled as she settled back comfortably in her seat. RB captured the left side of his bottom lip with his teeth to ease the carnal roar inside him.

Eboni leaned forward to plant a kiss on his cheek, pausing before her knees collided with his.

The sight of her perfectly round melons forced a charming smile to slip across his lips, and she wondered if he could see the naughty thoughts dancing around in her head.

The thought of kissing her made his mouth salivate. He lapped the juices pooling in the corners of his mouth.

Her nipples peaked as she moved closer to him. She didn't know what he was about to say, but whatever it was, her inner twin had decided the answer was yes.

"You missed a gift bag."

She pulled the paper out of the extra-large bag. Inside was lingerie with a gold pen and a sparkling notepad.

His voice was low and seductive. "I have a proposal. Spend one day and one evening with me. You can call it therapy, and you can be my sex doctor."

She chuckled.

"What makes you think I want to be your sex therapist?"

"You already are."

"Explain."

"You forced me to self-examine myself and pull out my charming classic man to make you smile. You are elegant and mature, and I wonder what else you could draw out of me."

"I see how this arrangement will benefit you, but I do not see the benefit for me."

"A wonderful day with me catering to your every desire and an incredible evening filled with multiple orgasms with no strings attached."

He paused and stared off in the distance for dramatic effect. "I'm asking for what I want."

"I see."

"One day and one evening," Eboni repeated. "I will see you in the morning."

"You don't want to hear more about the day or what I am planning?"

"Nope," she replied confidently. "I will see you around noon."

"More like seven in the morning. I only get one day and one night; therefore, I want all my time," RB countered.

"You only asked for a day." Eboni rose from the seat then bent over in front of RB to pick up some bags. She could feel his eyes burning her backside. She sashayed to the stairs then dramatically turned around, causing her hair to blow in the breeze.

RB swallowed hard.

"OK, see you at seven."

The smile curving his lips widened.

Chapter 14

The moment she stepped onto the yacht's deck, Eboni started taking control of the situation, asserting her authority. Being close to water gave her superpowers. RB quickly recognized the move because that was his first rule of seduction.

A slight seductive grin slid across his face, and the only thing that resonated in his mind was pure ebony seduction. She was pulling him towards her like a kid to a candy store. He tried to remind himself she was part of Raven's and Dr. Norwalk's scheme to shrink him.

RB was positive she went to the store and requested the sexiest bathing suits in stock. The first time he saw her, she wore a sheer flush color suit that appeared nude. Last night she had on an eyelet lace-up sheer mesh cover-up with a skimpy string bikini under it. Dental floss had more string than that suit.

Today's outfit was a one-piece suit with chain shoulder straps. A chain clasp restrained Eboni's ample breast. He was confident that the gold chains wrapped around her waist were accessories.

She twirled her hair around her index finger, and he swallowed hard. Everything about this woman was alluring and sexual to him. He didn't care about the circumstances that brought her into his life because he valued her presence. Plus, RB appreciated the chase. He didn't recognize the lion inside of him had missed the thrill of the hunt. These days women laid it out on a platter with no effort from him.

The notion of earning her trust and making love to her sparked a desire in him he'd never felt before. His biggest obstacle was figuring out how to out psych his psychiatrist.

RB took off his shirt, and the sun wrapped around his cinnamon complexion. Tattoos started below his collarbone and ended at the forearms and his chest. His chiseled abdominal muscles took center stage, and she could feel her pulse quicken.

The intensity of RB's stare rendered her speechless. She eased back into her seat. RB had planned this day in his head a million times last night, and he was not going to allow Eboni to alter his fantasies.

RB was unsure what prompted him to stroll over the ebony goddess speaking ill-suited, but he needed to stir the sex kitten inside of Eboni.

She placed the melon on her fork down and expelled a deep sigh of relief as he approached. RB had no expectations in his mind concerning this outing. He merely understood that her approach to therapy was less about sitting down and exploring his feelings. Her method of treatment was to psychoanalyze him using the technique of sexual seduction. He didn't know if this would stay in playful banter, lead to mutual flirtation, or go far beyond the point of sexual intercourse.

She swallowed the piece of sweet melon she had been sucking and focused on his thick juicy lips.

"Can I ask you a few questions?"

"Sure," she replied with no hesitation.

"Have you ever made love in public?" Before she could answer, he fired off another question. "Do you like oral sex? What is the most adventurous sexual position you have ever tried? Do you like masturbating? Do you get soaking wet when someone gives you a massage? If I say take off all your clothes and go skinny dipping with me, what would you say?"

Instead of responding to his questions, Eboni rose from her seat and removed her swimwear. The chains wrapped around her waist sparkled off her ebony skin as the sun graced her body with its presence. RB's body moved backward as he attempted to touch her skin before she jumped into the ocean.

Her magnificent response took his breath away. He thought they would go skinny dipping at night on the beach or in one of their pools in private.

RB threw caution to the wind, hurried down from the top deck to the lower deck, and joined her in the ocean.

He swam around Eboni then pulled her into his arms, pushing his tongue down her throat. A soft purr spilled into his mouth, and he delved deeper, tasting the sweet nectar of melon on her tongue.

Their naked bodies merged, producing braising heat, forcing Eboni to pull away.

Eboni swam around RB, attempting to cool the passion burning between her thighs. "I hope you have some silky lotion and essential oils for my skin. I am ready for my massage."

"I am sure they laid the best stuff out. It's not my masseuse, but Sir insisted she is great."

She grunted. He came across as a rich and arrogant snob who barked orders but never got his hands dirty.

RB wanted to let it go, but he had to ask what the groan was all about. "Why did you sigh?"

She splashed him with water and swam to the back of the vessel to get out.

RB refused to let it go. Once they both had showered, Eboni joined him in the room he had set up for their massages. She nodded her head in approval after examining all the products.

He looked intently into her eyes as he slid the robe from his body. "You still haven't told me why you sighed in the ocean."

"You keep naming all of these wonderful things you are doing or planned for me. When in fact you haven't organized anything, nor have you done anything except stalk me in the marketplace." She placed her hand on her hips, anticipating his reply.

Shock hopscotched across her face when he dropped his head in shame.

The masseuse's presence cut the tension between the two.

Fanning the massage therapist away, RB decided he would personally cater to Eboni Dream.

"Let me start with giving you a deep tissue massage."

"You are not about to have me visiting an emergency room." RB raised a skeptical brow at Eboni.

Eboni had witnessed many cases where massage therapists utilized inadequate pressurized techniques causing their clients to suffer from induced migraines, inflammation, nausea, bruising, and lingering pain.

The physician inside of her was not willing to accept the risk due to his lack of knowledge. However, the seductive twin in her was ready to risk it all to have his massive callous free hands explore her warm flesh.

"So, you're scared?"

"Never that! The doctor in me knows better."

"Well, I don't want the doctor right now. Let's press pause on the session. I want Eboni Dream, the woman."

Before Eboni could protest, her twin decided for them both by pulling the ties on each side of her red bikini, causing her entire outfit to fall to the floor like a pyramid of dominoes.

Chapter 15

Eboni posed in front of RB as he admired her petite frame and confidence. She was a stallion that never backed down from a dare, and her naughty twin had no boundaries. RB's mind was talking at maximum speed; however, no words escaped his lips.

"I assume you want me to lay on the massage table."

He nodded his head over and over, like a needle skipping over vinyl, unable to stop on its own.

Eboni's smooth nutmeg skin, narrow waist, perky breast, even her kissable button nose caused RB to lose his voice and pulse to escalate suddenly. He continued to swallow the lump in his throat.

"Either cover me up or start kneading my muscles already, black man." RB's esophagus let out a strange noise, causing Eboni to leap from the table.

"Do you need medical care," she asked, checking his pulse.

RB felt embarrassed. No woman had ever affected him in this matter. "I am fine," he managed to say, "you are so damn breathtaking."

Eboni didn't know if this was part of his seduction tactics or him spilling pure gibberish to get to the prize between her thighs. She touched his head and neck; his skin was a bit clammy.

"Can you stand up straight without leaning on the counter?"

He nodded.

When he struggled to stand straight, he faltered. He gripped the edge of the table to prevent himself from falling.

The doctor inside of Eboni kicked in, and she raced across the room, retrieving a water bottle, cheese, and fruit from a platter by the door. She was grateful the room was full of snacks and fluids. She opened the bottle and placed it to his lips.

"Please sip. You need to rehydrate."

RB did as commanded and took a seat in a chair. A naked Eboni dashed around the room, catering to him. He sat there for a couple of minutes, snacking and drinking. Eboni placed some ice in a towel then patted it around his forehead before putting it on the back of his neck.

RB wrapped his arm around her waist and kissed her belly ring. "Thanks for taking care of me, Doc." She nodded. "I was so excited about today. I have not eaten anything. You flashed all this physique, and my body malfunctioned and shut down."

A gut-wrenching laugh followed by a snort escaped the pit of Eboni's gut. She knew he wasn't lying or running a game on her. She also thought it was cute.

RB stood, and Eboni felt the full force of his 6'5" frame wrapped in 245 pounds of muscle. She closed her eyes and tasted the lip gloss on her bottom lip.

RB motioned for Eboni to lay down on the table. Once she was situated, he whispered in her ear.

"I foresee my body rub being horrible if you're giving me a disclaimer before you start, Mister."

RB playfully smacked her on her butt. The vibration of the hit sent ripples of pleasure soaring through her vagina.

He kissed her on the small of her back then hummed. "If I slid your panties to the side and touched you right now, what would you do?"

"I don't know because I am not wearing panties," she fired back with a chuckle.

"Shit, you have me all nervous and shaken up. I know I asked for one day, but if you allow me three days and three nights, I guarantee you will love me by the second night."

Eboni giggled.

"Mmhmm, I would love to bury my face between your legs and breast."

"That is lust, but I hear you."

"I said it would end with love, but it's starting with lust," he rapidly fired back.

"What if I give you three days and three nights of me and you fall in love, but I don't fall in love with you? What will I get?"

RB thought for a minute, and only one answer popped into his head.

"Shit, if you can do that, a damn ring. The one thing no woman has ever received."

"Some men give out rings like they are passing out mints. Marriage doesn't carry too much weight with me."

"I will profess my love for you then show you every day by being your loyal and humble servant. Look, I've only told three women I loved them in my entire life. My mom, before she passed away, my sister, and my middle school crush on her deathbed."

"Damn, man. Women have to die around you to hear I love you."

RB chuckled as he massaged warm oil into Eboni's tightly gripped shoulder blades. "My sister is still alive, and I try to tell her I love her every chance I get."

Eboni could hear the sincerity in his voice every time he mentioned his sister.

RB was better at giving a massage than they both grasped as he manipulated the back of her thighs. She moaned in pleasure. She didn't realize how much her body needed and desired this type of attention.

RB kneaded her voluptuous backside. She twitched when he applied delicate bites to her nutmeg skin. Her tense body melted as his strong hands circled the back of her head, then spanked across her shoulders and down the back of her arms.

Eboni went from groans of pleasure to a soft whimper. Her body was like silly putty when he flipped her over onto her back.

He started with her temples and scalp then eased his way to her shoulder blades and arms. She gasped when he caressed her breast and applied gentle pressure to her nipples. Next, he massaged the sides of her torso in a circular motion. Next, he ran his smooth hands over her flat tummy.

Eboni could feel her juices pooling between her legs, running down her buttocks. She was ready for him to reach her sweet spot. He applied pressure to her hips, rocking them from side to side.

"Stay right there," she insisted, lifting her head to stare into his eyes.

He did as she instructed. Once her head fell back to the table, he moved down to her thighs, rubbing her knees and legs before he reached her feet.

Eboni thought nothing could make this reflexology any better. Until RB washed her feet with his mouth, she swarmed on the table. Her breathing intensified as he moved back up her legs.

He bent her legs at the knees, placing her feet flat on the table. Her eyes flickered as he manipulated her inner thigh then moved to her pelvic bone. Chest heaving, she fought the ball of energy building inside of her.

She reached down and seized his hand. "You've done this before. Is this part of your seduction?" she managed to say, fighting to reclaim air back into her lungs.

"I swear on my mother's grave and my sister's life, you, my Eboni Dream, are the first."

Unsure of what to say next, she released his hand and relaxed against the table. He continued to rub down her pubic bone area then worked his way back to her inner thighs.

She glanced down as he turned the massage oil bottle upside down and allowed it to drench her yoni. He massaged the outer lips of her yoni.

She hollered in ecstasy when his hands captured her outer lips between his index finger and thumb. He applied gentle pressure as his oily thumbs cruised the inner flesh of her lips.

Her head tilted back into the table, and her back arched off the table. Her mouth flew open as he altered the pressure and speed.

Her body was a flaming energy ball. She was soaring through heaven, and her climactic bliss was over the horizon.

His thumbs glided across her clit like a windshield wiper. Her body was ready to expel her climatic energy into the universe, but she refused to let go. His left hand captured her clit between his index and middle finger. He rotated her clitoris. She gasped when his right middle finger dipped inside her vagina.

Powerful waves of emotion took over her body as he increased and decreased his hand's speed. Her body shivered as tears flowed from her eyes. Her energy exploded multiple times as she rode the wave of euphoria.

Chapter 16

RB didn't look at the time before deciding to run to Raven's villa. A groggy Kris answered the front door. RB pushed past her and darted up the stairs to Dr. Norwalk's room. Seeing her sitting in the office behind the desk pissed him off. All he could think was she was expecting him. Eboni and the good doctor played games with his heart and mind, and he wasn't going to stand for it anymore.

"Are you here to help me or harm me?"

"I'm here to help you, but I cannot do my job if you don't communicate with me."

RB paused from pacing the floor, leveling his gaze on Dr. Norwalk. "What do you women want from me?" She gestured for him to take a seat. He hesitated for a while, then took a seat across from the doctor.

He could not recall the last time he took a nap or slept through the night. Being next to Eboni, he slept. When he woke up this morning, he was ready to make love to her, only to discover she was gone.

Sir told him the lil doc left a couple of hours after they arrived. He continued to tell RB she warned him to stay quiet because RB was knocked out snoring.

"What do you think women want from you?"

Tired of their games, he shot daggers at her. It was five in the morning, and he was not in the mood for riddles or games. To break the silence, she asked another question, "When was the last time you told a woman you loved her.?"

RB's mouth flew open. He couldn't believe it. Eboni had already reported back to her boss about their conversation. "You already know the answer. I am sure she told you everything I said."

"Let's discuss your relationship with Raven. You show her so much love but no respect."

"You don't know shit about me. I left home to play baseball to take care of my sister. Baseball ensured me and Raven had a future and paid for my education. Leaving her behind was a tough decision, but I had to leave, for fuck's sake. I had no other choice but to turn to my shitty father for help. He was my only alternative. I couldn't let her stay in the foster system. I thought I left her in safe hands; he was our father, after all. Man, some foul shit happened to my sister. I carry that burden around every day. I know I don't deserve her forgiveness. Hell, I can't forgive myself."

The doctor noted something on her pad. A fire raged inside of him as her pen shuffled across the page.

"I had a part-time career as a baseball outfielder for eight seasons and a full-time job in the NFL. When I found out my sister needed me, I left it all and ran to her side. I stepped up and took full custody of my sister, and worked out the details along the way. I wasn't a picture-perfect daddy-brother, but I did my fucking best. Everything I do is for Raven, so get the fuck out of here with that bullshit you are selling because I am not buying it. I respect my fucking sister. I love her more than I love breathing."

Before the doctor could ask him any more questions, RB stormed out of the room.

He approached a wild-haired Kris in the kitchen. "Did you feel like something was going on between Raven and the doctor the night you arrived?

Kris sucked her front teeth and nodded. "I asked Raven how many times she and the doc ate popcorn and watched movies. They were snuggled in one blanket on the sofa like a fucking couple," Kris huffed. "Raven blew me off. The doc filled her head with some bullshit about me not trusting her and unsafe boundaries." She sucked her teeth again. "I also confronted the good old doctor."

Kris purposely didn't share the conversation details because she told the doctor she and Raven were a package deal, and a threesome was on the table.

"Keep an eye on them. I will not have a doctor fucking my sister's head up."

"I got you," Kris replied, walking RB to the front door.

Dr. Norwalk caught RB by the arm, gently pulled him back, and suggested moving forward with a therapy consisting of only her and RB. She would stop counseling Raven. She prided herself on professionalism, but her relationship with Raven was blurring the lines between personal and professional.

"Uncle Lou and the girls can remain here, and I will move in with you. This will give us an unlimited amount of time to communicate. This option is best for all parties involved."

RB shook his head. He wondered if Eboni was pissed about the reflexology. He never forced himself upon her, he thought. At any given time, she could have protested, and RB would have stopped. Each time she gripped his hand, he paused and waited for her to permit him to proceed. The dreadful screams of passion that ripped from her body didn't sound like a woman who was unpleasant and angry with him.

He didn't understand what he did to make her not want to work with him anymore, and he wasn't going to allow Dr. Norwalk to interrupt whatever they had going on.

"I do not want to do that. I will keep seeing the doc. If she doesn't want to see me anymore, then she can tell me, instead of hiding behind some bullshit concerning all parties involved."

RB's stormed out of the guest rental headed towards Eboni's bungalow.

As far as RB was concerned, he and Eboni were going to address this matter amongst themselves.

Dumais opened the door before he knocked. "She is in the room," he stated, stepping aside.

When Eboni arrived at home last night, she instructed Dumais to allow RB entry no matter the time of day. She did not intend to leave his bed, but she was scared for the first time in her life. Dakari was the only lover she ever bedded. The way RB made her body explode and pulled tears from her soul on the boat terrified her.

Eboni eased her back against the headboard when she heard Dumais giving RB directions to her bedroom.

RB walked into her room. Before she could wipe the sleep from her eyes or greet him good morning, he started barking at her.

"Why did you change your mind about spending the night with me? What type of person leaves while a person is taking a nap?"

"I don't want to ruin my reputation. My mother and father would be devastated by my behavior."

"I would never tell people about our escapades, especially not your parents. Why would I? How could I?"

She crawled over to him and sat on her back legs in the bed. "If you want to get to know me, you have to holster the arrogant man inside of you and allow me to connect to the real you. Are you ready to be open and honest?"

He nodded when she gestured for him to use his words. "So, you're saying you want Romello?"

"If that's the authentic you, then yes."

"Are you sure you can handle this?" His million-dollar smile finally received the response he was searching for previously.

She lifted to her knees and swayed from side to side with her hands on her hips. "Baby, I am therapy in a bottle and so much more. Once you open Eboni, I swear I will stroke all your fears away. Then I'll turn into ZzzQuil and put your ass to sleep. By morning I'll be a cup of strong dark coffee waking you up to the dawn of a livelier day. Before the sun hides behind the clouds and the moon rises high, you'll find yourself confessing your love for me."

"Well damn!" He adjusted the rim of his shirt. "I am a big boy. I think I can handle you."

"I'm not a boy's toy. I'm a mature man's blessing. A helpmate sent straight from God."

RB cleared his throat. "I see. Can this mature man unwrap his gift now?"

She scanned the room before speaking. "What gift?"

"You," he replied, running his long tongue across his thick succulent lips. "Do I pull the bow on the back of your panties to unwrap you?"

She blushed as she stood to her feet, twirling slowly before bending over in front of RB, wiggling the big satin bow in his face.

Chapter 17

Ogling into RB's ravenous upturned brown eyes caused Eboni to be nervous and excited. RB gently pulled Eboni between his legs, examining her entire body with the smooth palms of his hands.

Her bottom lip quivered, and her almond-shaped eyes slowly closed.

She was ready to tell him she wasn't prepared to have sex when her mind jumped, back to the conversation she and Lexi had after leaving RB asleep in his bed.

"Hey, ebony goddess," Lexi said after answering on the fifth ring.

An exasperated sigh escaped Naja's lips. Typically, she would have called her old roommate, Miya — the only BAE to have a front seat to her relationship with Dakari. Since Miya was a virgin, Naja decided her old roommate wouldn't understand her dilemma.

Lexi and Imani had been with their teenage sweethearts like her; therefore, she knew they would understand. She contemplated a three-way, but sometimes Imani could come off a bit judgmental.

Naja gawked at her fingernails as Lexi joked about her marrying some Caribbean lover to win the bet. When Naja didn't laugh, Lexi realized this was serious. Naja told Lexi how her father had found her four admirers he assumed would make decent husbands.

To obtain Lexi's honest opinion, Naja revealed her sexual attraction to RB and divulged what had happened on the boat and how it startled her that she didn't feel guilty. She thought it would be hard to be with another man, but RB lit her body on fire in ways Dakari had never done, and they still hadn't engaged in intercourse yet.

She closed her eyes and gulped air. "The guy's name is RB. He gave me a rubdown that made me cry tears, heffa, real tears. When we went back to his villa, I snuck out when he nodded off. I've never slept with anyone except Dakari," Naja admitted.

Naja's mouth flew open, and she covered it with her hand as if she were afraid to share the secret Lexi had revealed to her. She always thought Paxton was Lexi's first, and she had never been with another man. It turns out they separated just like her and Dakari. Lexi also had relations with another guy.

Lexi went on to reveal it meant nothing. She thought her relationship with Paxton was missing something. That summer taught her she already had everything she needed, plus it made her appreciate her relationship more.

Naja completely understood. She felt as if her relationship was lacking because Dakari was not a patient lover. He rushed her into an orgasm, and sometimes she faked it. Faking it was better than him telling her what to do to achieve a climax faster.

RB was different. He took his time on the boat. He made her feel as if her ecstasy was his only priority. Naja moaned into Lexi's ear.

"You are thinking about RB right now, aren't you?"

Naja blushed, tugging on a strand of her hair.

"Heffa, are you blushing? You are, aren't you?" Lexi asked.

"I want him, Lexi," Naja honestly admitted.

Lexi recapped that nobody was holding her back except herself. "Naja, remember your naughty twin, Eboni?"

Naja pretended as if she had no idea.

"Your silence speaks volumes, heffa."

Finally, Naja admitted she remembered how Eboni's antics landed her in hot water a couple of times. She always recalled feeling uninhibited when she allowed Eboni to take the wheel. The call ended with Lexi joking about Beyonce never taming Sasha Fierce, then why should she hold back Eboni Dream.

RB cut through Naja's thoughts by planting kisses on her fluttering belly. Arousal grew deep between her thighs. Naja pulled away and turned around to put some distance between them.

Before she could take two steps, Eboni decided Naja could waver all she wanted, but she would have fun with RB these last couple of days. Once they were back in Los Angeles, she would allow the good old doctor to take the wheel back.

Eboni sat on RB's lap. His hand massaged her melon-shaped breast, causing an involuntary shiver to coast over her body. His hands quickly journeyed down to her thighs. He gently kneaded her toned thighs.

She laid her back against his chest. RB kissed and gently bit her on the shoulder. She tilted her head slightly. He trailed kisses along her neck until he reached her earlobe, capturing the warm flesh between his lips.

A high-pitched moan worked its way up her throat when the heel of his hand ground against her clit right before he pulled her panties to the side, dipping a finger inside of her warm canal. Her only response was a sharp intake of breath. The clitoral pressure accompanied by his finger and yoni egg inside her vagina triggered neurons to combust in the pleasure area of her brain.

He pinched her blueberry nipples between his index finger and thumb and rolled it back and forth like a marble. He gently squeezed and tugged on her nipples as if he were trying to retrieve its nectar. A deep throaty moan escaped her lips when his fingertip scraped the yoni egg.

He released her from his grip and spun her around. The puzzling look etched on his face revealed her need for explanation. He steadied his gaze upon her, slurping her juices off his fingers as she struggled to speak.

RB couldn't wait to slide inside of Eboni's warmth once she explained the benefits of her jade quartz yoni eggs.

His eyes roved over her body. "Dance for me, Princess."

Eboni moaned in excitement before advising RB to instruct Dumais to keep Sir company for a while at his villa.

When RB walked back into the room, Eboni lay in the middle of the bed with a fruit basket.

"Thank you for my fruit and wine baskets." He nodded, never taking his eyes off her naked body.

She gestured for him to take a seat in the chair she had placed in front of her bed. The cigars and cognac she had Dumais retrieve were sitting on a table next to the chair.

"How did you know I like cigars?" Before she could answer, he waved his hand between them. "I forgot you know everything about me already."

"I don't know your inner thoughts or desires."

"I am willing to tell them to you." He hunched his shoulders as he clipped the tip of the cigar. "But how would that benefit me? You need to earn them."

"I see," she hummed. "For each dark secret you reveal, I will masturbate using whatever fruit you hold up in your basket. The catch is it must be in my basket as well."

"If it's not in your basket?"

"Then you have to reveal a secret only you and God share. Then you can toss me your fruits, and I will use it."

"How long are we going to play?"

"Until we run out of fruit or secrets," she revealed.

Chapter 18

Sir's annoyance for Uncle Lou sprouted with each inquiry about lil doc's true intentions. Sir restrained himself from marching onto the deck, asserting his precious doc was not a gold digger, nor was she trying to stage a coup for a hefty payday.

"All the women sign an NDA," Lou bellowed.

"Well, not this one. Frankly, Lou, I'm sick of telling you she is different. I respect you and see you as more than an employee of mine. You are my uncle in my heart, but respectfully speaking, this is my life. She would ruin her medical career trying to ruin me. Which I don't think she would do to herself or me."

"Boy, is the pussy that good?"

Sir's nostrils flared. He was not ready to hear RB talk about his lil doc sexually.

"I think so, but I don't know for sure. We haven't had sex yet."

Sir smiled. He was proud of lil doc. "Make that knucklehead work for your treasure," he mumbled.

"Well, before you do, I am going to talk to her about signing this NDA."

"Dammit, Lou! Leave it alone, go back to Raven's villa or Atlanta." RB hunched his shoulders. "I don't care, but leave Eboni and me alone."

Lou's eyes bucked. RB had never been disrespectful to him.

Sir felt it was time for him to spend some time with Lou and interrupt the conversation before it escalated.

RB eyed Sir and Uncle Lou as they whispered.

"RB, if you don't need anything else, we are going to go out for a while."

RB's eyes thanked Sir. He smiled and nodded at RB -- no words were needed.

Shortly after they left, RB heard a knock on the door. What did they forget, he thought as he trekked towards the door?

The words trapped in his throat prevented him from greeting the ebony beauty standing before him. He couldn't help but notice Eboni was standing as tall as him. His eyes trailed her body until they reached the six-inch heels gracing her feet.

"Your butler kidnapped mine. I figured since we're both alone, we might as well keep each other company."

He nodded, still unable to speak. He stepped aside, and Eboni sauntered in.

"Do you mind if I take off my coat?"

"Sure." Just as he found his voice, it was gone again when he saw the sheer bodysuit caressing her body. His manhood fought his zipper when he noticed her dark chocolate blueberry nipples pressing against the sheer fabric of her outfit. He was too afraid the lion in him would pounce if he glanced down, and the bottom was nude like the top.

RB mumbled in her ear, "Tell me what your body needs."

She eased back and stared into his eyes. "I'm the sex doctor, not you. So, tell me what your body needs."

She unbuckled his shorts and slid them down, then his underwear. She wasn't surprised to find his penis was already standing at attention.

She guided him to the first room she spotted. She noticed a stack of pillows on the floor.

"Princess, this is the movie room. Let's take this to the bedroom."

She shushed him, pushing him down onto the pillows.

He went to protest but hesitated when she gently rolled his delicate jewels in her hand as if they were stress balls.

RB always instructed women to concentrate on the tip of his penis. He was not the type of man who marveled in testicle stimulation until now. He could feel his eyes rolling backward.

Eboni pulled a bottle of oil from the basket she had brought over. RB moaned as she poured oil on his stomach muscles.

"I'm a tough act to follow," he warned her.

"I'm a doctor. I know every pleasure spot on your body." A low roar escaped his gut. "Yesterday, you agreed this was my show, and you would try whatever I wanted to do once, remember?"

RB was unsure what he had agreed to, but right now, he didn't care.

Her lips made their way down to his manhood. His grunts let her know it was ok to proceed.

She gaped at his penis and poked it with the tip of her tongue to gain its attention. "This massage is for relaxation, not for you to achieve an orgasm. You hear me, killer."

RB chuckled at her folly. Shit, he and his penis considered an orgasm to be relaxing.

She rained warm oil on the tip of his hardness; a harsh roar escaped his throat. She traced circles around the base of his penis with the end of her tongue.

His brow tightened in frustration, thinking she would tease him the way he had done her.

He kept thinking all she had to do was slide his shaft into her warm mouth, and he would be satisfied. She captured one of his jewels between her forefinger and middle finger and rolled her wrist in a circular motion. He was stunned when a grunt escaped his throat.

She raked her fingernails across his muscular thighs. Her movements were light and gentle, but the pleasure was intense and mind-blowing. She firmly gripped her left hand around his shaft, gliding it up the backside of his rod until it reached the top, where her open palm took a spin on his mushroom tip then sailed down the front of his penis. The entire time her right hand massaged his testicles.

Soft whimpers escaped his body.

Eboni captured his hand and guided it to his penis. He hesitated. He never asked her to do his job; why was she expecting him to perform hers. Her tongue traced the tip of his penis as she guided his hand over to his penis.

He stroked his penis as she kneaded his perineum with her mouth. The sensation was mentally frightening as neurons discharged in his brain, taking his breath away. He rubbed his penis faster. She placed her hand on top of his to slow his motion.

He didn't want to slow down. He was ready to explode, but he had promised this was her show, so whatever Eboni wanted to do, he vowed to try it once. His muscles tensed when she eased his legs up to his chest and captured his testicles in her mouth. RB could not believe she had his legs up like a female.

He was a puma who controlled everything between the sheets. He trusted Doc, but it was difficult relinquishing his power.

She rolled his testes gently in her mouth like jawbreakers. He quivered with excitement and decided to relax and allow her mouth to make love to him. He tapped his feet on her shoulders, clenching her outfit each time he flexed his toes. Her right hand eased over his, and she shoved his hand away from his penis. Before he could protest, she replaced it with her warm mouth.

Lifting on his elbows, a jolt of energy hit him as the doorways of their souls connected. He hungrily watched as her hands and mouth took turns on his penis. This was the sexiest vision he had ever witnessed.

He gripped the pillows. His backside tightened when Eboni's tongue caressed the raphe of his penis. Her tongue followed the line down until it met the soft tissue of his bottom. His entire body went rigid.

A couple more strokes and ecstasy would have been his to claim. He didn't know how to justify his manhood if he liked the way her tongue felt on his backside.

Sensing his uneasiness Eboni pulled away and sat between his legs, blowing on his damp flesh.

"Baby, do not allow the fire to burn out," RB grumbled.

She smiled mischievously. "If it does, I will ignite it again. I will make up for the discomfort I caused you." He shook his head, trying to pretend as if he was not bothered by her anal stimulation.

Eboni was a woman of her word. She lit him on fire and cooled him down three times before an intense orgasm wracked his body, incapacitating him.

Chapter 19

To evade everyone, RB and Eboni intended to explore the island all day. On the way out the door, he asked Sir if he could stay at Eboni's villa and keep Uncle Lou out of his hair. Sir assured him the estate would be empty when they returned and thanked him for making lil doc smile. RB had to chuckle because he had Sir calling Eboni "Doc" as well.

RB was ready to cancel all the excursions he had planned for the day when Eboni walked out in a dark blue fishnet mesh with a hooded cover-up dress accompanied by bikini bottoms and rose petal pasties covering her nipples. He caught his bottom lip between his teeth and slowly sucked it before he released it.

"Princess, I planned on us going snorkeling. Will those pasties hold up? I can't have you driving the other men crazy. I'm a lion, and I will protect what's mine." He marveled at his own words. He felt as if she belonged to him, but did she feel the same way?

"I have a bikini in the bag. I will put it under the dress and take these off."

"Can you wear the pasties and those bottoms tonight? Shit, I don't want you wasting a good outfit," he joshed.

While Eboni changed, RB wondered if she slept with all her clients. He quickly banished those thoughts from his mind. RB couldn't imagine her sharing her body with multiple men in the name of therapy. Wishfully, he prayed he was the only client lucky enough to have slept with the doc.

Eboni stood in the door admiring RB's body as he stood on the sundeck gazing out at the ocean. Thoughts of using his muscular shoulder to perform a seesaw motion on his dick invaded her mind. She had to admit it was more than sex. She craved to know everything about his present, past, and future.

She sighed in frustration. When she and Lexi chatted about letting her guards down, Eboni reasoned, whom would she be hurting if she allowed this man to spoil her for a couple of days? She figured she might even appreciate sex with a man that wasn't Dakari. Eboni wondered how a three-day fling turned into her catching feelings for the handsome man. This must be lust she felt because love took longer.

She quickly searched her mind for an article or study on love. She recalled reading a Harvard study about love and science dating. She snapped her finger and then smiled as she grasped this was merely her neurotransmitter being stimulated in the pleasure centers of her brain, which added a dash of obsession — and instigated the crazy, pleasing, stupefied, urgent love of infatuation. Realistically it's not like either one of them could fall in love in four days because that goes against the laws of physics and science.

She sighed heavily. Once they returned to California, RB would be a distant memory because she would be too inundated to entertain him anymore, and he would find another woman to proposition for sex. At least her parents would be satisfied. Her father would be happy she spent some time with his top suitor, and her mother would be delighted she didn't agree to be with a man that wasn't Dakari.

When they arrived back at RB's place, he had decided he would take control of the bedroom and blow her mind. They had engaged in days of foreplay. He was ready to feel her insides squeezing the life out of his penis.

When Eboni walked out in new pasties and a red thong, visions of thrusting her into the ceiling invaded his mind. He requested she dance for him. She agreed if she could give him a command next. He had to laugh at her haggling skills and the fact that he asked for a dance, and she commanded him. Instead of calling her doc, he needed to call her drill sergeant.

RB ran his tongue over his top lip. Eboni's dance moves were better than any stripper he had ever seen. He wished he could see her moves on the dance pole. After three songs, she insisted it was her turn to command.

Eboni enjoyed the foreplay because most men disregarded stimulation if they thought the woman was already wet. They assume the objective of arousal is to get a woman moist or a man hard. To Eboni, it was about sensuality and demonstrating you would take the time to satisfy your mate no matter how long it took.

Right now, she was ready for the foreplay to end and the sexing to begin.

She laid him flat on the floor. Once again, they never made it to the bed. She gripped his penis firmly with her left hand guiding his shaft to the entry of her warm yoni.

"Yes, baby, I am ready." RB's hands eased over her nipples. Lifting her brow in displeasure, she slapped his hand away.

RB scowled.

"You are not allowed to touch me until I allow you to." He pushed his bottom lip forward.

Is he pouting? she thought.

"I need to caress you."

She contracted her muscles around his shaft in a death grip. His penis thumped, so naturally, he propelled his hips upward. She wagged a finger in his face. Every time he tried to thrust upward, she lifted off his manhood.

The more dominating her stance, the stiffer his shaft strengthened.

He tried to help her balance on her feet, and she slapped his hand away and lifted off his penis. He relaxed as she raked her fingernails across his chest, applying kisses to any scratches she made.

She eased back down, and he gripped her hip. RB pleaded when she started easing off him again. He tucked his hands behind his head. He was confused by her passive-aggressive behavior. She blatantly ignored any request he made.

She smiled.

The sight of her resting all her weight on the tips of her toes as she rode the head of his penis drove him insane. RB grunted and moaned as she rode his penis like an elevator.

Eboni was pleased when all she could see were the whites of his eyeballs. She clutched the tip of his penis with the entry of her vagina for a count of fifteen before sliding down. Doc didn't stop until her ass kissed his thighs. She contracted her muscles as she slid back up to the tips of her toes for another count of fifteen.

Eboni whispered in his ear, "I hope you know Kama Sutra." Before he could answer, she had pulled his knees up until his feet rested flat against the floor, then she mounted him in a reverse cowgirl position.

"Goddammit," he muttered when she lifted her feet off the floor and clenched her ankles, seesawing on his penis. Eboni was everything he needed and deserved. He dared to say she was the female version of himself because she was an educated doctor in the streets with animal instincts in the bedroom.

The stimulation to her g-spot forced her to moan in pleasure. "Yes, RB," she cried, half out of breath. Strobes of rainbows danced around her head, triggering her to become unsteady.

RB gripped her by the calves, and when she didn't protest, he pulled her tightly closed legs up and down. Her gorgeous dark chocolate legs in the air drove him insane. His toes lifted off the floor, and he could feel an eruption nearby.

His mouth flew open when Eboni wiggled out of his grasp and placed her hands on his knees. She elevated her yoni up and down on his shaft. He cupped her ample backside and massaged the back of her thighs.

She pushed him off her, turned around, and dropped to her knees, snatching the condom off, yanking his arms simultaneously until he was on his knees in front of her.

Enthralled by her skills of seduction, he hardly noticed her aggressiveness.

His fingers enmeshed in her hair as animalistic grunts escaped his body. A rainbow of strobing lights flashed in his head as she sucked him into a vortex of pleasure. The sweet scent of lavender vanilla engulfed him. She plunged his entire shaft down her throat and didn't stop until it kissed her tonsils and played tetherball.

"Oh shit, Dr. Dream. What are you doing to me?"

His moans intensified as her tongue and hand took turns stroking his penis. She could sense he could not hold back any longer. She replaced her hand with his and leaned back on her left hand while polishing her pearl with her right thumb. Eboni's moans ignited RB's body.

His hand torpedoed up and down his shaft until he tied a pearl necklace around her neck. The earth spun rapidly on its axle as she jumped off the cliff of pure ecstasy, joining RB.

Chapter 20

The intensity of completeness RB felt in Eboni's presence was a pleasurable surprise. His heart knew he could trust her. He genuinely wanted to give this therapy stuff a try. He wouldn't stop spilling his secrets, feelings, and fears until his heart was empty and light. He even considered gifting Eboni with his heart once the process was complete.

Eboni extended her neck and kissed RB on the tip of his nose. He returned her affection by placing a kiss on the lovable hollow behind her ear.

"I only have one other man to compare you to, but this was amazing."

Contrary to her aggressive and brash bedroom mannerisms, RB was her second lover. She felt compelled to inform him of this naked truth. Eboni's confession astounded RB. She wheeled the level of skillset and control of a woman who had mastered the art of sex and seduction. He wouldn't have judged her if she revealed her sex partner number. How could he? He had plenty of women in his bed. Most of them were nameless bodies of pleasure. However, the fact that he was her second lover made his breath hitch in his throat. In his book, her status equated to that of a virgin.

"Why did you come to this island?" RB questioned.

Eboni reasoned she shouldn't confess she had been in a committed relationship since childhood which ended with her ex cheating three weeks ago.

"You asked me to be the therapist," she playfully spat, pecking the dimple in his chin. "Why do you need a sex therapist?"

"You know I am not a perfect man, but I've done my best." He sighed. Eboni was a bit confused by his statement. "Dr. Norwalk seems to think I don't love or respect Rave because she is always interceding for me with women."

A tiny sliver in Eboni needed to know more, but the fear of him turning out to be exactly like her father terrified her. It wasn't the sex that made her admire him. It was their day of adventure, from snorkeling to the clear water kayak tour.

She could still feel his muscular frame pressed against her body as they jet skied. She kissed and memorized every intricate tattoo engraved on his back. She admired how his eyes stayed glued on her. She could barely describe the intensity she felt when RB assured the tour guide, he was not missing a magnificent view and nestled his head deeper into the curve of her neck.

The entire boat ride, he repeatedly kissed the hollow void behind her ear and the angle of her collarbone. The banter they shared during their three-hour scavenger hunt reminded her of being carefree in junior high school. Once she reached high school, everything she engaged in was to get her closer to becoming a doctor.

"Does your silence mean you agree?"

"No," she replied, "tell me about the last two times your sister mediated on your behalf."

RB swallowed the lump in his throat. He reminded Eboni once again that he was not perfect. He described the incident with the young lady before they left for this trip but purposely left out the timeline.

He described another incident that sounded similar in nature, except the woman was different. He closed by reminding Eboni he was not married, so he had safe fun. He assured her he would spend all his time protecting his wife's crown if he were married. His homeboy, Malik, had told him this is what he would do for his wife. He agreed with Malik but downplayed it at the time.

His last statement eased Eboni's mind a bit. She understood that unless you were a virgin, like Miya, everyone had a past consisting of past lovers.

"I can see why she thinks you don't respect your sister, but I am on the fence concerning the love part."

It stung to hear Eboni's words, but he received them. He figured if he revealed the dynamics of their relationship, she would understand him better.

Eboni could sense he needed to get some things off his chest.

"What is your take on therapy?"

"I am not big on allowing someone to examine the raw parts of me or being judged by them," he honestly admitted.

"Mental health is a critical issue in the Black community, and it is not discussed enough. It takes a village to assist during therapy. A colleague of mine did a dissertation about sex being effective therapy. He hypothesized that most people allowed their guards to drop during sexual encounters to bond with their mates. Stating treatment could be beneficial if couples assisted each other in an intimate setting like ours."

RB thought about divulging his earlier thoughts. Instead, he stroked his chin in thought.

"For each suppressed emotion you share, I will replace it with a joyous feeling," Eboni proposed.

"This shit sounds crazy," he noted. "How will my dick get hard if I am dredging up painful thoughts?"

"You don't need to worry about that. Tap into that pain, and then I will replace that pain with mounds of joy. You are going to take charge of your healing."

Before she could say another word, he bellowed, "I do not know what it feels like to be in a committed relationship. I never slept with the same woman twice, so you should feel blessed."

She cuts a sharp glance at him. "Those are confessions, not emotions."

"I have a fear of something bad happening to my baby sister and me not being there again to protect her the same way I failed to protect my mom."

She kissed the whites of his knuckles that had clinched the sheets. RB could feel love soaring from her lips into his body, but it still hurt. He knew there was no way she could genuinely kiss away the pain. She laid his hand on her bare chest and held it there. It felt as if her heart opened the gate of his misery.

"Feel my heart with your pain, and I will give it back in love."

"My father dipped on my mother once my sister was born. He was not prepared to take care of four when he only agreed to a family of three. His actions forced me to become the man of the house. One evening I was supposed to meet my mother at her bus stop, but I was out with my girlfriend. I just wanted to be a kid for a night."

He dropped his head in shame as weakness flowed from his eyes. He tried to look away and erase his tears.

"Your masculinity does not diminish when you cry. That's a sign of a true King. It's hard being vulnerable. That's a sign of true strength."

RB nodded but was too ashamed to look at her.

Eboni lifted his head until their eyes greeted. She kissed his tears and licked them away. "Bitter and painful," she said, caressing her top lip with her tongue.

He nodded and dropped his head in embarrassment.

She lifted his head by his chin then forced her tongue into his mouth. Their tongues tussled. RB stopped fighting once the sweet nectar of melon saturated his mouth. He sucked all the delectable sap from her tongue. His mind conceded to the possibility that she could take his pain and replace it with happiness.

Eboni eased back when he continued his story. He confessed that a stray bullet intended for another passenger getting off the bus killed his mother. His tuff demeanor crumbled when he revealed Rave was taken by social services when the police came to notify them about their mother's demise. He swore he would have never left Rave in a situation where she would be mistreated, but he was a kid himself. He didn't know what to do.

Eboni wrapped RB in a secure embrace after he shared that his middle school crush died from lupus. She was stunned that so much guilt plagued his soul. He was blaming himself for things only God had control over, not him.

She advised him to seek God's love to fill all the empty spots he drained of pain. She recited Psalms 23 with RB.

Sadness etched across his face when Eboni told RB she agreed with Dr. Norwalk. He owed Rave an apology. It was a hard pill for him to swallow when she said, "Are you charging Rave for taking care of her?"

He assured her he would never. However, to the blind eye, it seemed that way. She helped RB view his situation from a unique perspective, but not once did she cast judgment upon him.

He couldn't believe the gut-screeching laugh that escaped his body when she said, "If you are bad enough to bed them, then be brave enough to wake them up and toss them nasty gyals out." He chuckled at her, imitating his Jamaican accent that only surfaced when he was angry or during sex.

"Now I see why you were mad when I slipped out while you were sleeping. Now you know how all those women felt. Karma was biting you in the ass."

RB flipped Eboni over on her stomach. "You mean this round chocolate Godiva ass?" he asked, applying gentle bites to her butt. She laughed until she snorted. To him, that was the sweetest sound he had ever witnessed.

That night RB cradled Eboni tightly with his right arm while his left hand remained plastered over her vagina. They slept in this position until RB heard knocking at the front door.

Chapter 21

RB elongated his frame nervously, anticipating the arrival of his ebony princess. The smell of the salty seawater faded to the tropical aroma of pineapples, mango, apricots, melons, guava, and fresh flowers. Pride swelled his chest as he revered his arduous work. RB had turned this secluded island into a majestic oasis.

Sir admired RB's hard work as he cut fruit and decorated the tent. He was stunned when the young man insisted he needed to retrieve the lobsters from the lobster traps in the sea. The lobsters sold in the fish markets were fresh, but Sir had reiterated this fact to RB last night.

RB darted around the tent, rearranging flowers. Sir halted RB's step when he started speaking. "Son, you can get dressed. I can finish getting this together. Lil doc will be here in two hours."

RB graciously declined his offer. Eboni's statement on the yacht invaded his mind the second he asked Sir to plan this romantic dinner on an isolated island. Before Sir could walk away, RB changed his mind. Lou teased RB about searching for instructions on preparing and decorating a romantic meal.

RB could hear the helicopter whirring overhead. He raced to straighten his tie, dashing from the tent to greet his princess.

The white silk fabric on the tent's canopy flapped as it fought the high winds of the helicopter propellers.

The crumbly soil nestled under Eboni's stilettos as she cleared the helicopter. A waft of air caused her long tresses to drift in the breeze.

RB filled his lungs with salty air and courage. The soothing swish of the surf, the waves crashing into the rocks, and the light R&B tunes vanished under RB's thunderous heartbeat.

Her silken mud oak skin caught the rays of the sun on her shoulder and sparkled. He didn't know if she would describe her complexion as mud oak.

To RB, mud signified viscosity, strength, intensity, and earth. This soil had been utilized as a natural medicine for centuries. Drawing out impurities, healing inflammations, and relaxing sore muscles and joints.

Oak is exceptionally durable, looks good in all-natural finishes, and its grain pattern is unique.

How could he not see mud oak when he looked upon Eboni's beauty? She was unique. She had drawn out his deepest impurities, relaxed his heart muscles, and empowered him to begin the healing process of his body, mind, and soul. When his cold, hungry eyes peered through her buoyant eyes, he saw a better version of himself with endless possibilities — the walls which caged him in were demolished.

When he went running this morning, it was to talk to God and his mother. He pleaded for his mother to forgive him, and he asked God to help him forgive himself.

He apologized to his heavenly father for abusing the most precious gift God has ever bestowed upon man, the woman.

When the clouds cleared and a beam of sunlight washed over his body, cleansing his soul, he grasped he was a brand-new man, and his old antics had to perish. After his run, he called Malik, admitting he was falling for the infiltrator implanted in his life.

Malik joked about meeting his future sister-in-law. RB smiled each time Malik called Eboni Mrs. Brooks. Flashes of her naked body and her hypnotic almond-shaped eyes and beatific smile evaporated all his apprehensions and fears. Sheer happiness filled his heart each time she giggled.

RB lived in the moment of possibilities as Malik dreamed aloud for him. However, in his heart, he knew he didn't have the time to cultivate a relationship. Hell, he didn't even know where she lived.

He refused to allow his heart to believe he could maintain a long-distance relationship if she resided in Florida as Dr. Norwalk. Doubt started to creep in his mind, and he wondered if she would be jealous of the groupies or leave him once she learned of his reputation in the streets of Atlanta.

RB bowed his head and mimicked the prayer Malik had said earlier that day. When his eyes flung upward and landed on Eboni, an endearing smile graced his face.

If Eboni was the woman God created specifically for him as Malik believed, then telling her all the things he had done in his past would not run her away; instead, she would admire his honesty.

The peach silk dress he selected caressed her curves, pulling him away from his thoughts.

His mouth flung open. Her stunning beauty proved she looked good in all-natural elements. Her beauty, splendor, and heart had him suspended between heaven and earth.

RB threw caution to the wind preferring to live inside the moment and cherish the memory for the rest of his life.

RB held his hands out, and Eboni placed her petite fingers inside of his massive palms. He pulled her in and pressed a kiss to the side of her head, afraid to mess up her make-up.

Eboni moaned as her body melted into RB's. Her mouth crashed onto his. He parted his lips, allowing her tongue to explore his mouth. She hummed against his lips.

RB could feel his manhood rising. He eased back to sever their embrace.

Eboni whimpered then closed the gap between her and RB.

She rammed her tongue into his mouth, taking over the kiss, and he didn't resist. He enjoyed the way she dominated him. She delved deeper, tasting the tantalizing sweetness of the pineapple lingering on his tongue. The nectar saturated her taste buds, and she moaned in his mouth.

A warm, tingly spark of desire blossomed between her legs as if there was a direct link from there to her mouth. She appraised his athletic physique. Prince, I want you right now," she moaned, causing a flood of wetness between her thighs.

Behind the large tent were two medium-sized tents. One was a private dressing room decorated with pillows and clothes for them both depending on how long they stayed out there. The other tent was a mini kitchen with enough food to feed three families.

Eboni kissed his earlobe. "You can send all these people home, then we go back to one of those tents and make love."

He pulled away; her chest heaved as he caressed her cheek.

"Princess, we have all night. I want you. I mean, I want you." Their gazes drank each other up for several minutes before his eyes journeyed below his waist.

Eboni giggled. Her angelic voice filled his heart. It was a sound he could hear for the rest of his life.

She ran her fingers down his bulging chest, hoping his alluring eyes would urge her further. "Allow your man to wine and dine you first. "Disappointment floated over her body, and her bottom lip slipped outward.

"None of that," he said, "I can't have my woman looking sad when all of this is for you."

Eboni perked up when she realized he had called himself her man and her his woman.

"You have been my therapist, so allow me to be yours tonight. I want to know what you fear so I can chase them all away. I want to know your dreams so I can make them all come true."

Eboni relaxed and absorbed the beauty encircling her. Vibrant and fragrant flowers decorated the tables. Floral arrangements adorned the four corners of the tent in pure white oversized vases, and purple orchids outlined the perimeter. Eboni noticed a rock iguana admiring the beauty surrounding them.

"Prince, a little bird told me you did all of this yourself."

The corners of his mouth curled so high that his eyes tightened into slits. "Damn, this man is sexy," Eboni huffed under her breath.

Eboni couldn't stop swooning at the intricate details.

RB took her hand and placed kisses on it. "Princess, I had to hire servers so that I can enjoy you. I hope that is all right?"

Eboni nodded.

A jolt surged through her body, producing more moisture between her thighs. She didn't know how much longer she could hold out. RB's debonair demeanor was seducing her.

Eboni was ready to explore his naked body.

She smiled as she observed his attire. Usually, he was in shorts. Yesterday he wore a linen pantsuit that clung to his muscular frame. Eboni blinked twice.

The man knew how to wear a suit was all she thought, drinking RB's statuesque physique as he modeled his black and grey pinstripe suit.

She noticed his lips tremble when she stepped closer, pressing her engorged nipples against his firm chest.

RB spun her around, engulfing her in his embrace. She could feel his manhood pressing against her butt. He sang lyrics of love in her ear, and he planted kisses on her neck. Eboni's heart lurched, and butterflies stormed in her belly when he lifted her off her feet and twirled her in the air.

She tossed her head back, laughing and snorting as the wind whipped through her tresses.

Her laughter was music to his ears, and her snort halted his heart.

RB thought he was infatuated with Eboni at that moment; his heart forewarned him to the possibility that this was so much more.

His eyes squinted, causing his nose to wrinkle at the prospect of him declaring the three words he swore he would never say to any woman.

Chapter 22

Eboni shifted in the bed, searching for RB's warm body. Disappointment drifted over her body as she thought about him not lying next to her. They were both leaving on Tuesday. Last night RB asked Eboni her views on marriage and if she foresaw herself being his wife one day.

If he had proposed last night, she would have said yes. Not to win the bet that she and her BAE's made one night in college, wagering which BAE would get married first. She laughed, thinking about how she insisted she and Dakari would be married first since they had been together since they were toddlers.

She hoped her parents and the BAE's would understand she was caught between heaven and earth when she decided.

The BAE's would think she married him to win the bet. Her father would be disappointed he wasn't present but would bounce back from disappointment because she picked his suitor. Eboni paused as she rubbed her head. Her poor mother would be disappointed she didn't marry Dakari.

The three days she and RB spent together were more profound than her and Dakari's years together. Once RB let down his guard, he was a giant marshmallow. Nobody in her life made her laugh the way RB did.

He accepted every challenge she threw his way with a smile. She admired the love that sparkled in his eyes each time he mentioned his sister, Rave. Most kids would not step up at eighteen and take responsibility for their siblings.

The butterflies she felt last night were present. She gripped RB's pillow and inhaled the mahogany teakwood scent. Her heart lurched again as a calm fell over her body. The butterflies, sweaty palms, and schoolgirl behavior meant one thing, she thought. She had fallen in love with Tata's choice for her.

Eboni clutched her eyes tight, trying to envision what her life would be like with RB. People in everyday business work a maximum of ten hours a day. She would be working and studying non-stop. Yet, in her heart, she knew she didn't have the fortitude to cultivate a relationship. As much as her heart desired RB, it aimed to become a pediatric oncologist more.

Each scenario that ran through her mind ended with RB cheating because she didn't prioritize the time where he was concerned.

Her heart wasn't ready to leave this fantasy behind right now — all she required was five more days with him. The jet was scheduled to arrive midday Tuesday.

Eboni contemplated calling her father and extending her time. She had two weeks before she had to report to the hospital. Her bottom lip eased forward because she didn't know RB's schedule or if he could take five more days off.

The notion of no more love sessions like the one she experienced on the secluded beach in their tent that spilled over to the ocean and concluded between RB's warm sheets plagued her thoughts.

She groaned heavily, pondering if RB went running, contemplating the same scenarios as her. Drained from last night and overthinking, Eboni decided to go back to sleep.

Her eyes fluttered close then shot back open when she heard RB and a woman's voice trailing through the walls. Eboni wanted to pull strands of her hair out as Tata's voice invaded her thoughts, pushing her over the edge.

"Yes, he is just like you, Tata," she mumbled.

Eboni eased out of bed, crept to the bedroom's entry, and quickly peeked around the corner. She hoped to spot a caterer setting up breakfast. She would even settle for Sir and RB hosting a woman.

"Please let it be a maid. It's a maid," Eboni reassured her heart.

She watched intently as RB's faint voice warned the woman at the door to lower her voice.

She could not see the woman, only her ivory hand clutching the door. Eboni leaned farther into the hallway.

"Look, I can't visit with you this morning, nor can you come in."

Eboni leaned in closer to listen to the woman's reply. Her heart stopped beating, a knot curled in her throat when RB promised the lady he would come by after he finished his errands.

She couldn't believe he referred to her as an errand. Eboni wondered if he was recruiting another woman to warm her spot, or was she keeping the ivory woman's spot warm?

Eboni's eyes bucked as she clutched her chest, attempting to diagnose the crushing feeling in her chest.

Chapter 23

Plopping on the bed, Naja continued to process what she heard at RB's villa. She couldn't grasp what had changed as they slept. What would make RB push her away to be with another woman? For a second, she thought her fears were manifesting this ruse until RB told her they would meet up later for dinner because he had planned a pamper-me-pretty day for her.

The words 'day for her' rubbed her uneasily. What about him? What would he be doing in her absence?

She tried to catch her mind before journeying to a place of jealousy, wondering if he would spend the day wining and dining the ivory woman from the front door.

Her heart dropped to her ankles at the thought of RB making love to another woman. She hated acting like her mother, shying away from the altercation, fearing the truth. Why didn't she ask about the woman at the door, she thought?

With RB, Eboni knew she would have a partner in her life, or was she imagining these things because the sex was astonishing, and the conversation was fantastic. She surprised herself last night when she blossomed for RB, revealing her petals of truth.

Even with him admitting he had indulged in women for his pleasure and never considered their feelings. Eboni didn't want to defend these women, but they were grown, and RB was honest from the time they spoke to him, but she wondered if his player days were indeed in the past.

He assured her that part of him died the moment he kissed her. Her heart fluttered when he declared his vision had changed, tunneling directly upon her.

In turn, she disclosed her fear of falling in love. Declaring she was terrified of becoming her mother. When RB asked her to explain, she revealed her father cheated on her mother, and her mother stayed because she loved him more than she loved herself.

RB pulled her into his arms planting kisses on her head and face before assuring her he would never take advantage of her love. She felt comfortable in his arms and could feel the sincerity in his voice.

RB kissed her earlobe and whispered, "If you were my wife, I would never cheat on you. Marriage is a big commitment. I would never taint a union blessed by God."

He made it so easy for her to trust in all the lies he whispered in her ears.

Last night as she and RB shared secrets, Eboni had left the building at some point, and Naja was the one driving; while at the wheel, she had fallen in love with RB.

She wondered if there was a difference between being in love with someone and loving them? She didn't think she could love anyone but Dakari.

She couldn't remember the article or study she read about kids needing to feel their mother's love and comfort when hurt, confused, or in pain, and right now, she needed her mother.

Naja picked up the phone to call her mother.

Ignoring her mother's rants about Dakari, she allowed her mother's soothing voice to stroke her confused mind.

Naja's body stiffened at the question. "Is RB just like your father?"

"Muma, I can't have this conversation with you right now. I'm not in the mood to sugarcoat anything or play dumb."

"Princess, you can always tell me anything. I am used to your candid responses."

"Muma, I hold back so much because I don't want to hurt you." Naja let out an exasperated sigh. "My greatest fear is ending up with a man similar to Tata."

"Why, Princess? Your daadi is a good man. He takes loving care of the family."

Naja closed her eyes, playing her response in her head. Everyone knew, including the BAE's, that her father was a bit of a lady's man, and her mother tolerated his antics in the name of love. Over the years, Naja observed her mother weeping on many occasions because another woman called their home or cornered her mother in a boutique, claiming her father was her lover.

Her mother never wavered in the presence of these women, but late at night, she could hear her mother crying in the bathroom or weeping to her father, pleading for him to stop embarrassing her in the community.

"He is a good father but a bad husband. I've heard the cries over the years, exhibiting ignorance to ease your fears."

Her mother had done a fantastic job convincing herself that her father was a great husband to her and assuming Naja was clueless to her surroundings.

"Why do men cheat, Muma?"

"Honestly, Princess, I wish I knew."

Naja recalled asking her mother this same question after Dakari slapped her across the face with the veracity of her father. Naja cried for hours after discovering her daadi had spawned three sons after her, and everyone knew except her.

Dakari convinced her the truths he shared were to strengthen her resolve, freeing her from the dark web of lies her family had spun around her.

Tears rolled down her cheeks as she remembered her mother's simple response, "That's what men do."

She reminded her mother that Dakari's father was not a cheater.

Naja was speechless when her mother divulged his father was no better than any other man. Her muma admitted Dakari's father had an estranged family across town, and they had three kids together, and he had another baby on the way by a young gyal.

Despite the reasons Dakari provided Naja with sharing the truth, she never washed his face with his father's dirty laundry to win an argument or debate. Tarnishing his father in his eyes wasn't love to her.

She rationalized that true love shouldn't hurt or tear someone down. It should uplift them.

"Princess, are you okay?" her mother asked, yanking her back to the present.

Playing oblivious to protect her loved ones was destroying her mentality towards love.

"Muma, studies have suggested we tend to choose romantic partners who are similar to our opposite-sex parents. The study went on to reveal that women don't necessarily choose to date men like their fathers. These men are merely familiar to her because it's the first type of man she learned to love. She is profoundly familiar with his temperament, actions, and presence."

"OK," was her only response.

"I don't want to love a man who can father three children outside of our marriage like daadi."

"Five," her mother replied. Naja could hear the crackling pain in her tone.

"Why do you stay?"

"He is a good provider, protector, and he loves me. Where would I go? How would I support myself? I have been with daadi since I was a young gyal. He is all I know, and I love him."

Naja rolled her eyes. "Does love prevail over pride and self-esteem?"

"I'm not a weak woman, Naja."

Naja remained silent. Over the years, she struggled to understand her mother, fighting tooth and nail not to become her or fall in love with a clone of her father.

"I left when you were a baby and went to Turks and Caicos to visit my godfather. I couldn't find the motivation to breathe without your father. I was lost. He punished me with silence. When he finally came to the island to retrieve me, I could live again."

Her mother cleared her throat. She could tell she was crying. "Forgiving him opened up a new door. He stopped covering his tracks after he cheated. I assumed he figured there was no need to lie since I knew the truth about his philandering ways. My kids and my 'usband are my life support. Without you guys, I would die."

Naja didn't know what to say. She never imagined loving a man like her father, but here she was, struggling to breathe without RB. A man she'd only known for a fleeting time.

How could she judge her mother?

Why did God make the bond of love so intense?

"Regardless of what studies show, Naja, follow your heart. Life is more than percentages and facts."

"But..."

"No, buts. The enemy will manifest your deepest fears to block your blessings. Tata's suitor may not be a cheater. Maybe your fear of becoming your dreadful parents is making you foresee things that are not there."

"Muma, that's Lexi. Can I call you later?" She hated fibbing to her mother, but she couldn't handle this conversation anymore. "Before we hang up, please know I don't think you and Tata are horrible parents."

"You are misinterpreting Dakari's action as well; I promise you. They both may have some of your father's similarities. It could be his protectiveness, kind heart, or the love he has for you. It doesn't have to be his negative traits, so stop hiding behind your fears and give love a chance."

"I hear you."

"Your Muma's data confirms love is what you make it. I don't expect you to settle for things as I do. You are too strong and confident for that. I don't care what statistics say. Be the one in a billion that breaks the cycle."

Naja nodded her head in agreement, pondering if her fears were manipulating her feelings.

Chapter 24

RB's hand nervously shook as he slid the engagement ring on his pinky finger. Sir placed his hand on RB's shoulder, and a smile crept across his face.

"Romello Brooks, are you sure about this?" Uncle Lou questioned RB.

"Lou, I've always tried to prove I deserve the blessings God has given me. Sometimes I even wondered why he protected me when I failed to protect the women in my life."

Lou opened his mouth to speak, and RB placed his hand up between them. Lou halted his speech, leaning back against the glass cases.

"I was mad when Raven brought me here under misleading pretense, and I know I shouldn't have fallen in love with my doctor, but I love her, Lou. I've divulged secrets only me and God share. Then, last night, she told me her fears and how she feels comfortable in my presence. I knew she was the one."

"But..." Sir placed his hand on Lou's shoulder to silence him this time.

He wanted to know how RB felt about his lil doc. He couldn't wait to call Titus and tell him their gyal was getting ready to jump the broom.

"When I went running this morning, the thought of losing her drew tears to my eyes. Tears, Lou, tears." RB placed his right hand on Lou's shoulder and kneaded it. "You've known me since I was a child. Have you ever seen me cry?"

Lou shook his head no. Instead of trying to convince RB not to propose to Eboni, Lou pointed to a better ring in the case.

After Lou, Sir, and RB had picked the perfect engagement ring for Eboni. He was ready to get ready for tonight.

Throughout the day, he fought not to join her on her pamper-me-pretty day. It pained him being away from her all day. He knew he couldn't walk away from her tomorrow. However, Sir and Lou instructed him to stop smothering the girl. Maybe if he had surprised her earlier today, things would have gone differently.

RB knew Raven had already met Eboni, but not as his girlfriend and future wife. He couldn't propose to Eboni without his sister-daughter present. Eboni would be marrying him and Raven.

He was hesitant about inviting Dr. Norwalk. But, at this point, if Dr. Norwalk fired Eboni, that would work in his favor, then she could move to Atlanta faster and find a job there if she wanted to work, he thought.

RB sat at the table nervously, waiting for Dumais and Eboni to arrive.

Lou and Sir were already somewhere celebrating. Guaranteeing RB, he would be fine alone, affirming doc would say, 'yes.' Sir declared he could feel the love floating between them.

He told his sister to arrive twenty minutes after instructing Dumais and Eboni to come. This way, he and Eboni would have had a drink and shared a couple of kisses.

He had sent her to get her nails, toes, and hair done. The last stop was to a boutique to pick an outfit for her first unofficial engagement party. He did not doubt in his mind that Eboni would say no.

RB bounced the ring box in his hands before returning it to his pocket. It felt as if time was moving backward.

RB glanced up, and Eboni was standing in the doorway, wearing a red, tight-fitting dress. Her hair was in an updo, with thin strings of curls bouncing on her bare shoulders. His hands shook a little as he moved closer to her.

RB didn't like the forced smile plastered on Eboni's face as he approached.

"Hey, Princess. Tell your Prince who did it?"

She hunched her shoulders. This was the second time a chill filled the room in Eboni's presence; he felt the same shutter grace his spine this morning when he entered the bedroom.

He had planned to make love to Eboni as they showered, then he would tell her about the plans he had made for her. But, before he could get a word out, she insisted she needed to go to her villa to freshen up before her day alone.

He could tell she wasn't excited about spending their last day without him, but he had no plans to let this be their last day together. As far as he was concerned, this would be the first day of the rest of their lives together.

"RB, deception is the same as lying. Probably worse because you are intentionally misleading someone."

RB's eyebrows drew together, causing his forehead to wrinkle. Again, he was confused by her behavior and statement.

"Have you been completely honest with me?"

"I think we both were deceitful in the beginning," he honestly admitted. "I pretended to be cold and hid behind my arrogance. You challenged me to show you Romello. I destroyed the task."

A grin played at the corners of his mouth, but Eboni's facial expression never shifted.

RB wrapped his arms around Eboni's waist, pulling her closer.

She flicked her eyes upwards until she met RB's eyes. The intensity of the gaze triggered her body to quiver. A single tear rolled down her cheek, and he kissed it away.

He tapped his hand on the ring in his pocket. He was ready to propose, but he couldn't ask her until Raven arrived.

"Princess, you pretended to be someone else, so what. I have forgiven you, and I hope you have forgiven me. I heard you last night. I will never deliberately hurt you."

He planted kisses on her forehead; her body shuddered as warmth surged through her veins.

"I don't want any other woman except you."

He leaned in to kiss Eboni, but she wiggled from his grasp, slipping off to the bathroom.

Eboni patiently watched as the two women hugged RB. One of the girls planted kisses on his cheek. The other young lady nuzzled her head under his neck. He placed her in the same playful headlock Eboni had grown to love. Then he placed kisses on the top of her head.

RB's head nodded back, greeting the woman she had met her first night on the island at the fish fry.

Eboni gasped for air when the woman approached RB. He released the girl kissing his cheeks, but he never let go of the woman nuzzled under his neck, occupying her spot.

Eboni's mind journeyed back to the night the ivory beauty introduced herself.

Eboni snapped her finger when she recalled that her name was Karan. The memory pushed through vividly. Eboni recalled Karan telling her she was here all alone but was a frequent visitor to the island. Karan admitted to not knowing anybody on the island because she came here for mental therapy.

After Eboni told her where she was staying, Karan suggested they get together for drinks and shopping. She joked about a fondness for haggling with the merchants, regaling Eboni with haggling stories, causing her to laugh until she snorted.

Eboni scanned the crowd checking to see if anyone overheard her snorting. That's when her eyes landed on a tall, mysterious man undressing her with his eyes. Now she wondered if he were watching them both, silently wagering which beauty he would bed first.

They were all liars, Eboni thought.

She rapidly stepped back when RB's body eased in her direction. He looked nervous and flustered.

Once he turned around, she watched as RB released the woman and guided them to a table that sat two tables over from theirs. RB reluctantly released the woman glued to his side. She watched as he bent down. Tears rapidly pooled in her eyes, and her heart dropped to her feet, halting her steps.

Was he going to propose to this girl?

Eboni's vision was distorted by her lashes sticking together. She tried to capture the kiss RB gave the girl. She reasoned it was too fast to be a French kiss. Eboni lifted to the tip of her toes, trying to see the woman's face. Unfortunately, her view was obstructed by an oversized plant with vibrant green Swiss cheese leaves.

Tears flowed down her cheeks, ruining her makeup. Knots formed in the pit of her gut as she watched RB sit at the table, cleaning lipstick off his face and wiping his lips.

She couldn't believe he was disrespecting her while she was in the restroom.

A breeze swept her backside. She rapidly turned around to see a side door marked employees only. Naja crept towards the door and peeked out. Two men talked as they smoked a cigarette. Naja easily bypassed them, went to the restaurant's front, and paid a buggy driver to take her to her villa.

Her dad had arranged for the jet to pick her up on Tuesday. She wasn't mentally prepared to explain why she needed to leave early, so she decided to get a room at a hotel by the airport.

She composed a letter to RB, telling him he was just like her father, and she could not believe how he disrespected her in the restaurant.

She didn't feel the need to write anything else.

Halfway out the door, she ran back to the letter sitting on the table, removed her panties, and wrote two more sentences.

Chapter 25

After twenty minutes, Raven came over to the table to see when RB's date would arrive. She was happy her brother met a woman, and according to Uncle Lou, they had been on a couple of dates.

Ignoring Raven, RB walked over to their table to ask Dr. Norwalk to retrieve Eboni from the bathroom. Instead, he was shocked to find Dr. Norwalk had left.

Raven spun a frantic RB around to face her. "What's wrong, Daddy-brother." He calmed himself because Raven only called him Dad when she was terrified or apprehensive.

RB gripped Raven's shoulders with both of his hands. "Where did Dr. Norwalk go?" he asked in a soothing tone.

Kris spoke instead of Raven. "She left. She was mad I didn't allow her to sit next to my fucking woman."

They both eyed Kris in disbelief.

Raven's head whipped in Kris's direction. "She went back to the house to pack." The sadness in Raven's tone of voice caught RB's attention. Clenching her by the chin, he eased her head up until their eyes connected.

"Do you and the doctor…"

Before he could finish his question, Raven cut him off. "No. Nothing is going on between us. I brought her here to help you, and she ended up helping me as well. I see the difference in you. I'm grateful for you meeting with her."

"Dr. Norwalk and Dr. Dream helped me."

Raven raised a questionable brow. She didn't know her brother ever sought therapy before this trip.

RB attempted to calm the pounding of his heart. He was worried about the women he loved; right now, his only concern had to be his sister.

"Kris, go check the restroom for a woman in a red dress. She's an ebony princess about 5'11 and drop-dead gorgeous." Kris nodded as she slid out of the booth.

RB walked Raven outside so they could have some privacy.

"I know I haven't been the best brother or parental figure, but I need you to know I did my best."

Raven nodded.

"I am sorry about what happened to you."

Raven forced herself to take a deep breath. "I was raped, RB. It's okay to acknowledge the facts. Dr. Norwalk helped me understand I was raped because my attacker chose to force sex upon me, and there was nothing I did to deserve sexual abuse. Mist filled his eyes. As much as he wanted to cry, he recognized she needed his strength, not his pity. He shielded his sister in his protective embrace.

"I never blamed you. You didn't create me, but you are my dad. For years, I felt as if I was a burden. You had to raise me instead of being a wild kid having fun. I blame myself for the way you treat women. You never got it out of your system because you were too busy raising me."

RB scolded, then huffed before speaking. "I blamed myself. I should have figured out a way to keep you close. Owen didn't treat you as if you shared his DNA from the day you were born."

RB ran his hand over his head then his face. Raven took his hands into hers.

"You couldn't have known, Dad. You have been taking care of me since I was born. That's why I call you Dad. I know you're my brother, but you're more like a father to me, and I love you unconditionally."

"I apologize for not respecting you. I will never ask you to interfere with me and any other woman again. Hell, there will never be another woman for me except Dr. Dream."

Raven shook her head in protest. "You do respect me."

"I do, but I wasn't showing you respect, Babygirl. I should have never asked you to interfere in my crazy antics. You've been parenting me as much as I've been parenting you," RB admitted.

"I love you," Raven said, elevating to kiss RB's cheek.

"I love you more," RB rapidly replied.

"If I knew you were seeing a therapist already, I would have sought her out."

RB rocked his head from side to side. "Dr. Eboni Dream works with Dr. Norwalk. She didn't tell you she brought another doctor here with her?"

"No, she didn't."

Kris interrupted RB and Raven before they could finish their conversation. "There was nobody in the bathroom. I searched the entire restaurant for a woman in red. She is not in there."

RB spotted Dumais leaning against the wall, talking to some men. He rushed towards him. "Have you seen Eboni?"

"I thought you guys left in a buggy. I tried flagging you down, but you guys kept going."

RB cleared his throat. "I was not in the buggy if I am standing here."

Before Dumais could say another word, RB took off in his buggy headed towards the villa.

Chapter 26

Dr. Karan Norwalk clutched the edge of the desk when the floor beneath her feet trembled. She thought an earthquake had hit the island. She jumped when her door flew open, and a flustered RB stood before her. She remained silent and relaxed her body, creating a safe environment for RB to share his feelings.

"What did you do? Did you send her away? It's not her fault. I crossed the line, not her."

Dr. Norwalk rapidly blinked, striving to decipher his ramblings.

"Who is her, RB?"

"Eboni Dream."

Dr. Norwalk sat up straight. "I don't know anyone named Eboni Dream."

Frustrated and hurt, he slammed his hand on the desk. When Dr. Norwalk flinched, he composed himself.

"This is not the time to pretend as if you do not know the other therapist. Your treatment plan worked. I opened up to Eboni. I shared my deepest secrets, and she assisted me in forgiving myself."

He scoffed. "Dr. Dream showed me you were right. I was disrespecting Raven. I never meant to make my sister think she owed me for raising her. It has been my pleasure to be her daddy-brother as she calls me."

RB flopped down in the chair positioned in front of the desk. He pulled the ring from his pocket and slid it to Dr. Norwalk.

"Dr. Norwalk, I never imagined I could love again. Hell, sleep. In three days and three nights, I fell in love and changed. We're supposed to be making love right now, not going through this. Not this. Please bring her back to me."

Tears poured from his eyes, and for once, he didn't care what Dr. Norwalk or anyone else thought about him. His manhood was intact, but his heart and soul were in pain.

Dr. Norwalk walked around to the front of the desk. Sitting on the desk, she passed RB some tissues. "I can see the change in you. I wish I had something to do with it. However, I don't know Dr. Dream. If I did, I would tell you how to find her."

"It's not in my mind."

"I never said she was a figment of your imagination." She kneaded his shoulders.

RB placed the letter in her lap. "I don't know what I did wrong to make her leave."

"Did you guys argue?"

"Hell no."

"OK," Dr. Norwalk said in a soothing tone.

"Who is Naja?"

"I don't know," he insisted.

"She signed the letter, love, Naja."

RB pulled the paper out of Dr. Norwalk's hands and reread the last two sentences.

I fell head over heels in love with you in three days and three nights, just as you predicted. You won, so all I got was mind-blowing sex and no ring. Love, Naja.

"I'm guessing that's her middle name."

"OK."

"Stop stalling, Dr. Norwalk. You see, she acknowledged she fell in love with me, and I love her, too."

"RB, I am truly trying to help you. As I said, I don't know an Eboni or a Naja."

He lifted his gaze until their eyes locked. "I know you know this woman. Y'all were laughing and talking at the fish fry, so please cut the bullshit act and bring her back," he pleaded. "I know she wasn't supposed to have sex with her patient, but we fell in love."

Dr. Norwalk remained silent, struggling to find the correct words.

"Did you fire her? Or threaten to fire her if she didn't leave?"

"RB, I am the only doctor treating you."

"Bullshit."

"I do recall talking to a woman at the fish fry. She was here to get some rest. We agreed to go out and explore the island. When I wasn't with you, I was counseling Raven. I never found any free time."

RB buried his head in his hands and bawled. He couldn't believe how much this hurt.

An ounce of hope lingered over him. "Maybe Sir knows her."

"Don't be upset, but Sir works for me. He is retired, and he helps me out sometimes. He owns a lot of property here. I felt you needed a man to talk to, and I wanted him to protect you from anyone who may have noticed you were the great Romello "RB" Brooks."

Dr. Norwalk hoped the stroke to his ego would pull him out of his frenzy, but RB didn't bite. However, Eboni had managed to do something Dr. Norwalk could not do, get RB to open and accept the prospect of change.

The man crying before her had accepted the possibilities of change. He was no longer the immature man she met six days ago.

RB pulled himself from the chair and decided to call Sir to take him to the airport to search for Eboni.

The airport was bustling with travelers, but Eboni was nowhere in sight.

Instead of going back to the villa, he booked a room at a hotel by the airport when he couldn't locate Eboni. Next, he tried to unearth Sir or Uncle Lou with no success.

Mind and soul rattled with love's loss caused him to weep in his sleep. He never saw Eboni again unless she visited him in his dreams!

Dipped In Deceit

Chapter 01

She didn't recall the name of the man drooling on her forearm or how long they had been spooning. What she did know was that her body had alerted her to rise and exit the premises.

It took her eyes a minute to adjust to the darkness. Then, she quietly eased her body free, slinging her right leg over the edge of the bed, allowing her frame to collide against the soft carpet gently. Finally, her visual stimuli activated, assisting her in locating her purse.

Ransacking her handbag, she paused when the tips of her fingers graced her cell phone. Placing the phone against the walls of her bag, she glanced at the clock on the dimly illuminated screen.

"Flawlessly on cue," Tamia mumbled under her breath.

It was four o'clock in the morning, which meant it was time to depart.

Gathering her clothes off the floor, she dressed while navigating through the darkness. His floor plan was the only thing she had etched to memory.

By the time she reached the front door, she was fully dressed. She had even combed her hair. She stopped at the door, contemplating if she should leave him a note.

"Naw, dump that. This isn't a relationship," she said louder than she intended.

Tamia had no plans to hook up with this guy again because he had no sex skills. He spat more juices onto her wetness than he licked off. Then, after poking her thigh and the crest of her hips, he finally stumbled upon the gates to her slice of heaven. Before she could grant him entrance, he screamed her name, collapsing on top of her.

She felt leaving him a note may give him false securities, and she detested misleading men when it came to their bedroom skills.

Pausing to examine his assets, she wondered if she should keep him as a sponsor. He had only known her two weeks before he dropped ten racks and paid all her bills for the month.

A soft chuckle played in her throat as she turned the doorknob. His horrible sex game made his wallet a deal-breaker.

As she was closing the front door, it swung back open. "Tamia, where are you taking my nectar? Why are you sneaking out at dawn?"

"Look," she paused, trying to recall his name.

"Shawn," he exclaimed with anger lingering from his tone. All she could think was that short men have the biggest bark and no bite.

She cleared her throat before speaking. "If I am anything, I am real. I never bite my tongue. Are you sure you want to hear my truth?"

"Hell yeah, I want to hear your warped logic," he voiced without hesitation.

"Last week, you did the same thing to me. I woke up ready to gaze into those almond-shaped eyes, and you were gone. I spent a ton of money on you that weekend, and I expected a morning blowjob or something after you fell asleep during the movie. After I licked you from head-to-toe last night, I didn't expect you to dip out on me again. Hell, at least bid a brother farewell or thank him for rocking your world."

He folded his arms and tapped his feet on the natural wood floor, waiting for a response.

Her brow rose to her hairline, and her solid square jawline stiffened, causing Shawn to step back. At five foot ten, her frame loomed over him.

Pressing her glossy, seductively luscious lips together, she searched her mind for a polite response. "Well, first off, Shawn, I don't owe you anything. You will never catch me in any man's bed when the sun rises."

"How many men are you fucking?" he rudely grilled. "Are you a gold digger?"

A powerful expression replaced her scowl as she tossed her long silky chestnut brown hair off her shoulder. Closing the gap between them, she gawked intently into his inexperienced eyes. "I am not a gold digger, although the only thing I am turning down is my damn collar."

He scoffed. "Then be woman enough to own the fucking gold digger title."

Leaning her head backward, clenching her flat stomach muscles, she roared from the pit of her belly.

Her laugh prompted anger to permeate his gut.

"Dear Shawn, I am an opportunist who never turns down any opportunity presented to her because men never turn down a chance to explore another woman's vagina."

She tapped her waistline with her hand. "However, I cannot help it if every man I encounter chooses to become a contributor hoping to get my wet-wet."

He applied pressure to his bottom lip with his teeth as he eyed her sweet spot.

"Unlike men, I am honest. I told you from day one I was not looking for a man, and you knew you were not the only man I was dating."

Tamia never understood why women placed themselves in monogamist dating ships. In contrast, men date multiple women until they are ready to enter a committed relationship.

As far as she was concerned, she would be single while walking down the aisle until the preacher pronounced her Mrs. Parkwood. The thought of marrying Mr. Parkwood made her giggle.

Shawn stood there looking like a hurt love-struck fool admiring her gingerbread skin. "Tamia, I like you." He shuffled his feet waiting on a response.

"You are the kind of woman a man would love to marry. You are independent and beautiful," he murmured.

Staring into his confused copper eyes, she felt sorry for his gullible ass, but she had to keep it one hunnid with him.

"You are not the kind of man I would like to marry to win a bet," she honestly admitted. "I am twenty-two years old."

Her mind drifted back to the night in college when Miya, the youngest member of the Black and Educated social group, proposed they wager on which BAE would get married first.

Imani, Naja, and Lexi assumed Tamia would be the fourth BAE married. Although Miya insisted Tamia would be last, and she would be first.

Tamia fought for a higher position not because she desired marriage or viewed herself better. The BAE's entire ranking system was based on knowing their boyfriends since they were teens. She had a teenage sweetheart like Naja, Lexi, and Imani; therefore, she felt she should rank higher than Miya by their definition.

One evening in college, the girls were kicking it in the student union, and Tamia was gearing up to tell her girlfriends about her teenage lover since the girls were sharing stories.

Before she could get a word out, her sisters slapped labels on her. She will never forget that day because she cried herself to sleep.

Under her tough exterior was a broken girl that needed an impenetrable shield to survive, and before she could lower her guard, the BAEs had already branded her like the rest of the world.

"Well damn," he said, clenching his chest, pulling her back to the matter at hand.

"I love my freedom, and I am having fun," she voiced with excitement. "I told you this before we started kicking it."

He massaged his brows. "I did not expect to fall in love with you this fast," he bellowed. "Do you think I go around licking all over women?"

Damn, that explains a lot. If you journeyed downtown more, you would have better skills and wouldn't have spit all over my body last night.

She snickered. "Y'all never do," she replied, shaking her best assets.

"And I appreciate all of them," he whined, eying her butt and breasts. "You will never find a man who appreciates you the way I do. I love you."

"Shawn, you are a naive man. You don't know me from Adam." She turned to walk away, but he caught her by the wrist, tugging her closer to him.

"You liked me last night when I was licking and dicking you down. You loved me the other day when I took you on a five-thousand-dollar shopping spree."

She could tell he was becoming emotional; she couldn't help but burst into laughter because he didn't lick and dick anybody down up in here last night.

"Shawn, it was more like spitting and missing."

She racked her bottom lip through her teeth then moaned. "God blessed you with a gigantic package, but you have no stroke. As far as the shopping spree goes, you bought me one outfit and a purse."

He smacked his lips.

Oh shit, here comes the bitch who lives inside of all men. But, of course, men always smack their lips before their inner bitch emerges.

"Please, Tamia. Didn't you have a wonderful time? I licked you into euphoria. Admit it," he whimpered.

"Why would I lie or thank you for a wonderful time when it was horrible?" She glanced at the watch. This exit was taking longer than it should.

"You timidly licked me like a cat licking on a bowl of hot milk, drooling all over my lovely folds." The sadness filling his face forced her to stop talking.

"No, don't stop now, you evil bitch."

She expelled the air in her lungs then replenished them. "You fuckin' child. How hilarious. You are going to insult me because you are an atrocious lay. Well, your stroke was stiff and had no rhythm. Plus, you lack confidence in yourself. On top of all of that, you exploded before you entered me, so you fucked my inner thigh."

"Bitch please! Ain't no woman ever told me no shit like that before."

"Another woman might lie to you; I never will. They were docile; I am not.

He hissed.

"Listen to me, twenty percent of sex is about confidence, and you lack that. Thirty percent is about skills, and you lack that. Thirty percent is about imagination, and once again, you lack that. All yo' ass gave was twenty percent, which was an extended thick dick. Would you continue to fuck a twenty-percent woman?"

He hunched his shoulders. "Exactly," she noted, "then why should I?"

"You are a crazy vindictive bitch," he screamed before slamming the door in her face.

There was a little regret lingering inside of her. She blamed it on her broken and contrite heart.

She wasn't always this way. She believed in people and love and dreamt of happily ever after until love crucified her because of her lineage. To protect her fragile heart, Tamia operated by a set of rules:

1. Never allow the sun to catch her in a bed that wasn't hers.

2. Never give her heart to another man.

3. No pillow talk.

4. Charge all men for her presence so they would appreciate her time.

5. Trust no one, only one.

By the time she reached her car, she had convinced herself she had told him what no other woman had dared.

Some people go through their entire lives thinking they are good lovers because no person had enough courage to say their sex was hideous.

Tamia had never been afraid to reveal a man's bedroom percentage. She figured we are judged on everything else in our lives. Why not our bedroom skills?

At work, when you do poorly, you receive a verbal warning. For example, when a woman never moans or talks dirty during sex, she's giving him a verbal warning and vice versa.

After your verbal warning, if you still do not improve, your supervisor or manager tries to shock your system. This write-up goes into detail, outlining the areas of your performance that require improvement. This is what your mate is doing when you claim they are nagging or bitching.

If you value your job, you make the necessary enhancements, thus securing your position. You get terminated if your progress doesn't improve, hence the layoff notice she served Shawn.

Tamia's steps halted in front of her newest model BMW SUV. The penmanship on the note wedged under the driver's windshield wiper blade caught her attention.

She clicked her teeth together as an emotional panic raced over her body.

Chapter 02

She didn't know her full name, where she worked, or where she laid her head at night. But Yasmine knew her nickname was Nectar, her number, and that she couldn't stop blowing up her fiancé's phone three nights ago.

Yasmine gawked at the disheveled woman staring back at her. Her raw umber skin was flushed, and her round black olive eyes were watery. She wiped her mouth with the back of her hand, running her damp hand along her high angular cheekbones.

She rinsed her mouth one more time for good measure. She retrieved another washcloth from the top drawer of the black and gray floating vanity.

Kneeling to wash the splattered food spots off the natural stone floor. In three days, she had used over ten washcloths to clean the guest bathroom; therefore, she decided she would do the laundry instead of the maid.

An exasperated sigh escaped her body as she examined the mess in the kitchen. She wished her fiancé would hire a full-time cook and allow the maid to come more than once a week.

Being Suzy Homemaker was wearing her thin.

She huffed at the three nails she chipped, gripping the toilet. She silently chastised herself because she knew ribs and sandwiches never came up smoothly.

She pulled a mint from the candy dish, hoping it would soothe her sore, inflamed throat before preparing dinner.

***

Craig strolled into his house, smiling from ear to ear. His fiancée, Yasmine, of two years, was in the modern white kitchen preparing dinner.

Leaning against the kitchen door rail, he wondered what was on her beautiful mind. The pungent smell of garlic roasted vegetables floated in the air.

He admired his future wife's strength; he could tell she was exhausted.

He'd asked her friend Monica and her cousin, Laura, if he should hire a full-time chef, and they both agreed Yasmine wouldn't appreciate anybody in her space.

Two weeks ago, he noticed a change in Yasmine. He constantly asked her to tell him what he needed to do to ease her stress. Her answer was always the same. "Take my clothes off and make love to me."

Craig crept up behind her, wrapping his arms around her narrow waist, startling her out of deep thought. "Hey, honey."

Tears trickled down her face. She didn't understand why every man she loved cheated on her. She didn't know what it was about her pussy that made men cheat. Craig was supposed to be over his cheating stage.

Craig kissed Yasmine on the hollow behind her ear, triggering her to whimper.

He intensified his grip, swinging his right arm in front of her to flaunt the beautiful bouquet in his hand. Yasmine leaned back into his chest, inhaling his smoky cedar wood scent.

"Hey to you," Yasmine finally managed to say.

"I missed you all day," Craig admitted, placing her flowers on the countertop. Yasmine shifted her weight, trying to wiggle out of his embrace.

She sighed and faintly replied, "Um-hm, thank you."

This was not the first time Craig sensed Yasmine's annoyance in him. "Baby, did you have a rough day?"

She hunched her shoulders, and he kissed the top of both. "Baby, if you tell me what is wrong, I promise I will fix it, but I can't fix it unless I know what is wrong."

Yasmine gently pushed down on Craig's hands, but he refused to release his grip.

If she answered his question, she had to admit she went through his phone, and she wasn't prepared to acknowledge that his cheating stemmed from her poor bedroom performance, which derived from her feel fat and unlovable.

Therefore, it was easier for her to blame him for the shift in their dynamics than shoulder any fault.

Yasmine gripped the edge of the stainless-steel sink, using it to pull her from Craig's embrace, but he yanked her back.

"I know you need to cook, but I just need to hold you a little longer."

She rested her hands on the white and gray marble countertop. He caught the tip of her earlobe between his lips, nibbed on it before whispering, "Am I losing you, Yasmine?"

She smacked Craig's hands, thrusting her butt backward.

"What type of question is that Craig," she barked. "How can you lose me when you already have me? Are you planning to leave me for someone else? Do you want to make love to someone else?"

Craig walked over to the table in the dining room and sat down, burying his head in his palms.

Yasmine walked over to her groom-to-be. Running her hands through his golden hair, she tugged at his head.

"Look at me, Craig."

Craig remained in the same position. His heart was heavy.

His friends constantly joked about him not keeping up with a thirty-year-old woman, but Craig was far from a walker and a cane.

He was athletic and enjoyed making love to Yasmine. These days she is always too tired. A couple of times, he knew she was faking an orgasm.

From the day they met, he showered her with gifts, affirmations, and affection. He knew the value of a good woman at forty-nine years old. Yet, he could feel her pulling away from him, and he had no clue as to why.

Yasmine squatted on the side of Craig. "You can always sit on my lap," he noted, easing back the chair.

Yasmine nestled her head on the right side of Craig's neck, planting gentle kisses on his collarbone. Craig moaned as he palmed her round derriere.

Yasmine wondered what happened to the spontaneous man that she met three years ago.

"Kiss me," Craig mumbled.

His fiancée did as he requested. Leaning back, gazing into his sky-blue eyes, she wished hers sparkled with the same joy as his.

She missed the butterflies that swarmed in her stomach at the mention of his name. Her life had become redundant and boring because her weight repulsed Craig, which meant her mother was right.

You couldn't tell her Craig was twenty years her senior because he was full of life and adventurous. There was a time where she struggled to keep up with him.

She missed the days when he called her at work requesting some hot chocolate for lunch.

His cockiness used to make her panties soaking wet. They would make love in the stairways of his office building, on her office desk, and in restaurant bathrooms.

He would gladly stroke her clit in any darkly lit restaurant or club. Plus, he gave her a mile-high card.

He crushed the myths about Caucasian men's penis size. God generously blessed him below his waist, and freaky C could get busy anywhere.

So naturally, when Craig asked her to marry him, she agreed. However, she was unaware that engagement meant boredom.

Their motto used to be anywhere, anyplace, anytime. Now, her life was set on a repeat of work, daily white roses, weekend shopping, boring sex once a week when she initiated, and him preferring to fuck his Nectar instead of his fatty.

"Yasmine, are you OK?" Craig asked again. A tear trickled down her cheeks, and she swiped it away.

"I will be," she replied with a hint of disappointment in her tone.

Chapter 03

P lain-colored walls decorated with pictures of company department leaders, logos, awards, plaques, and other markers of company pride and prosperity decorated the room. Some of the awards and plaques belonged to Aiden's father and great-grandfather. It was the perfect room to take his cover photo.

The young reporter placed a recorder in the center of the table between her and Aiden.

He ran his tongue over his lips, and the overly eager twenty-four-year-old interviewer swiped her sweaty palms on her skirt.

Aiden was a handsome twenty-seven-year-old man whose presence dominated any space he occupied.

He slid the oversized black leather office chair towards the cherrywood rectangular table and flashed the nervous reporter an encouraging smile.

His cologne filled the air, and the young reporter blushed as she twirled the tip of her sandy blonde hair. "You know I don't bite," he said with a slight chuckle.

She grinned then continued to fidget with her clothing. Finally, she closed her eyes, and Aiden noticed a change in her mannerism.

"Well, Mr. Parkwood, I hope you don't bite little ole me." She flapped her eyelids like the flashing yellow caution light.

Aiden noticed a few people walking past the conference room, peering through the stripped glass walls and door to see what was happening.

He wanted to scream, "the prodigal grandson has returned," but he knew Pop-pop would disapprove of that type of behavior.

"Before we talk about your family legacy, let the readers of the American Dental Alliance get to know Dr. Aiden Parkwood. Of course, we all know you are a dentist with the Division of Oral and Maxillofacial Surgery at Parkwood Memorial Hospital and Parkwood Medical Center, with a focus on oral and maxillofacial surgery, including dentoalveolar, orthognathic surgery, cleft, and craniofacial, and cosmetic surgery, as well as facial trauma and head and neck cancer."

Aiden's chest expanded with pride. He had accomplished a lot in a few short years.

He performed contract dental work in various cities obtaining licensing in multiple states, expanding his knowledge by working alongside fantastic dentists. Solely on his merit and not the family name.

"I have a couple of questions I would love to ask you. Then we would like to take a couple of pictures of you."

"Ask away."

"How/why did you choose the dental school you attended? Did your father or grandfather also attend?" His eyes broadcast emotions of doubt. He wasn't prepared for another boring interview. "Trust me, Dr. Parkwood, we will learn about that man, but it is a dental magazine."

On cue, they both chuckled.

"When I applied to dental schools, I knew that I wanted top-notch clinical training but also an excellent academic experience that would prepare me well for postgraduate training and make me a competitive applicant for residencies. UCLA suited both criteria perfectly, and I knew right after the interview that it was the right school for me."

"What surprised you the most about dental school?"

"It is difficult to understand exactly how challenging dental school is until you get there. To succeed and excel in dental school, a student must have a strong work ethic and willingness to study hard, excellent hand skills, and the ability to build good relationships with patients. The learning curve is incredibly steep."

He ran the back of his hand over hers, and her body shivered. "Do you think I have exceptional hands and the ability to build on our new friendship?" She covered her nose and mouth with her hand and laughed nervously.

She fanned herself before asking the new question. "Why did you choose to specialize in oral surgery?"

"When I was exposed to oral and maxillofacial surgery as a dental student, I realized very quickly that it was the right specialty for me. It combines dentistry, anesthesia, and surgery and has massive scope for a specialty, which provides many options for practicing oral and maxillofacial surgery. So, rarely do you see people of color dominate this field. I wanted to join the ranks of other extraordinary Black dentists."

"Your mother is Caucasian, and your father is African American, correct?"

"It's the opposite."

"I would think you would identify with Caucasoid."

Aiden despised the conversation of race. His skin complexion resembled rich molasses cookies, his nose was narrow and slightly upturned, but he had brandy-colored eyes and thick succulent lips. There was no way anyone would or could mistake him for anything except a Black man.

"No," I don't, he sharply replied. "Next question."

"Has being a specialist in your field met your expectations? Why?"

"Oral and maxillofacial surgery has been every bit as challenging and enjoyable as I thought it would be. The work is arduous as I had expected. Still, it has also been an excellent experience learning to provide a wide variety of procedures and services to patients and gaining exposure to many different areas of medicine and dentistry. The skills I have obtained will assist me in running my grandfather's empire one day."

He anticipated her first question would be: Why have you chosen to return to Los Angeles, CA. Then he could address the rumors about him taking over the family empire.

He was shocked when his mother called demanding he return home immediately, informing him that Pop-pop was ready to retire and pass the company to him.

He agreed because he was already nearby preparing a plan to claim his future wife. Plus, Aiden figured it was only fair for the company to stay in the family.

His great grandfather left his grandfather a small dental practice. Pop-pop took that one location and multiplied it within five years. His grandmother was an architecture major; therefore, she designed all the buildings. Eventually, other doctors sought his grandmother to develop their facilities, which created a new branch of the Parkwood brand.

Once studies showed that dental infections could increase the risk of heart disease, Aiden's father opened a private medical center to aid inner cities. Before long, the Parkwood family had opened numerous privately owned clinics and a privately owned hospital.

Aiden knew he had enormous shoes to fill, but he was ready for the perplexing task.

"Do you have a wife, fiancée, or girlfriend, and if so, do you have enough time to spend with her?"

She waited for a reply to her question with bated breath.

"I do not have a family yet, but I have a tremendous amount of respect for my co-residents who are married with kids and manage to spend quality time with their families." He flashed a mischievous smile. "I have no one. Do you know anyone that may be in the market for a semi-successful and debonair man?"

She adjusted herself in her seat because Aiden Parkwood was beyond handsome. When he winked at her, she could feel moisture building between her thighs.

If the photographer weren't in the room, she would have submitted her resume for the job. Instead, she made a mental note to slip Aiden her number before leaving.

"How would you and this new woman balance life outside of work?" She awkwardly winked at Aiden.

"It is challenging to achieve a good work-life balance in oral and maxillofacial surgery because free time is limited. Therefore, it is essential to set goals and priorities outside of work, whether to exercise, cook, maintain a hobby, or spend time with family and friends. If you aren't proactive, it is easy to spend your time off doing nothing but sitting on the couch watching TV."

He leaned in closer, and her breath hitched.

"Off the record. Any free time I have to devote to this lovely lady, I would spend making her scream my name."

When he eased back, the reporter's face was flushed a deep beet red.

Before she could respond, his mother barged into the conference room, demanding that they wrap up the interview because he had an appointment with his tailor.

Chapter 04

Yasmine gazed out of her corner office window while her cousin, Laura, rambled on about everyone's business except hers.

"Girl, guess who I ran into?" Laura asked Yasmine.

Yasmine turned her black leather executive chair around to face the wall.

"Look bitch, these white people are getting on my nerves, and your ass wants to call playing the guessing game."

Laura laughed. "The white people at your job or the white man at your home?"

"Both," Yasmine snapped. "When did my life become so boring and routine, best friend? I recall a time that Craig would call me three and four times a day for his sweetness. These days I am lucky if I get sex once a week."

She paused, debating if she should admit that Craig was cheating.

Laura cleared her throat, irritated by the dead air between them.

Yasmine expelled a long stream of air into the receiver. "Bitch, leave me alone right now. I am sexually frustrated."

"Oh, poor Yasmine is tired of playing with Massa. Didn't nobody tell you to get engaged to a rich white man with a dick like a horse."

Yasmine wondered how Laura knew Craig's dick was big. "Yea, OK, bitch."

"Are you afraid of becoming Massa's slave after marriage? I tried to tell your ass slavery was over. I would never marry nor fuck a white man."

"Bitch, please. You would fuck a dog if the price were right. Now, who in the hell did you see?"

"Fuck you, Yaz. Take a deep breath," Laura said, trying to build up the anticipation. Regrettably, the only thing that she was building up was Yasmine's frustration.

"Bye, bitch."

"Wait, I ran into Aiden."

Aiden was Yasmine's ex and her first love. They had dated through junior high and college.

She visited him a couple of times while he was at Princeton University. During one of her trips to see Aiden, his mother asked her to take Aiden his mail.

Once she arrived at his university, she discovered he was not there. Eating and crying in her hotel room, she knew she was about to invade his privacy by reading his mail.

That's when she learned that Aiden had been cheating with some young girl.

The next day, she slipped into his building. A cleaning lady was opening his dorm suite.

Yasmine was surprised because he told her the cleaning service wasn't responsible for cleaning the living quarters or private bathrooms. Moreover, how did she know his four-digit pin? She ignored the questions floating in her mind and focused of her mission.

The cleaning lady placed a wastebasket between the door and railing. Yasmine peeked into the room, noticing the cleaning woman must be in the bathroom.

She tiptoed into the room, searching his desk for a sign of where he may be. She opened his top drawer noticing the pink scented envelopes from T. Hill. She gathered every pink envelope and dashed out of the room, leaving the cleaning lady none the wiser.

On the way back to the hotel, she gorged on twelve hot dogs, then released them and her stress into the porcelain bowl and flushed the memory all away.

Instead of returning home, Yasmine stayed in New Jersey, binging and purging. She didn't know how to return the letters, so she took them home to her mother.

Her mother blamed her for gaining weight. Assuring her no man wanted a fat girl as a wife, declaring most men always look for younger, thinner models.

She worried night and day that Aiden was cheating which increased her gorging.

Hurt and angry, she had sex with her girlfriend Monica's boyfriend to get even with Aiden, not considering Monica's feelings. It's a decision she still regretted every day.

After Aiden returned to LA to attend UCLA, their relationship was almost perfect again.

Following graduation, they both tried hard to establish themselves at work which meant more time apart.

When Aiden's father suffered a deadly heart attack, Aiden left Los Angeles without saying goodbye.

After a year, Yasmine started dating. She could not take the lonely nights anymore, or her mother's constantly telling her to forgive Aiden for leaving, and if he cheated while he was away, don't get upset because that's what men do.

In his absence, Yasmine grew closer to her college friends, Niah and Monica. Ignoring Aiden's calls was effortless, and she wasn't overindulging in food anymore.

Once Aiden realized she wasn't going to answer his calls, he started calling Laura, her mother, and her father to ensure she was doing all right. Eventually, he stopped checking in and moved on as well.

Her cousin's high-pitched voice cut through Yasmine's thoughts.

"Girl, why are you acting as if you don't want to see that fool? Whether you are engaged or not, I know you want to see your first love. That's why we are going out for drinks with him and his boys tonight."

In the pit of her belly, Yasmine felt nervous. "Bitch, you could have asked me first. Craig and I have plans tonight, and I need to get my hair and nails done," Yasmine barked.

"I am not going to be too many more "bitches". Now, what are you doing tonight?"

Before Yasmine could answer, Laura chimed in, "Nothing! Just going home to cook and wait for Massa to bring your ass some white roses. Hell, don't you do that shit every night."

Yasmine hated admitting her cousin was right. Her life had grown highly dull. The truth was that she was scared to see Aiden. Besides Craig, Aiden was the only other man she had ever loved.

"I can't go." Before Laura could respond, Yasmine terminated the call.

Yasmine was determined to rekindle her and Craig's spark and stay the hell away from Aiden Parkwood.

Yasmine swung her chair around and buzzed her assistant, Stacy.

"Yes, Mrs. Brooks, what can I get for you?"

"Stace, can you please call my beautician to see if he will do my hair right now, then call Prive spa to see if I can get in there to get my nails done. Also, order a dozen yellow roses and send them to my husband."

"Your wish is my command," Stacy joked. "Mrs. Brooks, are you going to be able to do all this during lunch? I am only asking because you have a 3:30 PM conference call."

"Girl, please. I am good, but not that good. Clear my calendar for the rest of the day. I will see you tomorrow. Once you finish typing up those transcripts, filing, and preparing the deck for tomorrow, you can go home early."

Her assistant rolled her eyes with a list so long she would barely make it home before eight o'clock tonight.

Yasmine used to be a fantastic boss. These days all she did was politely bark orders and filled her assistant's desk with projects.

Yasmine's last three marketing campaigns were all courtesy of

Stacy's hard work and dedication. Yasmine would breeze in after her three to four-hour lunches to take all of the creative credit.

"You bet," Stacy replied dryly.

"Hey, girl," Stacy greeted Craig's receptionist, Grace. "Is he in his office?"

"Yes, he just got out of a meeting. Let me transfer your call. Hold on."

"Hello, my beautiful Queen," Craig excitedly greeted Stacy.

She giggled like a schoolgirl. "Let me transfer your call, Mr. Craig."

Craig greeted Yasmine with more excitement than he did her assistant. "How is your day going, husband-to-be?"

Craig was ecstatic that Yasmine appeared to be in better spirits. "Wonderful," he replied, "It would be better if I were looking at your beautiful angelic face."

Better for him but horrible for her, she thought. Yasmine loved him, but she hated the way he smothered her.

"That's wonderful, honey," she responded, blowing off his comment.

"Tonight, I want to do something different? I apologize for the last-minute change, and I sent you roses to help persuade you."

"Oh, how sweet, baby. Since I did not hear an invite, I take it that no men are allowed. That's cool. I will call David and see what he is getting into this evening. It's Friday night, and I know he is getting into something. Well, baby, I will see you when you get home tonight. I love you."

"I love you, too," Yasmine replied. "But before you hang up, I want to get into trouble with you."

Craig leaned back in his chair. The seduction traveling through the airway made his penis flex. "Sure," he stammered over his words.

"I will see you at home around six o'clock. I have to get sexy for my man."

"Do I need to arrange anything?"

"Nope," she replied.

She walked out to her personal assistant's desk and eyed all the photos plastered around her cubicle. She didn't say anything about the pictures, but Stacy caught her rolling her eyes.

"Stace, can you plan a romantic weekend for Craig and me. See if you can get a car to drive us to Vegas or San Francisco, or a flight to a Caribbean Island, or Florida, then we can take a weekend cruise."

"Do you have swimwear for a Caribbean trip?"

Yasmine scanned her body. She was looking a bit bloated. Thinking she should avoid any place where she had to wear a swimsuit.

Yasmine waved her hands between them. "I will leave the details to you and Grace. We will both need appropriate attire for the location you pick. Make sure you get me swimwear that will cover my fat if you pick something in the Caribbean."

Her subordinate started to question her boss. She was skin and bones. Yasmine told people she was a size four, but her assistant bought her clothes, and she knew her boss wore a size two.

She would wear a zero if she didn't have breasts and a little tight bottom.

"Inform Grace this is a surprise romantic get-a-way I'm planning, so she needs to keep her big mouth closed. I told Craig to meet me at home by six; therefore, the driver or helicopter must be there by five."

Her assistant dropped her pen after writing the last note on her pad.

"Thank you, Stace. Enjoy your weekend."

"What weekend?" Stacy muttered under her breath. Planning this trip would prevent her from completing her other task, which meant she had to work the entire weekend.

Chapter 05

Aiden arrived at Mastro's restaurant in Beverly Hill, CA, expecting a private dinner with his mother and grandfather. Instead, to his surprise, Pop-pop had bought out the luxurious place to welcome him home.

Aiden had been back in town for three months. Only his boy, Davis, knew he had returned.

It took him a week to track down Tamia. She was his first love. When he finally tracked her down, he was shocked to find the boisterous beauty was dating a few men.

He followed her to one guy's house a couple of times. He knew all her looks, and each time she emerged from his home, nothing on her face or in her strut registered he was killing the kitty.

Even when they were out shopping, he could feel their icy chemistry floating in the air.

Aiden knew he fucked up, but he wanted his girl back, and he would do whatever it took to make that happen.

His mother walked in dripping with class and money. Pop-pop gave his mother a disapproving stare.

"Now that Dominique Deveraux has arrived, I guess we can get started."

Aiden's mother smiled bright and twirled. She seemed to take no offense at being referred to as Diahann Carroll's Dynasty character.

"We are so happy because you are home, son," Andrea stated to Aiden, blowing air kisses in his direction while standing under the golden chandelier allowing the rays of light to capture her best angles.

Aiden took a deep breath. He knew sharing a table with his Pop-pop and mother would be tricky.

Aiden was surprised to see a young woman sitting at their table. Whenever they had a company event, the immediate family sat at his grandfather's table.

Throughout the evening, Pop-pop and his father would visit each table and chat with the employees. Aiden smiled because soon, that would be his responsibility.

His father always told him, "A great boss doesn't see himself as a boss. He views himself as head of a more prominent family. So, he must rule that family with rules and love, never fear and intimidation."

"I promise, I will," Aiden mumbled under his breath.

Pop-pop stood in front of the built-in wall-to-wall glass wine case clearing his throat before addressing the room.

"I want everyone to greet four people from another department and tell them one thing you like to do outside of work."

Aiden could not wait to introduce himself to the ivory beauty sitting across from him. He knew better than to eat where you shit, as Pop-pop would say, "that's a heavy, heavy mind thang," but he was willing to risk his peace of mind for one night with her.

"Hi, my name is Aiden, and I love making beautiful women smile."

"Well, OK. My name is Brooklyn, and I love going for long walks with my husband and two dogs."

Aiden noticed the way her timbre changed when she asserted husband.

"Congratulations on the two dogs," Aiden replied, moving on to the table adjacent to them. He ended up greeting over ten people. He smiled back at his Pop-pop when his pleasing smile landed upon Aiden.

Once they were seated, the director of events came out to greet the room and announced what was on the menu for tonight. She paused to walk away, then turned around and started speaking again.

"You work for a wonderful man. His only criteria was to make sure this night was memorable no matter the cost. Since my entire family and I go to Unique Smiles Dental & Orthodontics, Parkwood Hospital, and the medical clinics, I know he could afford top-shelf service tonight despite the cost. However, his heart and his son's heart make us give him the family discount every time he visits."

She paused and laughed under her breath. "Do you know Dr. Parkwood still gives us a bonus for our services?"

She pointed to the staff members wrapped around the room. "We are all here to serve you."

The owner stepped forward and raised a glass in Pop-pop's honor.

Aiden glanced around the room. He wondered if Pop-pop would announce his retirement tonight and that he was passing Aiden the keys to his legacy.

As the appetizers hit the table, Pop-pop got up to start making his rounds. "Aiden and Brooklyn, join me in greeting the employees."

Aiden froze as he was lifting from his seat. He didn't understand why this Brooklyn woman was joining him and his grandfather in a family tradition.

The kid inside of him wanted to stomp his feet, allow his bottom lip to protrude, then demand to know who this woman was exactly. Instead, he did what his Pop-pop requested.

Aiden visited every table on the left side, learning the employee's names, and listened to their families' stories. He entertained the tables on the opposite side of the room, finally attacking the middle tables. By the time Aiden reached his seat, the employees were eating their main entrée.

"Aiden and Brooklyn, I am not going to retire fully, but I am going to lighten my load and travel with this beautiful woman," Pop-pop said, eying Aiden's grandmother passionately.

"Aiden, it is a family tradition to pass the company to the next generation." Aiden's grandmother kneaded her husband's hand. "I am not sure if you are ready, son, to run the company."

The knot that had taken residence in Aiden's throat prevented him from speaking. Pop-pop raised his hand in the air when Andrea went to talk.

"I think Brooklyn should run the company until you are ready."

"How can she run a private family-owned empire?" Andrew asked, flinging his hands in Brooklyn's direction, never giving her the respect of eye contact. As far as Andrea was concerned, Brooklyn was beneath her and her son.

"A good dentist has charm, dexterity, empathy, he or she gains the trust of others, they have good listening skills, leadership, and have a knack for making money," Aiden's grandmother voiced.

Aiden's pleading eyes landed upon his grandmother. "Pop-Pop," Aiden said, "grandma described me."

"Aiden, um... that's a heavy, heavy mind thang."

"What's so fucking heavy about it?" Andrea questioned.

Aiden and Pop-pop whipped their heads in his mother's direction. Andrea hunched her shoulders at the table.

Aiden was feeling the magnitude of his grandfather's words.

He wished someone could turn off all the lights in the dimly lit restaurant and hit a reset button because this night was not panning out the way he imagined.

"Son, you have the entire summer to prove to me you are ready to run the family business, starting with a presentation on Wednesday. I was hoping you could provide your vision for this company. Each generation created a new revenue stream, and I will not allow this legacy to plateau with you. Where do you see the company in five years? What types of outreach/volunteer work will the company pursue?"

"I can do that," Aiden replied.

"I would love for you to get married so the family legacy can continue. We are a privately owned company, and four generations kept that going. Your grandfather and I will not see that destroyed. We would rather take the company public and allow the employees to own the company and allow Brooklyn to run the company. She is a happily married woman, and they plan on having a huge family."

Aiden couldn't believe what he was hearing. Were his grandparents trying to force him into marriage? Tonight was a heavy, heavy mind thang.

"I'm not saying you have to get married this summer, grandson, but I would like to meet the woman your mother said you moved back to LA to propose to?"

Aiden scratched his head.

He raised a disapproving brow at his mother. He couldn't believe she forced him to return under false pretenses. That explained his Pop-pop's bewildered look when he asked him when he was announcing his retirement.

"Aiden, when you returned and suggested I retire, I spoke to your grandmother, and she agreed it was time for me to slow down and grant you the opportunity to step up...."

"Every man must crawl from under his mother's thumb and etch out his path," his grandma asserted, cutting into his grandfather's speech.

His Pop-pop continued once his grandma reclined in her seat. He pointed at Brooklyn. "Brooklyn has been working with me, and I think with your help, both of you can run the company until you are ready to take the reins. Your grandmother suggested I give you the summer to prove you are ready to run the company by yourself, and Brooklyn has agreed to stand by your side in either capacity."

Aiden eyed Brooklyn suspiciously. He couldn't believe he briefly thought about sleeping with her job-stealing ass.

Chapter 06

A young pimpled face host dressed in a black tuxedo approached Yasmine. "Do you have reservations?"

Yasmine scanned the room, looking for her dinner companions before answering. "Yes, can you please check under Andrea Parkwood?"

The host scanned the list. "No, I don't see Andrea Parkwood, but maybe we can find you a table."

"Can you check once more? This time, please check under my mother's name, Jasmine Brooks?"

He scanned the list one more time. "Found it, Mrs. Brooks party of two, in the...."

Cutting him off, she quickly corrected him, "No, it should be a party of three." It was supposed to be her mother, Andrea, and herself.

Her mother was not enthusiastic concerning her marriage to Craig because he wasn't wealthy. She knew this was an ambush to question her about Aiden. She expected the call once Laura revealed her childhood lover had returned to California.

"I am sorry for the inconvenience, ma'am. Please come this way. You are in the private dining room," he said. "One of your guests has already arrived."

Yasmine loved Vito's in Santa Monica, CA. She and Aiden visited Vito so much they declared it their restaurant. She loved their tableside-tossed Caesar salad, but Aiden loved the enchanting setting.

The waiter led her to a private dining room, pulling the burgundy and gold curtain to the side, allowing her entry. She never recalled the curtain being drawn closed before.

Her eyes glanced around the room and landed on Aiden, standing in front of the wine rack, holding one red rose.

Yasmine was speechless. She didn't know if it was the spectacular surroundings or Aiden's elegant physique under the dim candlelight.

"I have it from here," Aiden told the waiter as he strolled around the table towards Yasmine.

"How are you, Ms. Brooks?" Aiden asked.

Yasmine extended her hand out, flashing her five-carat platinum Tiffany & CO. engagement ring in his face. "That's soon to be Mrs. Lawson," she corrected him.

Aiden chuckled. "I am sorry, Mrs. soon-to-be Lawson." He pulled out the green, cream, and gold striped Queen Ann chair. "I brought this for you," he said while handing her the rose and a light blue box from Tiffany & CO.

"You didn't have to," she modestly said.

"Just a little something to go with your engagement ring."

Setting the box off to the side, Yasmine inquired about their mother's whereabouts.

"I am not sure," he replied, "but she told me to tell you hi."

Those deceitful bitches, Yasmine thought to herself.

Their mothers had set them up. The reservation was for a party of two, her and Aiden. The host was right.

"I was under the assumption that she and my mother would be in attendance."

Aiden could tell by Yasmine's fresh from the beauty salon hairdo, the skintight purple Dolce & Gabbana stretch satin dress, and her six-inch fuck-me pumps dispelled the notion that she expected their mothers.

Nevertheless, he was disappointed in her weight loss. He wondered if she was still fighting her eating disorder. He decided he wouldn't bring up her past disease unless she excused herself after she ate dinner.

He smiled inside because his mother told him earlier that day, "If she comes dressed head-to-toe, then she still cares about what you think. If she comes in her work clothes, then she is over your bullshit."

In Andrea's eyes, Yasmine would be the perfect mate because she would obey and never challenge her stance in her son's life. Aiden wasn't interested in marrying Yasmine, but he would keep her for her stellar head game. No woman alive could match her sloppy toppy.

She laughed, and her breast giggled. He wondered if her breasts were still pillow-soft. Aiden traced his top lip with his tongue at the thought of his penis sliding between Yasmine's lips.

Although he and Yasmine dated off and on throughout his teens, Yasmine didn't have his heart.

Aiden's heart belonged to the first girl that punched him in the face, then kissed him, then hit him again in the arm and told him, "you like when I hit you, right." Mesmerized by her beauty, he foolishly agreed.

"Wonderful," he replied as he stretched his right hand across the table, stroking her hand with his thumb.

A fire ignited between her thighs, forcing her to sever their connection quickly.

She became extremely nervous about being alone with Aiden. He had this crazy sexual control over her, that always ended with her on her knees searching for her panties.

Aiden noticed the tension impeding Yasmine's muscles. "Are you afraid to be alone with me?" Her failure to respond was all Aiden needed to know. "Are you going to open up your gift?"

Yasmine glanced at the box, pulling it gently in front of her. She untied the white bow, slowly lifted the box lid, and gasped for air.

"That's the key to my heart," Aiden said. Aiden walked around the table and pulled out the platinum petals key pendant with brilliant round diamonds. Yasmine noticed that the chain was also platinum and had diamonds.

"Boy, you should not be spending this kind of money on me. I am not your woman."

"You're right, but you could be," Aiden replied as he placed the necklace around her neck, running his hand down her collarbone.

"Aiden, why are we here at Vito's under candlelight alone?"

Aiden had always been upfront with Yasmine, but he was unsure if he should use the straightforward approach or beat around the bush.

His mother intended for him to use Yasmine to dupe his grandparents into giving him the company. However, Aiden planned on reconnecting with Tamia and asking her to be his wife.

He only agreed with his mother because he needed a backup fiancée. Unfortunately, things between him and Tamia didn't end exceptionally well. Yasmine was the exonerating type, but Tamia could hold a grudge. He may need more than the summer to get her to forgive him.

"I am moving back to California. Pop-pop is looking to minimize his responsibilities and allow me to run the company. Now that I am back, I want you back in my bed." Aiden figured he had told no lies.

"Do I have a chance at burying my bone between your lips?" he asked in a kiddy tone.

Yasmine shifted in her seat. Her body and pussy wanted her to scream, "Hell yeah."

However, her heart and mind were in love with Craig. Her pussy stayed quiet because the romantic weekend she had planned was fabulous, but the sex was mediocre.

She wanted Craig to fuck her until she could not walk. Instead, he kept his head buried between her thighs. She wanted Craig to make her forget how to breathe or make her want to pull her hair out because it was so damn good.

Niah, her best friend, once told her that Jarvis's lovemaking was so good that it struck tears from her soul.

"Craig...I...I mean, Aiden, I am engaged. You had your chance with me, and you messed it up."

Before he could respond, the waiter walked in. "Sir, are you guys ready to order?"

"Yes," Aiden replied. "Bring her the Caesar salad and me the house salad. Then, for an appetizer, we will take the scampi a la grilia. For dinner, she will have the linguine alla pescatore and for me, the zuppa di pesce. We will also take a bottle of Chateauneuf du Pape."

Yasmine was overly impressed that Aiden remembered what she liked to eat at Vito's after all these years. "I am shocked you remembered all of my favorites," she said.

Each time Yasmine stared into Aiden's face, she bit her bottom lip. Aiden could see she was fighting the urge to taste him; therefore, he didn't address sex anymore. They drank wine and reminisced about their younger years.

"Can I get you something else?" The waiter asked as he opened another bottle of wine.

"Some privacy and no more interruptions," Aiden replied.

"No more wine for me. I am a little tipsy," Yasmine announced. She knew it was time to stop drinking because the more she drank, the wetter her panties became.

"Let's see. Stand to your feet," Aiden told her.

She sprung up from the chair and spun around. "See, I am not drunk, maybe a bit tipsy." When she veered around, Aiden was standing in front of her.

He pulled her into his embrace, ramming his tongue down her throat. He tugged at her sheer panties until he heard them rip.

He dipped two fingers inside of her vagina, grinding the heel of his hand against her clit, until he located the spongy cluster of nerves shaped like a lima bean. He applied pressure to her g-spot, milling the heel palm harder into her flesh.

"We can't do this," she protested. Yasmine fought his advances as long as she could before taking over the kiss. Lust filled her body as she danced on Aiden's fingers.

"No, don't stop. Yes, stop," Yasmine protested, pushing Aiden away, pretending to walk out of the private dining room. Aiden chuckled inside. If she had paced any slower, she would be walking backward.

"Wait, T-Baby! I am sorry." The mellow masculinity of his tone halted her steps.

Her body shivered. Aiden wrapped his arms around her petite waist. He pushed her up against the wall, kicked her legs apart, sprung his firm dick free from his pants, and thrust his stiff penis into her warm sopping wet pussy.

The form of his penis pressing against her blood-swollen walls astounded her. She openly welcomed each thrust.

Yasmine could feel juices running down her thighs. Aiden and Craig were the only men that could make her this wet. With other men, she had to use some form of lubrication.

Her pussy had a direct link to her heart. She could tell the level of affection she felt for a man by her moisture.

She wrapped her arms around his shoulders, pulling him in closer, concealing her face in the crook of his neck. Aiden eased out of her wetness and gazed into her face. He captured her protruding bottom lip with his teeth before pulling her lip into his mouth.

Yasmine placed both hands on the side of his jacket and exchanged positions with him. This session was not going to end without her and him exploding. Aiden could never resist her oral skills, and he needed a reminder.

She knelt before Aiden, casting her eyes upward until they locked with Aiden's.

She latched on to the tip of his penis, slowly inhaling his manhood inch by inch. Her ears rang when his breath hitched in his throat.

Aiden was pissed that her rusty-brown hair was in a neat French roll. He needed to entangle his hands through her locks to ensure she didn't stop.

He could never last long when Yasmine devoured his manhood. She hummed on his penis, concentrating on the thick bell of his penis. She moaned when sweet precum saturated her tongue. Aiden's body started losing strength as the blood flowed from his limbs, traveling towards his midsection. He jerked as a lightning rod of sweet cream coated Yasmine's throat.

Aiden yanked Yasmine to her feet, then before she could speak a word, Aiden lifted her in the air against the wall aligning her wetness with his tongue.

Her breathing became heavy and shallow as she struggled to contain the scream building in her gut. She arched her back against the wall. Soft whimpers escaped her throat as Aiden roared across her sensitive flesh.

The host eased the curtain open and rapidly closed it. Aiden's tongue torpedoed across her engorged clit faster, triggering her body to vibrate against the wall.

Ashamed, Yasmine pushed Aiden back and searched the floor for her shredded panties in pure disgust.

"That is my pussy and always will be," Aiden smugly said before exiting the room.

Chapter 07

Tamia pulled up to Aiden's beachfront Malibu home second-guessing her decision to come to Aiden's party. She shook her head, noticing there was only one more car and a van parked in the driveway in front of the white wrought iron gate.

The attendant opened her door and took her keys before escorting her to the entrance. Tamia adjusted her outfit as she traveled on the elevator to the lower second level per the attendant's instructions.

When the doors opened, a lovely Hispanic woman greeted her with flowers and a glass of wine before taking her coat.

"Right this way, Ms. Hill."

Aiden was nervous and terrified. He'd bought three outfits for tonight, but nothing felt right. He sensed he was overthinking everything. Yasmine and Tamia were different women. He couldn't bury his head between Tamia's legs to make her forgive him. Sex was never their motivation; it was honesty and unconditional love.

Tamia talked a good game, but she didn't sleep with half of the men she entertained. Growing up, Tamia always had his back, and he had hers. Scared of his mother's wrath, he dated Yasmine to appease her. However, he could never cut Tamia loose.

Somehow his mother discovered he was talking to Tamia while attending Princeton University. He pondered how his mother found out throughout the years because he didn't leave a money trail.

Pop-pop gave him emergency cash when he left for college, and his father and grandma did the same. He used that money to visit Tamia in Atlanta. When Tamia came to see him, he purchased her bus ticket with cash because she couldn't fly without an adult present.

Everything was going smoothly until he declined his mother summons.

He told his mother he was spending his memorial vacation with his frat brothers, and Tamia informed her grandmother she had to take a bus to Florida for a cheerleader competition.

When Aiden returned to school, Andrea was waiting on him. She knew he had been in Florida with Tamia, and they had been talking for years. His mother was livid. She hit him for the first time in his life.

Over the years, Aiden tracked Tamia's movements. He knew where she worked and how she spent most of her time with her social club, the BAE's.

He was jealous and worried when Davis sent him pictures of Tamia and a man hugging until he identified the man as Tre, their childhood friend.

Tre and Aiden visited Atlanta for the summer and some holidays; however, he was surprised that he and Tamia were still hanging out.

Aiden examined himself in the mirror one more time. He knew he couldn't go wrong rocking Tom Ford from head to toe.

He removed the tie, unbuttoned the top three buttons of his shirt, and wrapped a long black silk scarf around his neck to enhance his smoky gray pinstripe suit.

Stepping on the elevator to go up one floor, he nervously ran his hand over his head, tucking his scarf inside his jacket, buttoning it. Not because he was intimidated by Tamia. He knew she wasn't easily manipulated, and her presence always clouded his psyche.

An involuntary moan worked its way up to his throat when the doors opened, revealing Tamia's ample backside.

"Ooh wee, you came to step on necks," he said, stepping off the elevator.

She spun around, squaring her shoulders, standing a bit taller than he remembered.

A large gasp escaped his mouth, and he slammed his mouth close. He thought the back of her dress was lovely. The front was a two-toned color block cutout strappy sleeveless dress.

He ran his tongue over his top lip, then the bottom at the sight of her honeydew melon breasts, spilling out her dress. A cutout by her navel revealed a diamond belly ring, and a strap crossed her hip, caressing her bikini line, making him wish he were that fabric strapped around her body.

"Where are the rest of the guests?" Mesmerized by her, he hunched his shoulders. "The invitation stated welcome home celebration."

A few minutes passed as they basked in silence before he waved his hand between them.

"I see milk does an ass good, and the hills have grown," Aiden joked. Tamia's face twisted into a frown. "Girl, I popped those hips and ass out."

With a tongue as sharp as his, she barked, "Aiden, you have been gone for a couple of years. Did you think your Malibu house and sorry letters would grant you access to shoot up the club?"

She placed her hands on her hips. "You cannot and will not have a taste of my essence."

As she ranted, her dress shifted, allowing him a glimpse of her inner thighs. He wished the dress would inch up a tad more.

"I am trying to feed you, not fuck you, Mia Amor."

He could feel her sharp inhale.

"Thanks for paying off my student loans and for continuously depositing money into the bank account you opened for me when we were kids."

"Mia Amor, I have always been looking out for you whether you wanted me to or not. You're my future, girl."

"If you hadn't noticed, I am a woman now."

He pulled his bottom lip through his teeth and chewed on it before releasing it. "I have noticed."

Her stance lessened, and he stepped closer. She shook her head. "Do you know you are the reason I went into finance?"

"I was supposed to become a dental surgeon, and you were going to manage all of our money as we opened multiple Parkhill locations."

She scoffed. "Yea, Parkwood and Hill. To be a silly kid, believing in happily ever after."

A grin played at the corners of his mouth. "Why can't we have a happily ever after. Mia Amor Hill? I still love you. You were the first woman I ever made love to."

"You were the only man, not just the first." She hunched her shoulders. He went to speak, and she placed her index finger over his thick alluring lips. "You and my mother made me the woman that I am."

His shoulder slumped forward. He knew that wasn't a compliment.

Tamia's mother was dreadful to her growing up. Sometimes he wondered if he loved her or felt remorseful for her.

He never imagined a mother could be jealous of her child until he encountered Yolanda. He quickly grasped that all the stories Tamia told concerning her mother were factual.

At eleven, her mother kicked her out of the house, insinuating Tamia had sex with her boyfriend because her hips were spreading.

Over the years, Aiden blamed himself, and he always felt that if he never had sexual intercourse with Tamia, her body wouldn't have developed rapidly.

"If you are trying to get me back in your life, I need the peanut butter kid I fell in love with the first summer he visited his Ma'Dear, not the Fresh Prince of Bel-Air. And don't get me started on the rich, arrogant asshole who posed on the elevator. I never knew you came from inherited wealth, and I didn't care. And newsflash, I still don't care."

His heart leaped out of his chest into his palms, and he wanted to hand it to Tamia.

He guided her to the table where the chief had placed the appetizer. He pulled out her chair, pulled her in for a hug, and sniffed her hair.

He swept her hair aside, gracing her neck with wet kisses. She detested the jolt that shot through her body and landed between her thighs.

He tilted his head over until it reached her hands. She ran her hand over his shiny, thick waves.

"Are you trying to make me seasick?"

He cut his eyes up at her. "No, I'm merely trying to love you until the day we die. I want what my grandparents share."

She cleared her throat. "What about your mother?"

Aiden wished he could say he didn't value his mother's acceptance anymore nor follow her instructions, but he would be lying. "I will handle her," was all he could manage to whisper.

"I need a man that can stand up to his mother and put me first." He nudged his head against her hand. "Look, Aiden, I am more afraid of being miserable than being alone. So, I refuse to sneak around, hiding our relationship from your mother."

"I am not asking you to do that. There is a gala next week. I'm at my grandfather's table, but I bought you an entire table. Can you and the BAE's come?"

Her brows tightened, causing her nose to wrinkle.

"So, I can add stalking to your list." They both chuckled.

"I will even send a car for the ladies, but I want you to ride with me.

Aiden didn't know how this would pan out since his mother told him to invite Yasmine. He'd had tickets sent to her office.

His puppy dog eyes peered into her. "Are you trying to get me drunk with those whiskey brown eyes?"

He laid his cheek in the palm of her hand. "I could ask you the same question about your brandy-colored eyes."

She smiled, and he felt hopeful. She lifted his head. "You broke me once. I will never allow that to happen again."

He nodded and apologized.

"Are you seeing anyone else?" He opened his mouth to speak, and she stopped him. "If you are, stop. Let me clarify the question," she said as he attempted to speak again. "If you are sleeping with any women, tell me now. Revealing the truth means you're done."

Tamia's head whipped in the direction of the chef. She could have sworn she heard him say, "Don't do it, player."

"We are adults now, and I can handle the truth -- lies make me flip the fuck out. So, please don't come back into my life with lies."

Aiden figured there was no need to tell her about smashing Yasmine because he wasn't planning on doing it again.

He gazed into his future wife's eyes and lied.

Chapter 08

Despite her name plate being fastened to the beige cubicle's soft-sided wall, Yasmine continued to call her administrative assistant of six years the wrong name.

"What did I tell you about all of these personal pictures?" Yasmine barked, flinging her hand towards pictures of Stacy and her fiancé.

Her cousin kept telling her to quit, but Yasmine had a lot to teach her. Last year Stacy enrolled back in college. One day she would take Yasmine's place. Until then, she was determined to learn all she could from her.

"Stace, I feel like I am missing something important today. Do I have anything on my calendar?"

Before Stacy could pull up Yasmine's calendar, she threatened to write her up if she didn't take her pictures down. "Nobody needs to be reminded you have a loving boyfriend every minute of the day, and why do you guys look so damn happy?"

Pretending to look at her schedule, Stacy replied, "No, Mrs. Brooks. You don't have anything scheduled for today."

"Stace, are you positive? Maybe it's my mother's birthday or something."

"No, Mrs. Brooks, I have yet to miss any of your loved one's special days."

"OK, Stace! Girl, I trust you. I know you are always on your J.O.B. because you know I would fire you in a heartbeat."

Once Yasmine was in her office, Stacy called her cousin and divulged her plans. As she hung up the phone, a delivery guy handed her flowers.

"Mrs. Brooks, you have a delivery."

"Well. Bring it in."

When Stacy walked in holding a box of chocolates and a summer array of flowers, Yasmine gasped.

"Thank you, girlfriend." She rolled her eyes before handing her boss the chocolates.

"You have one more gift. It's a gift basket full of treats."

Stacy shook her head as she walked out. What a waste. She knew Yasmine would eat all those treats, then go to the restroom and give it to the porcelain gods.

Yasmine admired the lavender and gold bath essential basket. Spinning the basket, she gasped when she noticed a bottle of wine, flutes, and sweet treats. She knew all these gifts had to have come from Aiden because all Craig ever sent was dull white roses.

"Stace," Yasmine yelled instead of using her phone's intercom.

"Yes, Mrs. Brooks."

"Please clear my schedule for the day. I am going home early," Yasmine lied. She did not want Stacy to presume she was going to see Aiden even though she was.

Yasmine picked up the phone the minute her assistant exited her office to call her temptation.

"Hey, sexy," she greeted Aiden. "You were on my mind, and I just wanted to say...."

"Thank you," he blurted out before she could express her gratitude.

"Exactly. I need to come to thank you physically." Yasmine giggled, smoothing her hair.

Aiden paused for a second. When he told Tamia he wasn't smashing anyone; he'd meant from that point moving forward. However, he was sexually deprived.

He and Tamia had hung out five times, and she wouldn't even allow him to sniff her underwear. He ran his hand over his head then swiped his face.

"Aiden, are you there?"

"Yes. Meet me at the Loews Santa Monica Beach Hotel." He couldn't take her to his house because he had given Tamia full access to his home to pop in whenever she desired.

She smacked her lips. "Why so far away? It will take me some time to get there." The truth was the first time she adorned this lobby was after Craig proposed.

"Well, if you leave now, you will get there faster."

Yasmine walked into the beige and blue decorated room. Aiden was lying in the middle of the king-sized bed.

A gust of wind blew in from the balcony; she shivered, wondering if the wind was warning her to leave.

"Bring me that sweet pussy," he beckoned her.

Aiden sat on the side of the bed as Yasmine slowly undressed for him. He pulled her close and inhaled her alluring scent.

The smell of her sweet ecstasy made his dick hard as steel. He kissed her belly as he made his way to her sweet spot.

"No," she protested, "tonight, it's my show. I am thanking you, remember."

Yasmine laid down on the bed across from Aiden, spreading her legs far apart, propping her head on two pillows. She twirled two fingers in her mouth, then plunged them between her lips, teasing her clit.

Peering Aiden in his eyes as she seductively played with herself. "Ooooh, Lawd," she moaned.

Aiden slowly stroked his dick as he watched Yasmine get lost in ecstasy. She could feel Aiden pushing her hand out of the way and replacing it with his tongue.

Gazing down at him, Yasmine laced her fingers behind his head, pulling his face into her wetness. She figured if he couldn't breathe, at least, he would die happy.

Yasmine's legs began to quiver as a massive orgasm stirred inside of her. She braced her feet on Aiden's shoulder and kicked him off her.

She enjoyed seeing the same disappointment he left on her face at Vito's.

She gripped his penis and led him over to the chair sitting at the table.

His body trembled in anticipation. Yasmine slid her warm mouth over his dick until she gagged. She viscously sucked his penis, taking occasional breaks to apply pressure to her tongue to produce more saliva.

The veins in Aiden's penis exaggerated. She traced the swollen lines with the tip of her tongue. His penis knocked against the roof of her mouth before coating her throat. She sucked every drop of nectar from his body.

Aiden pulled away. "Baby, enough, he is sensitive."

She slid up his torso, rubbing her breast against his lips. He latched onto her breast like a newborn baby starving for a taste of her sweet nourishment. Aiden licked, slurped, and nibbled on her pudgy breast until his penis was fully erect and ready for round two.

She could feel his penis tapping on her tummy; pulling away, she eyed him seductively.

"I see you are ready for round two," she joked. Before he could respond, Yasmine adjusted her warmth over his erect penis and slid down.

"Damn, T-baby! Put it on me, girl."

"You haven't said nothing at all," she whispered in his ear. Aiden placed his hands on her waist, trying to get her to move. She was great at oral sex, but her bedroom skills lacked.

Aiden kissed her on the back, thrusting his hips upward. He guided her hips in a circular motion, clockwise, then counterclockwise.

The tight grip of her walls added to the excitement. Aiden pulled on her nipples, and she exploded.

Her head fell back in exhaustion. "No, no, my turn. I want to fuck you on the balcony," he moaned in her ear.

Yasmine followed him onto the balcony. As she attempted to ask him how he wanted her, he pushed her over the rail, ramming his penis inside her.

Aiden smacked her on each ass cheek as he pounded away. "Give it to me, big daddy," she screamed in bliss. A moment later, Aiden's sweat-soaked body collapsed onto her back. He panted in her ear, trying to catch his breath.

"I put it on you."

He arched a skeptical brow but didn't respond.

When Yasmine stepped out of the shower, she thought her eyes were playing a trick on her. It was eight o'clock at night.

She nervously chuckled then texted Laura, Niah, and Monica telling them she enjoyed her day with them, and she would text once she made it home.

She walked straight out of the bathroom to the entrance. "Wait, T-Baby, come swallow my playground one more time."

"Boy, you are talking crazy. My fiancé has called ten times. I must go. He is probably wondering about his dinner."

"Tell him I ate all of his pussy up," Aiden joked.

Yasmine smacked her lips. "Yes, you did," she replied. "I have to go."

"OK," Aiden yelled as Yasmine walked out the door.

The gentle breeze of the California night whispered cheater in Yasmine's ear as she ran from the hotel exit to her car.

Chapter 09

Flying down Pacific Coast Highway, Yasmine practiced the lies she would tell Craig. It felt as if she would never reach her house, which was a stone's throw away from Escondido Beach.

Her Benz felt like it was on two wheels when Yasmine skyrocketed into their mid-century three-bed ocean view Malibu driveway.

She hoped her fiancé was on the bottom level in the cigar room, enjoying a stogie and a glass of burgundy Merlot, with an open concept house that would be the only way to avoid him.

The California winds now sounded like Craig's whimpering cry when his father passed away.

Yasmine recalled the pain her fiancé suffered when his father died. Nevertheless, she tried to convince herself that her affair could not be compared to Craig's father's passing. Craig crying or hurting because of her dalliance with Aiden was too much for her heart to endure.

Yasmine loathed the pleasure she felt with Aiden and the sudden rush of guilt after she climaxed was ripping her soul apart.

Regretful tears slipped down her cheeks.

"I am going to stop this, Lord. I truly mean it this time. I need your help," she whispered as she peered skyward, hoping to see a star blazing.

Tiptoeing into the house, she jumped backward when she noticed Craig on the decorated deck off the kitchen. She knew she was missing something important today.

She wished she had listened to his messages or even Niah's. Normally her phone would connect to her Bluetooth, but tonight it didn't, and she didn't want to risk getting a ticket coming from Santa Monica.

Once she was near their house, she picked up her cell phone to listen to Craig's messages. When a police officer pulled behind her, she nervously dropped the phone on the side of the door.

Yasmine stood there with tears strolling down her face as she looked into Craig's eyes. She took a seat at the dining room table decorated with candles — which had burned utterly out —, salad, and a bottle of Moët.

"Happy Anniversary," Craig yelled once he looked up at Yasmine.

Her heart leaped from her chest into her throat, and she was speechless. She knew she had forgotten something important today.

"Baby, what took you so long to get home?" he questioned. "Didn't you get my gifts and invitation?"

Heartbroken, she slowly nodded her head. She had just thanked the wrong man for showering her with gifts.

"I am sorry, baby," she muttered.

She didn't know why she felt ashamed when Craig was fucking some tramp name Nectar.

Her grandmother always said, "two wrongs don't make it right."

Before the text and Aiden's return, she was somewhat satisfied with her relationship in and out of the bedroom. She had her mother and Aiden's mother in her ear talking about how Craig couldn't provide for her in the same matter as Aiden.

Her mind zoned out as Craig talked.

She wondered if Aiden was chasing after her because he was ready to be a power couple or their mothers pressured him. For as long as she could remember, their mothers controlled their lives.

Because their fathers were friends naturally, their mothers became friends. Many people thought their mothers befriended each other because they both were married to Caucasian men.

After her father left, her mother turned bitter and obsessed with her and Yasmine's weight because the young ivory beauty he left her mother for was thin.

By the time Yasmine was ten, her mother was feeding her chocolate ex-lax right after each meal to ensure she didn't gain any more weight.

If she gained a pound, her mother only provided her water with one vegetable and fruit shake for an entire week, threatening to punish her if she ate at school.

Aiden had to force her to eat when they were at a carnival because she had passed out.

Fearful of her mother's wrath, she purged. It felt liberating as she gained some form of control over her eating tendencies.

It was the only power she possessed in her life, and she asserted it as needed. So, she gorged herself then liberated herself from that day forward.

During a visit to Princeton, Aiden caught her in the bathroom, expunging her guts. He demanded she stop, and if she didn't, he would leave her alone.

Worried about losing Aiden, she told her mother and asked her to take her to get help. Her mother assured her she was fine and that there was nothing wrong with wanting to stay thin.

She told Yasmine, "Do whatever you have to do before some white woman steals Aiden from you."

Once Aiden returned to attend UCLA, he noticed her hair was brittle.

He inspected her teeth once a week. She didn't realize the acid from her stomach was corrosive and could wear away the enamel protecting her teeth. He even started to weigh her.

Her mother advised her to fill up on water before each weigh-in to trick the scales then take the diuretic she gave her.

Aiden threatened to end things with Yasmine if she didn't eat. She had started eating and was keeping it down.

Then one day, she caught Aiden arguing with a woman on campus. She will never forget the way he held the crying female in his arms.

When the girl pushed him away, Aiden plopped down on a bench, and she could hear him crying.

Instead of confronting him, she went on a massive binge. Whenever he was around, nothing in the world mattered except them. When he wasn't near her, all she did was eat, cry, and purge.

Once Aiden left town, she moved away from her mother. She didn't need to purge unless she had a pressing deadline or after a breakup. Until the text, she had stopped altogether. Now, she was back at it again.

"Will you make it to the engagement party? I'm only asking because you haven't been assisting me with the planning."

Planning her autumn wedding had slipped her mind lately. "I have been planning things with Laura, Niah, and Monica." Fibbing was becoming easier with each white lie.

Craig knew she was lying because he coordinated with her friends to plan her engagement party and honeymoon due to her hectic schedule. "If you lie, you will cheat. If you cheat, you will steal," he uttered to himself.

Noticing the pain tensed in his facial muscles broke her spirits. "I love you, Craig. I will do better."

"I know, honey. Thanks for having Stacy deliver my gift and some red roses." He lifted his wrist, admiring his watch.

"I love this watch. I guess I shouldn't be disappointed since she explained you had a business meeting. However, honey, I don't understand why you did not wrap it up early or have it canceled altogether to celebrate our anniversary."

At a loss for words, she did the one thing that permanently halted any man's questions. She dropped to her knees and freed his penis.

Craig stopped her as her mouth hovered over his erected penis. "Honey, do you still want to marry me?"

Punishing her tonsils with the tip of his penis, she allowed her sloppy toppy to answer the question.

Chapter 10

Facing the elevator, Tamia fixed herself in the oversized cream leather chair. She wanted her face to be the first thing Aiden laid his sexy eyes upon when he walked through the door.

She wasn't sure if the summer heat or her replaying the rude things her egg donor implanted into her head caused her heat to rise.

Tamia slid out of her studded cage bra, restrained garter panties, and laid them neatly on the chair before going to the pool to skinny dip.

"Miss Independent" by Ne-Yo blazed from the house intercoms.

She swam laps in the saltwater infinity pool, flashes of her disapproving parent's face slammed against her skull. Finding Yolanda sitting in her driveway was the last thing she needed after deciding she would make love to Aiden tonight.

Before stepping out of the car, Tamia vowed to give Yolanda whatever price she placed on giving birth to her today.

"Aiden is back," was the first thing her parent said. Tamia greeted her twice, hoping she would change the subject and move on.

"Has your fast ass seen him?"

"Mom, how much money do you need?"

Yolanda sucked her back teeth before speaking. "I don't need nuttin'. My numbers hit. I am so glad I moved to Los Angeles."

Tamia found it ironic that her parent didn't want her around as a teen because she resembled her father and possessed the body her parent claimed she had before birthing five kids. Since she was the second oldest sibling, she didn't see how any of this was her fault. Since none of her other kids wanted to take care of her, she moved to Los Angeles.

Tamia assist Yolanda with living arrangements, but Yolanda's thirty-day timeline stay at her house had expired. Yolanda tried to play the mother card, but as far as Tamia was concerned, her mother died when her grandmother closed her eyes. She was the one who raised her, even when she stayed with Yolanda. Yolanda used her as a punching bag after her father left or whenever she was angry, which was all the time.

"OK, cool. So how can I help you, Yolanda?"

"First, you can show me some damn respect. I am your mother."

Tamia flipped her hair in frustration.

"Bitch, you are not gorgeous. Back in the day, my ass was bigger than yours and my hips were wider. Men nicknamed me Cola."

"Cool, Yolanda."

"Is Aiden still swimming in cash? Did he give you some money?"

Tamia shook her head. Her mother stopped surprising her with the stuff that flew out of her mouth when she was fourteen. "I guess. It's a shame I am not a kid anymore, and you cannot place a price tag on my body."

"Bitch, I got us paid. Just stay away from his ass. You are not good enough for his family, and do you truly believe he loves you? I bet he is somewhere fucking some rich bitch as we speak."

Tamia stopped swimming to admire the crystal blue Malibu ocean. "Hey, my little mermaid," Aiden said, eyeballing her from a beige and brown lounge chair on the deck.

"Diva" by Beyoncé echoed as Tamia stepped her wet naked body out of the pool. Aiden puffed on a Cuban cigar, blowing smoke rings into the air.

"Fuck being a Diva, Mia Amour. Be my wife."

She heard Yolanda in her head. "Aiden is rich, and he doesn't love you. White boys fuck hood bitches; they don't marry them. Let's imagine his lily-white grandparent's face when Aiden brings a burnt bitch home."

Tamia was the second lightest out of her siblings, but Yolanda's nicknames for Tamia were burnt bitch, tar baby, and asphalt slut.

Whoever said, "sticks and stones can break your bones, but words will never hurt," didn't have Yolanda as a parent. She believed Aiden adored her, but his drunken lovestruck eyes and the way he showered her with gifts and affirmations screamed unconditional love.

"Why can't I be a female hustla and a wife?"

"You can be whatever you want as long as you are mine."

His eyes started at her feet, raping her body until their brown liquor irises connected. Was this his best friend and first lover standing before him?

Her naked body– gingerbread skin, five-foot-ten-inch frame, dark berry nipples, curvaceous Coca-Cola hips leading to an ass which could hold a cup and a saucer on it– was the type of shit that adorned every man's fantasies.

"I'm assuming the panties at my front door mean I can have them?"

A mischievous smile bounced across her face. "Only if you don't want the cookie that comes in them."

"You have to wear that outfit later tonight." She nodded. "I was trying to envision how you would look with it on. I didn't see any pumps." She pointed to the stiletto close to his feet.

He ran his skillfully silk tongue over his top and bottom lips, causing her to do the same.

He undressed, then led her to the jacuzzi. Aiden pulled her body close to him.

The heat surging from his body warmed the space. He pinned her to the wall and rocked his hips against hers, inciting a moan from her heavenly lips.

Aiden drew her nipple into his mouth, stimulating a whimper from her throat.

She curved her hand around the nape of his neck, dragging him in closer, nipping his bottom lip, then sucking on it to soothe the pain.

"Aiden, please don't hurt me again." A tear trickled down her cheek, filling his heart with a warm, clenching pain. He dropped his head in shame.

She rested her chin on his head. "You broke me down to the studs. It took a long time to build myself back up. If you are not ready for this, step away and come back when you are. I cannot go through that again."

Tamia cradled his head in her palms, wiping his tear-streaked cheeks with her thumbs.

Tamia's stern demeanor crumbled at the sight of his tears.

"I will never deceive you again," he declared. "I will never do anything to hurt you again."

She smiled. Aiden's tears were evidence that Yolanda was wrong.

Aiden murmured in Tamia's ear, "You're so damn sexy. I love you, Mia Amour."

She could feel his hard penis pressing against the small of her back. She eased her body back into his, resting her head on his shoulders.

One hand cupped her breast. Her only response was a soft whimper as she dropped the fluffy white towel in her hands.

He teased and rolled her left nipple with his forefinger and thumb while his right hand found the moisture between her legs, making her gasp for air.

Aiden always bragged that Tamia was the only woman that could make him ejaculate more than four times in one night.

Three and half years might have passed, but he still knew the ins and outs of her body. She wasn't Yasmine. He couldn't fuck her happy.

She didn't care about his money, so gifts were off the table.

To win his Mia Amour back, he needed God on his side because his actions, words, and heart had to be genuine and sincere. Therefore, he could not imagine doing anything else except making love to her, savoring each stroke and kiss.

Since they were teens engaging in sex, he never had to play teacher or guide her hips because they were each other's first everything. They knew what the other craved and desired without any words spoken.

Tamia parted her thighs a bit more, hooking her right arm behind his head, raking her hand through his hair.

His eyes rolled to ask his brain if this was happening.

She slanted her head to the right. Aiden knew that meant to devour her neck with kisses.

Overwhelmed with desire, he picked her up. She wrapped her legs around his waist, nestling her face under his right jawline as he carried her to the elevator.

Aiden laid her down on his California king bed.

She sucked in a gulp of air as Aiden lingered over her, admiring the soft hill at the junction of her thighs.

Her umber skin sparkled under the moonlight. A cool ocean breeze swept across his back, indicating it was time to feel her warmth wrapped around his penis.

However, the heat and wetness from her pussy summoned him there first.

He massaged the junction of her thighs, securing her leg over his shoulder using his right arm, gripping her waist, yanking her body until his meal kissed his lips.

He curled his tongue around her delicate skin, inciting her body to squeal in pleasure as he savored her sweetness. He repeated the motion, attempting to gain the same response.

Once she hollered his name, he eased back and continuously blew on her engorged flesh.

She tried to return the favor, but he refused her gesture, gently pushing her back onto the bed, fastening her leg back onto his shoulder.

He hitched her knee over his elbow, guiding his penis towards her hot entrance. Waves of pleasure lurched through her body.

"Still fits like a cozy glove," he whimpered in her ear.

She drew her bottom lip into her mouth and nibbled on it as he expanded her flesh.

Rocking her hips, she flipped him over. Her tongue slid into his mouth.

A deep roar escaped his throat when her rhythmic motion hurried.

He sunk his fingertips in her buttocks, smacking her on the ass.

Ripples of pleasure soared through her body, triggering her vagina muscles to tighten.

He lifted his head, capturing her swollen nipple between his teeth, moaning as her nipple sprouted in his mouth.

Then, the dam broke. Her juices flowed, pooling in the crest of his thighs. He thrust his hips upwards, sailing deep inside her, sending a lightning bolt of electricity through her body, prompting her back to arch.

Pleasure built deep inside her gut. She threw her head back, enjoying the tension of his warm flesh pressing against her walls as they screamed each other's name into the ocean breeze.

Chapter 11

The sound of the shower door caused Tamia to steer in the bed. Aiden sat on the top step of the steam shower in deep thought with his head hung low. He needed to confess.

The last six weeks they spent together reminded him of the old days. They went to movies, dancing, and he even found himself yelling on a roller coaster at Magic Mountain. His life with Tamia was carefree and easy. He felt like she could sense when he needed her.

For example, the other day, his street team didn't show up to help promote his community event. On cue, Tamia popped up sporting white Nike Airforce 1 sneakers paired with jean shorts and a white Parkwood T-shirt.

He still doesn't know where she found all those volunteers to help. A few times that day, he had to chase off some young boys trying to holler at his future wife, but he couldn't blame them. Tamia was an amazing woman, and her beauty was alluring to a blind man.

When his mother suggested using Yasmine's company to handle the marketing and promotions for the community event, he met up with Yasmine, and his dick slipped into her mouth. As great as Tamia made Aiden feel, his dick kept getting him in trouble.

He hoped Tamia would forgive him because he hadn't seen or touched Yasmine since he and Tamia made love.

Yet, the guilt of his past actions was killing him, and he still hadn't told his mother that he wasn't going to wed Yasmine or play games with her life because he was marrying Tamia.

He hoped Yasmine would be happy with Mr. Lawson.

Tamia watched Aiden, speculating what was on his mind.

She entered the shower and sat on the lower step laying her head on his thigh.

A million thoughts shot through his head. He had his Mia Amour back, and he didn't want to risk losing her again.

She was the woman he wanted to present to his grandparents as his fiancée. He didn't know how to satisfy his heart without disappointing his mother.

The entire time he was gone, he slept with a handful of residents. However, he never spent the night, nor did he engage in pillow talk after sex because he wasn't trying to create a bond with anyone since he was bonded to his Mia already.

If he and Tamia compared stories, they would be similar. Tamia indulged in men's attention and money, but not their bodies.

Although Aiden broke her heart, forcing her to vow never to take him back again, her heart saw it from a different vantage point.

Her heart recorded the tears he cried when she walked away, constantly reminding her that she had loved him since she was eleven, pointing out how he had been financially supporting her since he was sixteen -- sending her his allowance to buy school clothes, stationery, and anything else she needed.

She didn't even mind when he stopped sending her money.

He accidentally forgot to add his usual two hundred dollars in a rush to mail Tamia her special month-end letter. To amend his mistake, he immediately sent an apology card with three hundred dollars when Tamia didn't thank him, he found it odd but brushed it off.

The following month he only sent one hundred instead of the usual two hundred. Again, Tamia didn't complain. The following month he sent a letter with a note stating no more cash for you.

During their weekly call, she asked him why his letter was so crumbled and covered with tons of masking tape.

He surprised her shortly after that, and while he was visiting, he opened her a banking account.

He didn't have any proof, but he was sure her mother or sister stole her cash gifts.

Since she was only fourteen, he had to be the primary account holder. He also acquired her a PO Box to send his letters, explaining he would deposit money in her account at the beginning of each month.

When she graduated from junior high school, Aiden deposited a ton of money in her account as a graduation gift and to buy her prom dress. She was the only student whose escort was about to graduate high school and head to an ivy league college.

Most of her friends already knew Aiden. He was the big-headed boy from California that Tamia slapped because Yolanda told her that when people like you, they hit you.

After her graduation, Yolanda asked Tamia to give her five hundred dollars for her rent.

Before Tamia could lie, Yolanda revealed that she knew Aiden sent her money monthly. Admitting to taking the money, Tamia owed her for rent when she lived with her.

Tamia always wondered why her egg donor came over to Ma'Dear's house the first week of the month. She was waiting on Aiden's cash envelope.

When Tamia became outraged, Yolanda asserted Tamia should thank her for giving her the other letters and not putting Aiden's rapist ass behind bars.

Everyone knew about her and Aiden. She reasoned their relationship was acceptable when she was ten and he was fourteen.

Once he turned eighteen, it was no longer suitable. Tamia had to pay Yolanda three hundred a month to keep Aiden out of jail from that day forward.

She always thought Aiden knew about Yolanda's bribery fee until she realized Aiden increased the amount each year.

To this day, she still had the bank account, and Aiden still deposited cash in their joint bank account on their anniversary, Valentine's Day, her birthday, and holidays- constantly reminding her heart that he was thinking about her.

"A penny for your thoughts?"

He expelled all the air in his lungs. "Pop-pop doesn't want to give the company to me if I'm not married."

Her head popped up, and he immediately knew what she was thinking.

"That is not why I asked you to be my wife. I love you, Mia. I was out there running from the pain of losing you, my dad, and avoiding my mother's outrageous demands."

She eased her head back down, deciding to hear him out.

"My mother wants me to sabotage my competition by destroying her marriage. Mother believes they are pretending to be happy." He hunched his shoulders.

"I caught him eyeballing your ass at the gala, but that doesn't mean their marriage is fractured."

"Why because men can look as long as they don't touch?"

"Exactly. We are not blind, for fuck's sake."

"I know your grandfather's only requirement was not marriage."

"He wanted to hear our vision for the company's future."

"And?"

"Her ideas were to have a mobile free dental clinic, have doctors volunteer their time, and students serve as dental assistants and hygienists."

He paused, brushing his hand across her cheek.

"Mine was to treat hospital patients out of Parkwood and go into prisons. We need to be in the community promoting dental health and teaching about the importance of oral care to reduce heart disease. I also suggested a college scholarship in my father's name, offer sponsorships for international students, and to host a global student exchange."

Pride filled her heart, and words of affirmation flowed from her mouth. "You don't need to fight dirty. You have a better plan. Your community event was amazing."

He kissed her forehead.

"Aiden, I cannot agree to be your wife. I'm still learning to trust you again. I enjoy the gifts, the outings, making love, and I may laugh as we reminisce, but some stories cause anguish because I can still feel the pain connected to the memory."

Aiden decided it was not the right time to confess.

"Then there is your mother. You play me whenever she is around. So now you are going to destroy a marriage for her?"

He huffed in frustration. "I don't want to destroy her marriage, only see if she is lying to Pop-pop. A nasty divorce or scandal can destroy the brand."

She could hear the sincerity in his voice.

Tamia rolled her eyes and rumbled loudly. "I will see if she is playing Pop-pop."

"OK, but what do I tell my mother? She wants me to...."

She cut him short, pushing him away. She despised his egg donor as much as she did hers. They didn't deserve the title of mother. What more could she do to prove she had his best interest at heart without him always running to his mother?

Aiden gripped her towel as she tried to leave. Yanking away, she tossed the towel in his face.

"I can't do this shit again. You are a mama's boy, and you cannot cut the cord and stand on your own feet."

Aiden rose. His presence filled the earth-tone oversized sauna shower. The heat in his seductive gaze beckoned her body to come back.

"I love you. I would walk barefooted across hot ass coals for you." He sat on the shower bench, opening his arms, waiting for her to fill the space.

Tamia turned her lips upwards. Yolanda and Andrea's words played in her mind creating doubt.

"Come here, sexy. Don't make me beg," Aiden pleaded.

She shook her head. "I have to go. If you want me back in your life, you must break the hold your mother has over you. I don't mean put her on the back burner. I mean, evict her from the damn stove."

Stepping towards the entrance, Aiden gripped her waist, lifting her in the air, placing her on his shoulders, burying his head between her thighs.

She tugged at his hair. Everything inside of her warned her to resist and demand he release her. Instead, she relaxed and enjoyed the ride as his tongue explored her sugar walls.

"Ooooh damn, Mia Amour," Aiden moaned, "I was crazy to leave you. I promise never to abandon you again. I will set my mother straight. Stay the night and every night after that, baby. I need you."

"Uh-huh, I'm about to explode, Aiden, ooh-wee..."

Tamia buried her face in his hair. Tears rolled from her eyes. She didn't know if the tears came from pure pleasure or the fear of being caught in his mother's web again.

Chapter 12

His eyes scanned the dimly lit room. "Why are we here?" Ty questioned Tamia as they walked through the doors of 4play.

She knew where to find Tre, the third member of the trifling three or the creep squad to others. Ever since he started dating the virgin BAE, he lived in strip clubs.

"Bring me a shot of Patron," Tre yelled at the waitress from a table.

"I am sorry, but we don't serve liquor in this place," she advised Tre.

"This fool visits so many clubs he's beginning to confuse them," Ty said to Tamia.

"The trifling three in the house," Tamia said to Tre, patting him on the back. He gave her a head nod. "Do Miya know yo' ass up in here?"

"I don't have to get pre-approval from my girlfriend. Shit, she ain't my wife, and I ain't got no plans to wife her ass."

"Damn, motherfucker, be easy. She is my girl."

"I am still trying to figure out why you hook this nasty motherfucker up with her," Ty joked.

Tre flipped Tamia and Ty off. "Join me in the back. I need a favor from you guys."

"Bitch, can you bring me a soda to the back table?" Tre barked at the waitress.

"Damn. Show some respect."

Tre scoffed at Ty's comment. "Every woman you talk about you call a bitch. Tamia is the only person with a pussy I ain't heard you call a bitch," Tre countered.

Ty smacked Tamia on the ass, and she giggled. "This my fucking sister, I got mad respect for this hustla."

Tamia rolled her eyes. Tonight was not the night to piss her creep squad off.

"Aiden is back in L.A." Tamia watched the trifling two's responses. Tre's face turned sour, while Ty maintained his bright white smile.

"His grandfather is thinking about giving the company to some white girl because she is married."

She decided not to tell them that she and Aiden had been sprinting around Los Angeles like lovestruck teenagers. Aiden was inviting her to Parkwood events. When she received his invitation and the Parkwood T-shirt, she chuckled at his old-school tactics. It had been years since someone sent her a letter.

She quickly gathered her volunteers to support his community event. She was speechless when Aiden sent her a black car to escort them to Magic Mountain.

She was surprised he remembered all the adventures she desired to try in her letters when they were kids.

She once wrote that she wanted to do an under-the-boardwalk tour. Aiden sent a car for her, and when it pulled up to Venice Beach, he was standing there waiting with a dozen red roses.

They spent an hour enjoying the pier attractions before the driver took them to the next boardwalk beach.

She was caught inside of a fairy tale, and Aiden was slowly chipping away at her protective shield. She couldn't even recall her rules anymore because she had tossed her rulebook out the window.

Not interested in any conversation about Aiden, Tre ran his hand over his jet-black fade then gazed at the stage.

Tre and Aiden hung out each time they came to Atlanta for the summer. Tre had planned to make Tamia his girlfriend, but Aiden's peanut butter ass claimed Tamia as his girl.

"Tre, pay attention," Tamia barked. "You see these loose tramps all the time. Your baby sister needs a favor."

Tre rolled his eyes. Tamia hated when the bitch came out of him. Besides, he owed her a favor for hooking him up with Miya.

She knew Tre hated Aiden because he wanted to be with her.

After Tamia caught Aiden kissing some bitch on his college campus, Tamia remembered seeing a picture of the girl in his bag when he visited her in Atlanta after leaving California.

Aiden swore she was his cousin. The knot in her tummy knew it was a lie, but she was desperate to believe her man.

After catching them kissing, he confessed to dating Yasmine while dating her because his mother forced him. He pledged he didn't love her.

While crying on Tre's shoulder, he dropped to his knees. Before her mind could register what was happening, she was saturating his face. They never told Ty what happened, and they remained the trifling three.

"I need you to see if Aiden's competition will sleep with you, but don't smash, Tre. If there is a crack in her foundation, one indecent proposal will crack that foundation wide open."

"Why didn't you ask this Chocolate Adonis motherfucker?"

Ty threw his hands in the air as if he were being arrested. "Everybody knows Chocolate Ty doesn't fuck for free." He glided his tongue over his thick L.L. Cool J lips.

Tamia thought about it for a minute. Women did love Ty's low-cut fade, square chiseled jaw, almond sliced coffee bean eyes, and dark chocolate skin that made their panties moist. However, Tre was rude in public, but a gentleman while trying to get the cookie.

Ty was a gentleman in public and a disrespectful asshole when he was killing that monkey. She knew her creep squad.

"I need you to work those hazel brown eyes and baby face. Leave this hoe dreaming about your smooth chocolate skin and your perfectly trimmed goatee."

She pointed to Ty. "This fool will smash her, make her pay for the privilege, and blame it all on Chocolate Ty like they are not the same damn person."

Ty contorted his face. "We are not that same. I'm mellow and laid back. On the other hand, Chocolate Ty is a fucking dick."

Tamia and Tre shook their heads at Ty.

Tamia could not understand why an intelligent, educated Black man would choose to be a male escort. She figured his mother must have messed him up the same way Yolanda fucked her up.

Tre traced his succulent lips with his tongue. "You know these bitches can't resist the baby face," Tre said, running his hands over his smooth skin.

They all chuckled at Tre's cockiness.

"I saw her husband at Aiden's gala. His short round ass isn't hitting it right. His dick is probably hiding under his fat ass gut. If white men have a small dick, I am quite sure he can't afford to lose an inch."

This comment caused the entire table to erupt in laughter.

"Regardless of what white women say, they all want a taste of a chocolate dick," Ty announced. This time the whole table high-fived each other. "Eighty percent of my clients are white."

"Plus, I caught her eying Aiden, so I know she wants some chocolate."

Tre turned his palms upward. "Technically, that fool ain't Black."

"If he got pulled over by a police officer, they would call him a nigga. They don't know he has a white father; therefore, that motherfucker is Black," Ty declared.

They all stared at each other because Ty told no lies, but the truth still slapped them all in the face.

"Camera Phone" by The Game broke the silence at the table. "That's your girl."

"Motherfucker, you are too damn old to have a song as your ringtone."

Tamia snatched his phone, answering it, assuring Miya, the youngest BAE, that she and Tre were out clubbing and she would send him her way soon.

She passed Tre the phone with a joker smile plastered on her face. "So, I guess you're going to blackmail my ass into this scheme? And if I don't, you are going to tell Miya we were at the strip club."

"I wasn't, but that ain't a bad plan." Ty chuckled, slapping Tre across his back.

"Coming to the stage tonight is your girl, Candy Licker. Tonight, she is going to show you why they call her Da Candy Licker and how to enjoy a piece of delicious candy."

They all smiled, making their way towards the stage. "You better remain faithful," Tamia sang to Tre and Ty.

"Shit Tatiana knows who the fuck I am."

"I'm not married, and me and Miya ain't fucking." Tre paused his thought.

"You have a lot of damn nerves, Tamia. First, you tell me to propose an indecent proposal to Aiden's competition, and then you tell me not to fuck a stripper."

"Exactly. One is an offer, and the other is an action."

"Damn, Tamia. Did you see what that bitch just did?" Ty asked in amazement.

She nodded.

"Can you do that," Tre questioned with his mouth agape.

"Fool, if I could do that, I would never leave my house. I would be a lovely fold's eating fool," she joked.

Tre clicked his teeth, causing Ty and Tamia to gawk at him. "See how that white boy is changing her. Now, she is saying shit like, 'lovely folds' instead of pussy. Next, she'll be saying figgy pudding or some shit like that."

Ty chuckled. When Tamia gawked at him, he stopped. Tre gazed into Tamia's eyes. "I bet that bitch is at home eating her p.u.s.s.y all the time."

"And men jack off. Shit, I wish all women could please themselves, then we would have all the power."

"God knew better," Ty voiced, slapping palms with Tre. "Well, men have most of the power right now."

Tamia's eyes batted rapidly. "You guys stay with us for sex. But we can please ourselves. We have hands, showerheads, and an adult market that caters to the needs of a woman. We have more power than you men realize. We don't flex as you guys do. We tend to fall and stroke your damn fragile egos because we stay with you for love."

She folded her hands over her chest, waiting for their replies.

"Men are the rulers in the bedroom and boardroom," Ty expressed.

"For now, but shit, this world is slowly changing because more women are waking up and evoking their power. So, you better read Proverbs 31: 10-31 better than ask yourself if God knew more and better," Tamia noted.

Chapter 13

She spun around twice, scrutinizing her curvaceous body. "Here, try this one on," Tamia said, flinging a purple strapless draped dress by Bebe under the dressing room door for her friend girl, Miya. "I am getting these. My ass looked fluffy and delicious in these pants."

"Come out, let me see you," Miya requested.

"Too late, I already switched outfits," Tamia revealed, stepping out of the dressing room sporting a pair of linen-stitched hot shorts, a gold sequin racer-back tank, and gold five-and-half-inch leather strap peep-toe shoes.

"I want to cheat on myself with myself. Damn, boo, you are thick." She blew a kiss to her reflection.

Miya chuckled.

"I wish I had your body," a raw umber beauty stated to Tamia, but she didn't respond.

"You both look beautiful," Miya stated. "I wish I was a stallion like you."

"You look so familiar," the woman said to Miya as Tamia continued to model in the lengthy mirror.

"Do you work in marketing?" Miya shook her head from side to side. "Do you live in Malibu?" Before Miya could answer, the lady fired off another question. "Are you in banking? My fiancé, Craig, is in that field, and I attend many events with him."

Tamia eyed the ladies as she returned to the dressing room, mumbling under her breath. Tamia halted her steps when the lady asked Miya if she was at the dental gala.

"I remember seeing you there. Laura, come here," the lady called out to her friend. "Do you remember her?"

"Yes, she was at the gala," Laura recalled. "We both said we wished we had her Natalie Cole look. Brown hair, brown skin, and brown eyes with the cute beauty mark above your lip."

Miya blushed at the compliment.

"All of the women at your table were gorgeous," Laura admitted.

Before Miya could say another word, Tamia screamed for Miya to help her in the dressing room.

Tamia debated if she should tell Miya about her past with the woman. Shit, she had never informed the BAEs about her relationship with Aiden.

Instead of riding with Aiden to the gala, she rode in the truck with her girls, convincing a sad Aiden that she had to ride with her BAEs since she'd invited them.

He agreed that it would be rude if she didn't hang with her girls.

Each time Aiden attempted to make his way to her table, his mother pulled him back.

After his mother whispered something in his ear, he gave Tamia a lost puppy dog gaze.

Anger brewed in Tamia's gut when Aiden didn't approach her table.

The BAEs kept joking that Tamia was dating some wealthy married dentist. Instead of correcting them, she played the bad girl.

Once she spotted Ty at the gala, she was relieved. Finally, someone who knew the real her and not the opportunist shield of herself.

Jealousy stung her heart as the women threw themselves all over

Aiden. Like a good mama's boy, he allowed his mother to flaunt different women in his face.

Andrea smiled in Tamia's direction each time Aiden hugged a woman. Tamia thought she was the childish one, but it was Andrea.

Tamia refused to fall for Andrea's bait. She wasn't a fourteen-year-old girl anymore who didn't know how to conduct herself in public.

She would never embarrass Aiden publicly. She would wait until they were at home to act a damn fool.

When Tamia started laughing and talking with Ty, Aiden fixed his eyes on her every movement. She could feel his eyes tracing her curves.

Coming out of the restroom, Aiden pulled her to the side.

"Why are you laughing all in that man's face?"

She shoved him in the chest.

"The same reason you up in here looking like Chester the cat as Andrea pimps you out," she replied.

Of course, she could have told him that it was Tyrik.

The last time Aiden saw Tyrik was in Atlanta when Aiden was seventeen. Back then, Ty was a tall wafer-thin boy walking around sucking his thumb.

"I fell for all of your bullshit promises this week. You love me so much, right? So why are you sneaking to talk to me, looking over your shoulder afraid of the devil who birthed you."

As they were talking, Andrea walked up and addressed Aiden as if she didn't see Tamia.

Tamia pushed her finger into Aiden's temple. Pissed he didn't check his warden, she left with Ty to hurt Aiden.

Aiden called her all night then showed up at her doorstep. He burst into her condominium only to discover she was lying in bed eating Doritos and chocolate frozen yogurt.

He crawled in the bed next to her, apologizing for his behavior. She made him open his mouth and eat her signature treat. She held his mouth close, ensuring he didn't spit it out. Since that night, they'd experienced a ton of beautiful moments.

Now she was wondering if Aiden invited Yasmine or was it Andrea's doing. She loved Aiden dearly, but she refused to be with a man who couldn't stand up to his mother and proclaim his love for her.

"You should get those black leatherette leggings. Your body would look good in those."

Tamia placed her index finger to her lips to hush Miya as she listened to Yasmine and her friend in the next dressing room. Miya looked around bewildered, wondering what was going on before taking a seat on the stool in the dressing room to answer some text messages.

"Cousin, Aiden has fucked me a couple of times, but he still hasn't invited me to his house." Tamia heard Yasmine say.

"Bitch, I am not going to hell for you. Craig called, looking for you on your anniversary. Girl, you are going to lose Craig. Don't you want to become Mrs. Lawson?"

"I was in Santa Monica, having mind-blowing sex with Aiden. Bitch, it took me forever to get back home."

Tamia wanted to cry, but she held it in because Miya was in the dressing room with her. She couldn't believe Aiden was cheating on her after the seven weeks they'd had together.

"Miya, can you step out for a minute?"

As soon as the door closed, Tamia plopped down on the seat and silently whimpered.

She wasn't sure before, or maybe she didn't want to believe this was the same Yasmine from her childhood when she spotted her at the gala.

"If a man wanted you, he would fuck you in his house. Instead, Aiden has fucked you in a restaurant and a parking lot," Laura reminded Yasmine.

"I gave him head in the parking lot. Before that, we fucked at Vito's and the Lowes in Santa Monica."

Yasmine hated the way her cousin stared at her and downplayed her and Aiden's relationship. She hadn't seen Aiden in weeks, but he was busy trying to save his company.

"The night of the gala reminded me of the debutante ball, making me want Aiden instead of Craig."

Laura rolled her eyes at her stupid cousin. Craig was a good man, and Aiden was a dog if you asked Laura.

"Aiden didn't even hug or dance with you at the gala. Bitch, you are picturing shit in your head that did not happen."

Yasmine ignored her cousin's comment and continued to talk. Her mother and Andrea had been blowing her phone up, wondering how long it would take her to execute their plan.

"Cousin, do you recall the stocky young man sitting at the table with Aiden next to the thick white woman?" Laura nodded her head, and Yasmine continued. "If you sleep with that fat guy and destroy their marriage Aiden has agreed to marry me."

Tamia couldn't believe what she was hearing. Aiden had sought Yasmine's help as well. She had already tasked Tre with seeing if Brooklyn's marriage was happy.

There was no need for anyone to be destroying homes and having sex. Tamia rolled her eyes so hard it hurt.

If Aiden asked her to do some shit like that, she would have slapped the shit out of him, then had Tre and Ty beat his ass.

No company position should be worth a man's most prized possession.

All these years, she wondered if Yasmine was better than her and why Aiden dated them both. It was clear he dealt with Yasmine because he could control her.

Tamia wondered how Aiden would feel if someone manipulated him and toyed with his heart the same way he dallied with theirs.

"Bitch, I will think about it," Laura replied. "What's in it for me?"

"I will pay you ten grand," Yasmine replied. "Marrying Aiden would be a dream come true. I cannot put a price tag on happily ever after."

"And Craig?"

"I will call off the wedding. Andrea and my mother are already planning my wedding to Aiden."

Laura laughed. "Bitch, all of you are crazy. Craig is a good man. I would stick with him."

Yasmine fanned the air between them, blocking Laura's words.

A knot formed in Tamia's throat, trapping a dreadful scream in her chest as tears flowed down her cheeks. She covered up her mouth as Miya knocked on the door.

"I'll be out shortly," Tamia finally managed to say. She applied fresh makeup and walked out with her head held high and a new armor built around her heart.

Tamia paid for her clothes, hugged Miya goodbye, and trailed behind Yasmine and her cousin.

Tamia didn't know why she followed Yasmine to her car and was trailing behind her on the freeway.

When Yasmine cruised down Pacific Coast Highway, she wondered if Yasmine was meeting Aiden at his house.

Tamia scratched her head as Yasmine passed up Aiden's home.

Twelve minutes later, Yasmine pulled into a beachfront home's garage.

Tamia wondered if the zip code was the only thing Yasmine and Aiden were sharing.

In bed that night, Tamia asked Aiden again if he had smashed another woman since he returned to LA, and he nervously lied to her face again.

Chapter 14

Yasmine sat at her desk, trying to understand what had happened the other day. When she came out of the beauty salon, her car was on four flats.

Ever since Yasmine slept with Aiden, her life had been spiraling. Still, she had no clue how she would destroy Aiden's co-worker's marriage if Laura refused her offer.

"Stace, can you come in, please."

"Sure, Mrs. Brooks," Stacy responded.

"Stace, how did you remember my anniversary if it was not on the calendar?"

"Well, Mr. Lawson called and asked me to get you out of the office early because he was at home fixing you an anniversary meal. I called your cousin, and she said you were with her, and you guys were out shopping, then headed to your house."

Yasmine didn't recall receiving a message from Laura that night. She couldn't justify why that night was still annoying her after all this time.

"Since I told you there was nothing on the calendar. I felt like it was my duty to go out and get Mr. Lawson a gift, and when I delivered the gift to your house, I told him you had a late business meeting when he asked where you were. I hope that was all right," Stacy meekly replied.

"That was perfectly fine, Stace. I just wanted to know how you remembered after I left the office."

Yasmine didn't know why she felt her assistant and cousin were attempting to sabotage her engagement.

"Ms. Brooks, Mr. Parkwood is holding on line two for you," Stacy announced through the phone intercom. "Do you want me to clear your schedule for the day?"

Embarrassed, Yasmine barked, "Why would I want you to do that? Stick to answering the damn phones."

"No reason at all, ma'am." Stacy felt Yasmine should show her some respect. She completed her current projects, worked on Mr. Parkwood's mock-up, and ran errands to buy her fiancé gifts while she was out eating and drinking.

"Put him through, Stace," Yasmine barked.

"Hello, sexy," Yasmine greeted Aiden. "I am missing you like crazy. Do you think we can get together?"

"Damn, can you at least ask me how my day is going before you ask for cock?" Craig joked. "You haven't been frisky like this in a while, but I love it, Yaz."

"Craig," Yasmine said, realizing she answered the wrong line. "How is your day going?"

"Better now, I have an appointment that I cannot cancel. After that, I can meet you at home, or we can get a room."

Disappointment sailed across Yasmine's face. She was looking forward to digging her nails in Aiden's back. "A room would be great. I will send you the details."

Yasmine hung up with Craig and noticed line one was no longer flashing. She called Aiden back.

"Hey, we were calling for an update on the project, but the meeting is over, and I am busy. I hope you can complete the plans soon," Aiden said in one breath.

Aiden had taken Tamia's advice and spoke to Brooklyn.

Brooklyn agreed that Aiden had a better vision for the company and complimented him on his global travel. In turn, he promised to support her mobile clinic idea and added a few upgrades to her project plan.

Next, Aiden called Yasmine's office because she was the best at what she does. Her assistant Stacy assured him Yasmine would send a mock-up soon.

He informed Stacy that Brooklyn would be the point of contact.

Aiden was relieved when Yasmine didn't call him whining. He preferred not to work with her directly.

He didn't want to cross the line with her, and although he could not rewind time, he could ensure it never happened again or placed himself in a situation that could hurt Tamia's feelings.

Brooklyn had informed him that Yasmine's assistant was terrific, and once she finished school, they should hire her for in-house marketing.

Stacy had already sent over the first deck for their approval. He and Brooklyn thought the deck was good, but they were looking for something extraordinary.

Aiden couldn't wait to show Tamia the completed project. With Tamia by his side, he felt as if he could slay Goliath.

When Andrea complained about him working with Brooklyn, he politely told her to mind her business. His mother didn't press the issue when she discovered Yasmine's company was handling the marketing strategy.

Andrea felt proud that Aiden had some of her characteristics and not all his father's weak genes.

Aiden picked up his phone to call Yasmine back but ended up calling Tamia.

Lately, they had been playing phone tag. He left her another message briefly, questioning if she was with the tall, muscular man from the gala.

Each time he asked her about the guy, she would tell him, "If you concentrate, you will figure out who he is."

The only thing that came to his mind was competition. He tilted his head to the side to expel the thought, acknowledging it was his own guilt manifesting.

After work, he decided to pop up at Tamia's door with wine, Doritos, and chocolate froyo.

Yasmine called Laura to confirm she was going to seduce Brooklyn's husband. Yasmine's ears perked up when Laura said Aiden's name.

"I think you should leave Aiden alone and focus on your engagement to Craig."

Yasmine puckered her lips as if she were sucking on Lemonheads.

"You are the one who suggested I should go see him."

Laura launched into a long rant before Yasmine calmed her down.

"How is it my fault? I told you that we should go out to eat with him, not let him eat you out," Laura replied, smacking her lips at the end of her statement. "Poor Craig, he worships the ground you walk on. This shit will kill him. Did you think about him?"

"Oh my, Lawd, now you care about Craig. Are you not the person that is always calling him Massa and shit?"

Laura popped her lips.

"Those are jokes. Girl, I am just messing with you. Craig is a good husband. Bitch, if he weren't with you, I would be riding his big white dick," Laura exclaimed.

"Bitch, now you got jokes."

"Well, I have to go. I am running late for an appointment. I will call you later."

Before Yasmine could say another word, Laura disconnected the call.

"Well, I am going to the mall for lunch to buy sexy lingerie for Craig," Yasmine said in a sarcastic tone to the dial tone.

Coming out of Macy's, Yasmine's heart fell into her shoes like cement bricks. Her eyes narrowed, focusing on the couple standing in front of a jewelry store.

Yasmine's lungs felt as though they were shriveling as Craig wrapped his arms around her cousin, pulling her close to his heart, rocking her from side to side.

Yasmine stumbled backward. She didn't see this coming.

How could her flesh and blood laugh in her face and fuck her fiancé behind her back?

She refused to believe what was happening mere steps from her.

Craig could not be flaunting his affair in broad daylight. Laura would not do this to her.

She scanned her memory. Neither one of them ever mentioned hanging out with each other, Yasmine thought to herself.

Yasmine retrieved her cellphone from her purse and dialed her cousin's number. Her cheeks burned hot as she watched Laura hit the ignore button on her cell phone, pointing to her phone while laughing with Craig.

Pacing in a circle, all Yasmine wanted to do was eat and purge.

She inched towards them, but fear of confrontation locked her muscles.

Yasmine dialed her fiancé. To her surprise, he answered. She watched as he placed his index finger to his lips, pointing at the phone.

"Where are you?" she asked frigidly. "Are you ready for tonight?"

"Oh, umm. I am stuck at work, ruffling through paperwork," Craig lied. "I can't wait for some of your sweet nectar."

Tears slipped from the corners of her eyes. Was he alluding to Laura's nectar? Yasmine's eye snapped wide with surprise when Laura blushed.

She spun around, attempting to build up the courage to walk over and confront them. She wiped the tears from her eyes, and when she turned around, Laura had disappeared, and her future husband was hugging and talking to another woman.

Yasmine quickly remembered the girl from the store Tags and the dental gala.

Laura couldn't take her eyes off the tall Chocolate Adonis wrapped around her arm. Shit, if that were her man, she wouldn't allow him to go to the bathroom by himself, she thought to herself the night of the gala.

Craig turned to walk away, and the woman walked in her direction.

Yasmine's throat thickened with emotion.

"Hi, Yasmine," the woman greeted.

Yasmine blinked several times before responding. "I see you know my name, but I don't know yours."

Yasmine may have been afraid to confront her loved ones because she feared them hurting her, but she didn't have any problems facing a stranger. However, she did wish Niah was there because she was the fighter, not her.

"Tamia, but Aiden calls me Mia Amour."

Acid and bile filled Yasmine's throat. She gulped it back down.

"I see your brain is connecting the dots," Tamia said, tilting her head back to laugh.

Yasmine went into a long speech using fancy words, assuming she'd talked over Tamia's uneducated head.

Tamia ran her middle finger down the brim of her nose. "Nothing you said has anything to do with me, and before you assume I didn't understand you, I am a college graduate with dual degrees. You and Aiden went to UCLA. I went to USC."

Yasmine smacked her lips.

Tamia giggled. "Let me speak your language since coinage is all you understand. This ghetto strumpet's wallet can crush your pretentious bank account any day of the week."

"You don't know what the fuck I make," Yasmine fired back.

Tamia's lips turned up into a smile. "I am in banking like Craig. I have worked with him before," Tamia admitted, which was not a lie.

Craig was her mentor during a retreat she attended, and they stayed connected. Craig's submitted Tamia's name as a potential contender for any program that landed on his desk.

"OK, so now what? You mad because Aiden is fucking me, and he doesn't want you?" Yasmine nervously giggled, but Tamia's facial expression never altered.

Tamia's smile widened. "I figured since we are sharing one man-" Tamia paused before landing her deadly heart blow.

"I figured why not share our nectar with two? I am sure Craig loves my nectar best, just like Aiden."

Before Yasmine could regroup from the lethal blow, Tamia strutted off.

Chapter 15

Yasmine burst through the front door of her mother's house. "Who in the hell is coming up in my house like the freaking police," Jasmine screamed from the kitchen. "Don't be slamming my damn front door, either."

"It's me, Mom," Yasmine shrieked, darting into the kitchen, fastening herself around her mother's waist, tugging on her arms, struggling to force her mother to hug her back.

Slamming the door did extraordinarily little to ease the pain swelling in Yasmine's chest. Yasmine's soul needed to feel the safety she felt before her father abandoned her and her mother.

Her mother bent her elbows and lifted her hands in the air, rolling her eyes. Then, craving affection, Yasmine cried, "I need you, Mom. Please hug me."

It wasn't that Jasmine didn't love her daughter. She didn't know how to give her child something her mother never instilled within her. Jasmine's mother taught her how to remain in her pretty box.

Her mother lectured on the importance of appearance, reprimanding

Jasmine when she gained weight, forcing her on water diets and coffee enemas to maintain her size two, which was overweight in her mother's eyes.

Yasmine's grandmother didn't educate her mother on God's word. She preached on the importance of marriage, noting she was raising wives, not single, independent women. Therefore, Jasmine infused the same core values into her child.

"Craig is sleeping with Laura." Yasmine felt like a vice was crushing her chest.

"Ok, who cares," Jasmine replied. "Did she sleep with Brooklyn's husband?"

"Mom," Yasmine whined.

"Child, stop all that damn crying and yelling. Her mother slept with my third, fifth, or seventh husband. Shit, my sister undoubtedly fucked your father," her mother voiced coldly. "Laura is a hoe like her mother. Now, did you get her to fuck that chubby man?"

"No. Laura fucking my fiancé and Aiden fucking Tamia threw me for a loop. Hence I didn't have a chance to follow you and Mrs. Andrea's directive."

Jasmine's demeanor softened. She awkwardly stroked her daughter's hair while patting her on the back. "Honey, you tend to exaggerate sometimes, especially when you are not getting your way. Are you sure Aiden is cheating on you with a woman named Tamia?"

"Yes. Aiden has been cheating with that ghetto bitch since we were kids. Andrea swore she got rid of her when we were in college. Mommy, I cannot lose Craig and Aiden."

Jasmine rolled her eyes when Yasmine retched. "Do you need to go to the restroom and heave? Will that help you calm the hell down?"

Talking in a baby voice, Yasmine lied. Although she desired nothing more, she didn't want her mother to know she was still purging.

Her mother always supported her retching to lose weight but not to manage stress; that was a form of weakness in her eyes.

"If you stop worrying about Craig and help Aiden obtain his family empire, Andrea will force Aiden to marry your weak ass once you complete her task. Aiden and Craig are like diamonds and cubic zirconia."

Yasmine felt that Craig was more like moissanite, not cheap as cubic zirconia.

Jasmine popped her daughter in the head. "Craig wears New Balance and suits off the rack, while Aiden wear's Tom Ford. If you marry Aiden, I will never have to worry about money again."

Yasmine smacked her lips, muttering under her breath. Jasmine tried pushing her daughter away. Yasmine applied a death grip to her mother's waist.

"Can you be a mother to me for once? Please, love me."

Halting Yasmine in mid-sentence, Jasmine forcefully shoved her daughter to the floor then took a seat at the kitchen table.

"Do whatever you have to do to help your future husband take over the Parkwood empire. Even if that means you take one for the team. You're your father's child. I'm sure sleeping with one more man once won't kill you. Just be smart about it and never let Aiden find out."

"But Mom —"

"But Mom," Jasmine whined, mimicking her daughter.

Yasmine eyes bucked at her mother.

"But Mom, my motherfucking ass. I am tired of getting married. Do you think I wanted seven estranged husbands? Nope! I did it so you could have the best upbringing and stay in Beverly Hills with your friends. Now get your fat ass off the floor."

Defeated, Yasmine dropped her head, turning on her heels.

"Try to get your weight under control before you marry Aiden," her mother yelled as she opened the front door.

Chapter 16

The clock ticked slowly for Tamia but not sluggish enough for her to sketch out her next steps. She wasn't sure how she should approach Aiden.

She had promised she was through with love the first time Aiden cheated and again after he casually strolled out of her life. Now Aiden had her dipped in deceit yet again.

After Tamia followed Yasmine home the other day, she called Miya and asked her where the woman from the gala said she worked. Miya recounted their entire conversation.

Tamia hung up the phone and googled Yasmine. She found tons of pictures of Yasmine at marketing events. She stumbled across a picture of Yasmine and Aiden's mother with another woman.

Tamia reasoned she must be Yasmine's baby sister because she was a younger version of her.

Shock etched across Tamia's face when she stumbled upon pictures of Yasmine and Craig.

Bumping into Craig at the mall during work hours, she thought the universe was messing with her until she spotted Yasmine eyeballing them.

Tamia didn't plan to reveal her hand, but she needed to put Yasmine on notice.

She wasn't about to allow Yasmine to take her spot next to Aiden.

Anger filled Tamia. She retrieved Aiden's laptop, searching for more info on Yasmine until she dozed off.

Soft lips, gracing Tamia's outer thigh, stirred her from her slumber.

She turned onto her back, and Aiden planted a kiss on the sensitive mound between her legs.

His fingers skimmed to her wetness, dipping two fingers deeper into her warmth as his mouth covered her exposed flesh.

Her mouth flew open in a soundless gasp. Aiden's signature aroma of birch and fruity undertones engulfed her body then sailed in her nostrils, making her insane with desire.

She wished her mind had no recollection of the man that her heart had loved her entire life. She refused to tuck her tail in anger and serve Yasmine, her soulmate, on a silver platter.

Tonight, she would remind Aiden that she wasn't a young, inexperienced girl.

"Oh, Aiden," she moaned. "Stick your tongue deeper inside of me." She gasped as Aiden gripped her ass cheeks, forcing his tongue deep inside her wetness.

He curled his tongue upward until he graced her little bean. Aiden applied pressure to her g-spot with the tip of his tongue as his nose tickled her clit.

Emotionally overwhelmed, she tugged at her hair as tears flowed from her eyes. She tried to twist away, retreating towards the headboard.

"Bring that sweet pussy back here," Aiden mumbled, yanking her back down onto his rigid tongue.

"Mmmm," she whined, rocking on his tongue. She locked her legs behind his head, clenching her thighs tightly, while Aiden drank her sweet juices.

Aiden eased up her trembling body. "Fuck! I missed you like crazy."

His whiskey eyes were drunk with lust. "Your essence is syrupy sweet I can still taste it on the tip of my tongue."

Tamia eased over, and Aiden laid on his back, she eased down his frame, and he pulled her mouth to his. Their tongues seductively waltzed.

He forced her to straddle him.

"Dominate me, baby," Aiden moaned.

Tamia sank onto his penis. He growled while tugging at the sheets.

He placed his hands on both sides of her face, pulling her mouth to his again. He gently captured her bottom lip with his teeth, then wedged his tongue between her lips, relishing the taste of her kiss.

Soft whimpers escaped her throat.

Aiden's mouth gaped open when Tamia churned her hips in a circular motion. She would rise off his penis every couple of laps, allowing his mushroom tip to tease her clit, before slamming back down on his manhood.

Aiden's mouth gaped open, heavy breathing and the echoing sound of entangled juices filled the dimly lit room.

She rode his penis faster. He smacked her on the ass, and she increased her speed. He gripped her waist to slow her pace. He wasn't ready for this to end.

"I've been eating my Wheaties," Tamia joked.

Aiden clutched her ass cheeks, spreading them apart, thrusting deeper inside of her, then smacked her ass again.

"Baby, this isn't a Wheaties booty; this is a collard green, oxtails, and cornbread fed ass."

He edged his hand to her breast, teasing her nipples until they were sturdy peaks. Aiden could feel the tension welling in her body as her orgasm approached.

Tamia threw her head back as she geared up to escort Aiden to the same wave she was riding. He lifted her off his manhood.

"I'm not ready yet. Are you ready to tap out?"

Depleted, she swayed her head from side to side. Aiden flipped her over, pulling her to her knees, and wedged a pillow under her hips. Tamia curved her spine, floating her bump in the air.

Aiden pulled her cheeks apart and traced her starfish pattern, allowing his tongue to caress the rim of her bottom. He rotated between his tongue and thumb, trailing circles around her perimeter.

"Oh, shit," she hollered when Aiden's thumb applied pressure to her backside, breaking the barrier, while his other hand flicked her soft folds.

Aiden stopped when her moans of pleasure turned into a sobbing cry. Her diaphragm spasmed as she laid on her back.

He captured her earlobe with his lips. "Did I hurt you?"

"No," she replied, which was half truthful.

The pleasure ripping through her body stumbled upon trapped grief buried deep inside of her. The more she tried to stop crying, the harder she wailed.

Aiden knew this cry. This was the same cry she cried when her Ma'Dear passed away and the one he wailed at his father's funeral.

To this day, he felt he could have made it through that day if Tamia were by his side, but Andrea had forbidden him from inviting her. Seeing the pain his mother was in, he didn't want to cause her more anguish.

After his father's funeral, Aiden felt trapped inside that moment.

He didn't have Tamia and Andrea nagged him daily about taking his father's seat in the company, demanding he withdraw money from his trust fund for her.

Running away from home helped him breathe a little.

If Andrea hadn't called to tell him about Tamia's grandmother, he would have never returned to the states.

Once he laid his eyes on Tamia, his restricted lungs opened.

When they made love that night, Aiden grasped what was missing in his life and whom he needed.

They agreed he would go tidy up some loose ends then join her in Los Angeles. Before he could book his trip back, Tamia had changed her number.

He sent Davis to the address she gave him, but Davis said she didn't live there. He had Davis hire an investigator to find her.

Aiden traveled statewide, learning from different doctors until Davis located Tamia.

Aiden followed Tamia around for months, trying to see if she was serious about anyone. However, Tamia spent most of her time with a social group called the BAEs.

He had met two of her club sisters, Lexi and Naja. His father had done business with Naja's dad, Titus. He met Lexi at an MLB game. Lexi's boyfriend was Paxton Young.

He aimed to win Tamia back before he informed his family of his return.

Someone saw him out and told Andrea. His mother showed up at his house demanding he move into the family estate. He refused because that would interfere with his plans.

"Mia Amour, I know this cry. It stems from pain. Talk to me."

Aiden applied soft kisses to her shoulder while professing his love. He rolled her over, placing his index finger under her chin, lifting her head until their souls connected.

"Do you forgive me?" Aiden whined.

She nodded. "I am sorry, I don't know what happened. Please continue to make love to me." She tugged on his arm until Aiden laid on top of her.

She ground her hips against his, kissing him passionately. She felt his penis nudge her thigh. She widened her legs, and Aiden slipped inside of her.

He buried his head in her hair. "I fucked up, baby. I'm not perfect, but I promise I will never mess up again."

Tamia wondered if he was referring to smashing Yasmine or leaving her all alone when she needed him the most.

Tears flowed freely from her eyes, gliding down his back and arm. Her cheeks stung. She slammed her eyes close, focusing on the pressure erecting inside of her.

"Say you forgive me," Aiden demanded, plunging deeper into her wetness.

"I am sorry. I won't fuck up again."

Her body quivered, producing a new round of tears. She dug her fingers in Aiden's shoulders, pulling his heart closer to hers, hoping to ease the pain crushing her chest.

"I will never hurt you again. I vow to provide and protect you always. Mia Amour, say you forgive me."

"I forgive you," she murmured in his ear. "Now, make love to me as if this is the last time."

Her tears graced his cheek, triggering Aiden to cry as well. They both felt depleted by regret and pain as their bodies climaxed in unison.

To ease their pain and atone for past mistakes, they made love until they both were happy and optimistic.

Chapter 17

After what happened at the mall, Yasmine had been spoiling Craig, hoping to remind him that she was better than her cousin, Laura and that hoodrat Aiden was sexing. Her mother was correct. She needed to mend fences with Laura, then pay her to sleep with Brooklyn's husband.

She buzzed Stacy. "Can you come to my office?"

Stacy grunted as she gathered her boss's deliverers stacked at her desk. "Yes, Ms. Brooks."

"Did you send Aiden the new deck? I called him, but he hasn't called me back." Before Stacy could answer her question, Yasmine continued to talk.

"What's all this?" she asked, pointing to the items Stacy placed on her desk.

"Ms. Niah dropped off her keys to her house and instructions for you. You promised to let the contractor in while she and Mr. Jarvis go on vacation. Remember you told me to put them in a safe place once she dropped them off and add it to your calendar."

Yasmine snapped her fingers. That explained why Niah had been calling nonstop. Yasmine meant to return her calls, but she had too much going on right now.

Stacy pointed to a brown box.

"That's from your mother." Yasmine rolled her eyes at the package. "Mr. Aiden called, but you were on the phone with Craig. I would have interrupted you, but you made it clear not to interrupt you when you were talking to your fiancé."

Yasmine teeth broke the barriers on her tongue. She could taste the salty crimson in her mouth. She felt Stacy didn't put the call through on purpose. She knew how vital Aiden was to her.

"He told me to tell you, 'You are almost there. A couple more tweaks, then the deck will be perfect.'"

"When did he say this?"

"Yesterday," Stacy rapidly replied.

"OK, did you redo the damn deck?"

Stacy wanted to remind her boss of her job title and responsibilities, but she forced those words back down her throat since she needed her job.

"The deck is done."

"Perfect, Stace," Yasmine said, knowing it made Stacy's skin cringe. "Call him and tell him to meet me at this address."

Yasmine wrote Niah's address on a post-it.

Stacy raised a skeptical brow as she recognized the address. She started to reveal that Monica had called and left a message about coming by Niah's house tonight to prepare for the contractor. Instead, she kept the information to herself, hoping Monica caught Yasmine in a compromising position and told Mr. Craig because she did not deserve a caring man like him.

Stacy wondered if Yasmine understood how much Monica hated her. Stacy grasped this fact a long time ago.

During a marketing event, Laura divulged the tension she felt between her boss and Monica was due to Yasmine sleeping with Monica's man, then warned her to keep her man away from her boss.

Yasmine could feel her vagina salivating as she imagined tonight in her head.

Last night she swore Aiden's penis was summing her. To smother the flame between her legs, she mounted Craig and rode him frantically as she pictured Aiden in her mind.

Yasmine called Craig's cellphone and left him a message informing him she had an off-site meeting. Then she called Kym, her Vietnamese friend; she needed a Brazilian wax.

She boxed up Aiden's deck and headed out.

Stacy tried to advise Yasmine that her mother was waiting on line one, but Yasmine fanned her off.

Stacy tried to tell Jasmine her daughter was gone for the day, and she needed to call her cellphone. But her mother insisted she knew where her child was going because she was her assistant.

Stacy had no issues with Monica catching Yasmine sleeping with Aiden, but not her mother.

Stacy's eyes watered when Yasmine's mother cursed her out and belittled her appearance.

"She went to Niah's house," Stacy blurted, then hung up on Jasmine.

She finally understood why her boss was a bitch because she was birthed by a psycho bitch.

Yasmine laid the new lingerie she had bought on the guest bed. Then, she went to Niah's room to get perfume and bath essentials, but the master suite and Jarvis's office were locked with a deadbolt.

Yasmine recalled a mixture Niah made once getting ready for an erotic night with Jarvis.

She went to the kitchen and blended a mix of honey and peaches. Once Yasmine washed the mixture off her body, she massaged her kitty with the same concoction, allowing it to air dry. She repeated the process three more times, wanting to be extra sweet for Aiden tonight.

She looked at the clock then placed a call to Stacy to see if Aiden had confirmed.

Stacy confirmed that Aiden had confirmed. Stacy was gearing up to tell her boss he called back to cancel when she heard a doorbell chiming.

Yasmine hung up on Stacy.

Yasmine checked the items on the dresser. The ice in the bowl with the whipped cream hadn't melted, and the peaches were still chilled.

She rotated the bottle of Moët in the ice bucket before dashing to the front door, praying she didn't slip on the pricey tile.

Yasmine's intestines twisted up in a painful knot.

She was instantly pissed she hadn't closed the gate and made Aiden use the entrance intercom.

"Oh my," Semaj said, gawking at her naked body. He licked his bottom lip hard, causing a sucking sound to escape his mouth.

Yasmine wished she had on a robe to slam it close. The thin white fabric left nothing to the imagination.

"I have the wrong address," he managed to say.

Yasmine started to let him walk away, but it was clear that Aiden would not give her any more attention until she broke up Brooklyn's marriage, securing his seat in the company.

She caught him by the wrist.

"No, Semaj, you are in the right place."

He appraised her shapely figure again. "Come here, sexy," she commanded. Semaj slowly walked past the threshold.

"Do you know Brooklyn?"

"Yes," Yasmine lied.

"I can't believe she is granting my birthday fantasy," he stammered, eyeballing Yasmine's butt as she ushered him to Niah's guest room.

Yasmine gulped hard as she unbuckled his pants, yanking two mints off the nightstand, popping them in her mouth.

She hoped her voluptuous, pouty lips didn't swallow up his penis. She clutched his penis with her thumb and index finger.

He grunted as she struggled to wrap her tongue around his dick.

She never used her hand, but she had no other choice. She ran her index finger and thumb up and down his penis, saturating it with her saliva.

"Yes, like that, sexy? Gag on it."

Yasmine wanted to laugh in his face, but she could not gag on a cocktail wiener.

"Oh shit," he bellowed out. "I am your bitch! Do your damn thang, gurl."

She couldn't grasp why he was talking to her in such a condescending manner.

"Big Daddy is about to cum," he warned her.

Her eyes watered as she struggled to force his thick semen down her throat. Semaj's sperm tasted bitter, unlike Aiden and Craig's, which was sweeter than any candy she had ever eaten.

She shook her head as if it were an Etch-A-Sketch trying to rid her thoughts of Craig by focusing on Aiden. He was the primary reason Yasmine was sleeping with Semaj.

She wrapped her lips around Semaj's penis again. He pulled away, she knew his tadpole was sensitive, but she needed to do something to occupy her mind.

"Ease up," he huffed.

Semaj took off his shirt then seized the bottle of Moët from the ice bucket sitting on the nightstand.

"I can't wait to taste a black cunt."

He drank from the bottle then pushed Yasmine on the bed, spitting champagne on the mounds of her folds.

He ran his tongue over her stomach, licking and slurping the champagne from her body. He latched onto her nipple with his teeth tugging until tears rolled from her eyes.

She yanked her breast from his mouth, but she missed the pain that surged through her body.

He smiled, then yanked her legs apart, spreading them full eagle.

He placed peaches between her lips, placing an ice cube between his lips. The ice cube fought the slippery peaches for access to her swollen clitoris.

The tip of his tongue pushed the peaches away. He latched onto her clit, sucking hard.

He grazed her clit with his teeth then soothed the pain. She swarmed in the bed as he admired her splendor.

He filled his mouth with ice, pushed the cubes inside her vagina with his tongue, and then sucked on her clit.

The pain and relief drove Yasmine crazy. Her despair turned into pleasure as moans escaped her throat.

"Now, that's the sound that Big Daddy has been waiting to hear."

"Oh, Lawd," she screamed as he manipulated her anus with his forefinger.

She clenched her thighs tightly around his head, not caring if she suffocated him as she came.

Semaj sat on the bed and patted Yasmine on the thigh.

"I know this is a one-time treat, but I have an offer that can benefit us both if you are willing to sneak behind Brooklyn's back. A house this big has to be expensive. I know you need money to help pay the bills."

Yasmine sat up and looked him in the face. "This is a friend's house, and this was a one-time thing, Semaj."

Semaj hunched his shoulders. "Your lost, sweetheart."

Semaj lifted off the bed to walk into the bathroom. The tires of flesh hanging from his side and pancake ass made her want to vomit.

Craig was muscular and fit, and so was Aiden.

She couldn't believe Aiden sent him over. She tried to force a smile upon her face. At least this was over.

She picked up Semaj's underwear and hid them in the drawer. She planned to call her mother and Andrea on the way home and advise them that Laura finally slept with Semaj and gave her his briefs to send to Brooklyn.

Tomorrow she would have a carrier deliver them to Brooklyn's office and demand she resign. She made a mental note to threaten to reveal her unhappy marriage to Dr. Parkwood if she does not quit.

The last thing she wanted to do was mess up Aiden's directive or for Andrea and her mother to discover she screwed up.

"Tomorrow, this will be a distant memory," she mumbled to herself.

She couldn't wait to see the joy on Aiden's face after she told him she had completed the task he entrusted to her.

Chapter 18

Yasmine had been calling Aiden's phone non-stop since yesterday. She even crept out of bed with Craig to leave Aiden a voicemail.

Tamia stirred in the bed and inched closer to the end of the bed each time Aiden's phone buzzed in his nightstand drawer.

Finally, Aiden turned his cell phone off without saying a word and pulled Tamia into his arms, apologizing for disturbing her sleep.

Tears filled Tamia's eyes, as she nuzzled in Aiden's arms. She knew it was Yasmine calling.

Back at Yasmine's house, she continued to call Aiden's phone, but it kept going to voicemail. She was about to leave another message when she heard Craig searching the house for her.

She emerged from the bathroom, led Craig back to their bed, and took her frustrations out on his penis.

Yasmine's face lit up when Aiden's number flashed on the LCD screen. She yelled hello a couple of times, but her cellphone always received horrible reception in the elevator.

The second she stepped off the elevator, her phone buzzed with a text. She quickly typed an affirmative response then stopped at her assistant's desk.

"Stace, Aiden is sending a carrier over with a package. Please bring me the item the second the carrier drops it off."

Stacy signed for the cookie basket, the floral bouquet, and some packages. She tossed the packets to the side and read the card attached to the basket. It was from Aiden, thanking Yasmine for doing a fantastic job on his account.

Stacy figured that since she did all the work, she should keep the flowers and cookies. Stacy stuffed the thank you card in her purse then took Yasmine the remaining mail.

Yasmine held the black and red invitation in her hand. The corner of her lips curled upward.

"Damn," she mumbled, glancing at the clock. She had to meet him at the hotel in two hours, and the invitation stated on time is late. She chuckled softly to herself. "Thirty minutes early is on time."

Yasmine felt around the envelope and pulled out a door key.

She knew it was for the Loews Santa Monica Beach Hotel. She couldn't wait to watch the sunset on the balcony in Aiden's arms.

Yasmine showered then laid out on the bed that anchored the suite he had rented. Her heart leaped from her chest when the door swung open. She could feel his eyes skimming her body.

She ran her index finger down her frame and buried it between her thighs. Her mouth hung open as her body arched off the bed. A lustful moan escaped her body.

"Bitch, crawl over here and suck my dick," he demanded.

Yasmine mounted to all fours and crawled towards the end of the bed. She halted. Her jaw tightened in anger.

"Yasmine, what are you doing?" He pointed to his rock-hard penis. "Bitch, get down here and suck this chocolaty lollipop."

Slamming her eyes closed, Yasmine performed the one task she knew she did well.

Tears rolled down her eyes as she wondered how many men Aiden needed her to fuck to prove her love.

Chocolate Ty pulled away from Yasmine. Her head game was no match for his well. If she continued, he would explode.

"Climb farther in the bed," he instructed.

He got on his knees in the bed behind her and slapped on a condom. He smacked his penis against her buttocks a couple of times, grunting in anticipation. Then, he pushed inside of her in one swift motion, and she groaned.

Her rigid body froze in place. Ty gripped her hips and rotated them in a circular movement on his penis.

"Come on, girl, move for me. You were eye-fucking me at the dental gala. Now that I'm here, you are going to be a lousy lay."

Yasmine faked moans of pleasure. Ty could feel her moans and vagina were not on one accord due to the rough friction as her juices slowly dried up.

He pulled out, drenching his condom with lube, then entered her again, slamming her backside viciously.

Something triggered inside of her causing her to thrust back into Chocolate Ty.

His L.L. Cool J lips, low-cut fade, square chiseled jaw, almond sliced coffee bean eyes, and dark chocolate skin brought her back to the night of the gala.

Yasmine became furious with herself. She was more focused on Aiden sending another man to smash her that she didn't realize Chocolate Ty was a gift from her mother. Fucking him was the sweetest revenge since Tamia had messed around with both of her men.

Yasmine tugged at the back of Chocolate Ty's thighs, forcing him deeper inside while bouncing her backside on his penis.

"Shit, bitch," he grunted.

He intensified his stroke, gripping her shoulders, pulverizing her insides.

"Oh yes," Yasmine screamed. The excitement of revenge made her wetter.

Chocolate Ty eased off Yasmine's back and went to the bathroom to clean up.

She wasn't the best in the sheets, Chocolate Ty thought to himself, but she could be a client on his roster because her head game was better than Superhead's.

"That will be two grand," Chocolate Ty demanded, walking back into the room.

"Two grand for what?" Yasmine rapidly replied.

"For the dick, I just gave you," Ty answered with no shame in his tone.

Yasmine moved to the end of the bed. Her face contorted before she asked, "You charge two grand for dick?"

"Hell no."

Yasmine was relieved but wanted to know why he asked her for money if he didn't charge for his penis. Was it a betrayal fee, she wondered?

"I charge five grand for this chocolate lollipop."

Yasmine's eyes bucked.

"The woman who hired me paid three grand, arranged for this room, and told me to ask for the key for Yasmine's suite. I assumed you were Yasmine, and you would pay the remaining balance after I provided my thick long service."

"What fucking woman?" Yasmine thought her mother had sent him, but why wouldn't she pay the total amount?

Maybe it was Laura because she saw Tamia and Chocolate Ty at the gala. The harder Yasmine thought about who hired him, the more her head throbbed.

"I don't know, but you can't find me in the yellow pages. I only fuck rich housewives that can afford my fee."

Yasmine let out an exasperated sigh. It was her mother. She could always depend on Jasmine to solve one issue while causing another.

Yasmine bit on her bottom lip. She wondered if Tamia knew her man was a male prostitute.

"Do you take credit cards or checks? Can I give the money to Tamia later?"

"Does it look like I have a fictitious business statement, an LLC, or a damn corporation? I deal with cash transactions only. Besides, my girl doesn't get involved in my business. We don't have that type of relationship. You need to pay me now."

Why couldn't her mother have shortened him by five hundred? She could have withdrawn that from any ATM.

Excitement bloomed inside her as she thought she could withdraw money from her checking, savings, and two credit cards to pay him. It didn't matter because she had juicy dirt on Tamia, and she couldn't wait to tell Aiden that Tamia's other man was a male hooker and he better get his dick checked out.

Chocolate Ty snapped his finger in her face. She rolled her eyes.

"Well, you need to form a consultant company to help manage your money. Then you can take checks and credit cards--a nice bogus business will help you camouflage your money. You are providing a form of sexual therapy. Maybe call it a life coaching business."

Ty clenched his chin. That wasn't a bad idea.

"The head was superb, and you gave me decent business advice. So, let's call it even." He passed her his card. "Call me if you ever what to suck and fuck. I only have two rules, no kissing, and you suck, I fuck. I don't eat pussy."

Yasmine shook her head. All his card stated was his name and a number.

Yasmine couldn't wait until tomorrow to talk to Aiden. Since Niah was still out of town, she decided to spend the night over there so Aiden could come to visit in the morning. She assumed Aiden stayed in Beverly Hills with his grandparents.

As Yasmine drove to Niah's million-dollar Brentwood home, it dawned on her that she desired more than an eight-bedroom home. She craved the love Niah and Jarvis shared when he wasn't cheating on her friend. She knew what she had to do.

Yasmine pulled out her cellphone and sent Aiden a 911 text with Niah's address, informing him she needed to talk tonight.

Aiden felt his phone buzz in his pocket as he was exiting Davis's house. Since he was already in the Brentwood area, he figured he would stop to thank Yasmine for the marketing campaign. He also needed to extinguish any notions of them hooking up again and ask her to stop calling him in the middle of the night.

He refused to hide his phone or turn it off when Tamia was home. He didn't want to give his woman any reason to doubt his love or loyalty.

Yasmine's hand nervously trembled as she tried to key in the security code for Niah's gate. The realization of the things she had done in the past few weeks weighed heavy on her heart.

Craig would never ask her to do the things that Aiden had demanded of her.

When Aiden pulled up to the house, he had to pat Mr. Lawson on the back because their place was gorgeous from the gate.

He couldn't wait to see the inside. Aiden pulled into the winding driveway, noticing a guesthouse to the right of the entrance.

Before he could stop, he saw Yasmine standing in the middle of the driveway. He pulled alongside Yasmine.

He noticed her red-rimmed eyes when he stepped out of the car. "Yasmine, what's wrong?"

She fell into his arms. "Why don't you respect me?"

Aiden was confused by her statement. He respected her and admired her work, and he stated those facts.

She pulled out of his embrace.

"Impossible. If a man respected you, he wouldn't allow other men to fuck you for his profit."

He pulled her hand into his. "Is Mr. Lawson forcing you to sleep with other men?"

She smacked his hand and stepped backward as if the question blew her away.

"Craig is the best thing that ever happened to me. Because of you and our mothers, I have risked my perfect life for a fantasy."

Aiden listened to Yasmine's babbling gibberish. The more she ranted, the deeper his confusion settled.

Finally, he placed his hand in her face to stop her ranting.

"I am not following. Start from the beginning as if I don't know anything."

She walked into the guesthouse. "We don't need to go to the main house. You missed that opportunity the other night."

Aiden's brows rose as he stepped into the guest house.

Yasmine decided to reveal everything to Aiden because she could never tell Craig what she had done to win the heart of a man who loved another woman.

Chapter 19

Stacy attempted to warn her boss that Craig was storming towards her office. The scowl on his face terrified Stacy.

Before she could buzz Yasmine's phone, he had passed her desk. She sprung from her seat, trying to cut him off before he reached Yasmine's door.

"Hold all her calls," Craig demanded, slamming the door in Stacy's face.

"Craig," Yasmine called out when a gust of wind shuffled the papers on her desk. She hurriedly covered up the contents on her desk.

"We need to have a serious conversation, and this could not wait until tonight -- that's if you came home."

Craig's statement dripped with contempt, and Yasmine wasn't accustomed to hearing him make snide remarks.

Tears immediately streamed from Yasmine's eyes at the thought of losing Craig. She had already lost Aiden. If he swore to stop sleeping with her cousin and Tamia, she would forgive him and never mention it again.

Craig opened his mouth to speak, and Yasmine cut him off. "I know you are cheating, and if you stop, I will forgive you, and we can move on with our wedding plans."

Craig scoffed. "Cheating with whom?"

"You're cheating with Laura, and before you lie, I saw the text message on your phone. You refer to her as 'Nectar.'"

"Monica sent that text to my phone by accident. I called her office and left a message with my cellphone number to solicit help with wedding planning. I called Niah's office and Laura's as well. Somehow your crazy friend sent me two texts meant for someone else. When we all met up to discuss plans for your bridal shower, wedding, and honeymoon, we all had a good laugh. I figured by now, you and your girls would have laughed about it as well. Niah wanted to be the one to tell you what happened."

Damn, that explained why Niah had been blowing her up. Niah knew how Yasmine's fear of being cheated on drove her over the deep end.

Her frown deepened.

Although that sounded like some dumb Monica shit, she couldn't believe it because that would mean she was the only cheater in her relationship, and she grasped at the idea of Craig cheating on her to justify her desire for Aiden.

"I bet you did," she replied coldly.

"I love you, Yasmine, and I thought you knew me better than that." He contorted his face as his own words resonated in his mind.

Craig slid his phone across the table to Yasmine.

"Please read all my communication between your friends and me."

Tears spilled from the corner of her eyes as she read the text messages.

Her voice cracked as she spoke. "But I saw you and Laura at the mall. I called you, and you lied about being at work. You're the liar, not me."

She slammed her hand down onto the desk. Craig didn't flinch. He remained calm and levelheaded.

"You saw your cousin, who loves you dearly, assist your future husband in getting your ring designed."

"But... but you hugged her."

"A friendly sister hug. Our bodies never touched, only our arms rocked each other."

He huffed, then closed his eyes. He didn't want to lose his composure.

"I didn't know you undervalued me."

Yasmine refused to believe she had made all of this up in her head. He could explain Laura and Monica. But how could he explain Tamia?

"That same day I saw you with Tamia?"

"I didn't know you knew my old mentee. Tamia was an excellent protégé. I think we both were surprised we bumped into each other. She is an investment banker associate. Tamia will be amongst the top twenty women on Wall Street if she follows my guidance in eight years. This industry is in dire need of African American women. Last year Edith Cooper joined the ranks of the most powerful women on Wall Street. She's worked for Goldman Sachs since 1996 and led their commodities business in Europe and Asia since 2002. It's 2009. I want to see more than one Black woman gracing the ranks. I hope Tamia joins Cooper one day," Craig said, beaming with pride.

"Black women are extremely undervalued," Yasmine noted.

"I never devalued you." Craig ran his sweaty palms over his hair. "Enough of this. I want to discuss us--no more deflecting."

Yasmine's body jerked as the contents in her stomach demanded to be set free.

"You changed my life, and I wanted to change yours. If you weren't ready, you could have told me."

"I'm prepared to be your wife," Yasmine cried.

Craig patted the large vanilla folder in front of him. He slid it across her desk. "This doesn't appear to be a woman eager to be my wife."

Four hours earlier, his assistant passed him the envelope resting in front of him. The expression on Grace's face prompted a feeling of impending doom inside of his soul.

Once he saw the first picture, he was mortified. She apologized for opening his mail.

He couldn't be upset with his assistant for executing a task she had been performing for fifteen years. If the package didn't say confidential, she was authorized to open his mail and sort it based on precedence.

He felt Yasmine was cheating, but he refused to believe it. He couldn't ignore the images trembling in his hand.

Yasmine didn't need to investigate the envelope. She was sure Craig's folder stored the same compromising pictures that were in her envelope.

When she walked into her office, she found the envelope lounging in her office chair.

Ashamed of the photos in the folder, she shoved them back in the folder then unfolded the letter.

She held her hand over her mouth when the letter informed her she had slept with her boss's man, Chocolate Ty, and if she didn't stay away from Aiden, they would reveal her secret to Destiny.

Sick to her stomach, she ran to the bathroom to relieve the sour bile in her tummy.

Yasmine was about to finish reading the letter when Craig busted through her office door.

"I counted three men in these photos. Are you a sex addict or a cheater?"

Yasmine didn't know how to explain why she had slept with Semaj and Chocolate Ty without revealing the truth.

How could she admit to Craig that she slept with two men to satisfy a man that didn't want to marry her?

"Only three," she whispered.

Craig couldn't hold the emotions inside anymore as a couple of tears slipped down his cheeks.

"Honestly, you don't need to explain, Honey. There was a letter in my envelope from a woman named Yolanda. She recounted a story about two girls in love with the same boy. But when the man opted for her daughter, your fiancée set out to destroy my child to win her teenage crush, Aiden, back."

Yasmine attempted to interrupt Craig. He silenced her with a raise of his hand and a glance to her office door.

"I remember you telling me about how he hurt you in college then vanished, leaving you heartbroken. You wept as you revealed that every man after him cheated on you. I promised never to be those men.

She closed the letter stating nobody messes with her baby, and she felt I deserved to know the type of woman I was marrying. After all, I did for her child. The complimentary close was, 'Sincerely, Tamia Hill's Mom.'"

"Craig, I am sorry. I've already lost everything. I cannot lose you, too."

"What is everything? You still have your job, health, and strength. I was not grouped in your everything bucket; therefore, I am inclined to believe Aiden is your everything," he countered. His voice rose louder than he intended.

"No, no, no. You are twisting my words. You are my everything. I need you."

He shook his head. There was no way he could forgive her or marry a woman he did not trust.

"I cannot forgive you and move on."

"Men cheat all the time, and women forgive them. So why can't men exonerate women for our indiscretions?"

"If I stepped out on you, I wouldn't expect you to absolve me."

She swiped her nose with the back of her hand. "I would, Craig, because I love you. You don't understand the pressures of being a Black woman in a relationship with a white man or your mother forcing a rich Black man on you because she is afraid a white man can't protect a Black woman's crown."

His lungs expanded with a deep intake of air.

"My love is unconditional; therefore, you would never have to forgive me for such a repulsive transgression. Yasmine, you never asked me about my finances, but you don't have to work. I am a Managing Director. I clear fifteen million a year. I would have taken care of you and your mother if she had given me a chance. I don't need to flaunt my money to prove I have money."

"My love is real, but I am flawed. Please help me, Craig. Do not abandon me."

Craig shielded his face with his hands.

"I have movers at the house packing your belongings. They will take them to your mother's house. I am sure that will make her day. I hope you know that Jasmine doesn't want you to be happy because she is unhappy. But I guess you are your mother's child."

Yasmine hurried from around the desk, dropped to her knees, and wrapped her arms around Craig's legs.

"I broke it off with Aiden because I love you. I don't know why I slept with those other men. If you leave me, I will die. I'll indulge and purge day and night. Before the nectar text, I had stopped. Help me, don't crucify me," she pleaded.

Craig closed his eyes as tears streamed down his rosy cheeks.

Yasmine's words broke his heart all over again. Instead of pulling Yasmine into his arms, he kissed the top of her head and eased away.

He placed his hand on the doorknob and turned towards the woman he still loved.

"When I took your clothes off to make love to you, I tried to take your problems and burdens off with them. I didn't have to be a Black king to protect your crown."

Chapter 20

The elevator door opened, and Aiden quickly hid something in his closed fist. He swallowed hard, willing himself to stay composed.

When Tamia didn't exit the elevator, Aiden beckoned her with a curl of his forefinger. Aiden and Tamia stared at each other as awkwardness filled the space between them.

Aiden didn't imagine the night going this way. Tamia was supposed to get off the elevator, swoon over the flowers and the glimmering candles scattered throughout the room. And then smile joyously at the melodic sound of Beyonce, her favorite artist, playing softly throughout the house's intercom.

Aiden searched for the words to express how overwhelmed he felt--dragging his eyes over her body, aligning his eyes with Tamia's before he spoke.

"You are so damn beautiful, Mia Amour. I've loved you for fifteen years. I am ready to elevate our relationship to a new level by changing your last name to Parkwood."

Tears pricked at his eyes. "Only death can ever separate me from you."

He sheepishly stared at Tamia, waiting for her to react. Aiden closed the space between them as he lowered to one knee.

"Then die already."

He knew Tamia was joking. He wanted to run outside to inform their family waiting on the deck that she was joshing.

When she placed her hands on her hip and demanded he get his cheating ass off his knees, a clenching pain restricted his movements. He raised a confused brow at Tamia.

"Mia," he reached his hand out to her, and she slapped it away. Hot tears of grief replaced his tears of joy. "Why are you doing this? Are you scared?"

She held her belly and laughed. Something about the sound sent tremors up Aiden's spine.

"Scared is being pregnant at fourteen years old while your boyfriend goes off to college, leaving you to fight two evil demons."

"Pregnant," he repeated.

"Yolanda sent a letter to your mother demanding money, or she would send you to jail. Your mother flew to Atlanta and paid my shitty parent to get me an abortion. Your mother told me you knew I was pregnant and was worried it would destroy your future." Tamia looked up, hoping to slow the stream of tears flowing from her eyes. "I didn't want to get an abortion, but Andrea said a baby would ruin your life since you had just started college, and if I loved you, I would do it."

Aiden got off his knees and reached out for Tamia, but she slapped him away.

"Those bitches forced me to kill my baby. After it was over, Andrea confessed you didn't know, and if I ever told you, you would leave me and hate me forever."

"I can never hate you. I would have done whatever I had to do to take care of you and our child," he assured her. "Is that why you stopped writing to me for a while?"

"Yes," she confessed, wiping her face with the back of her hands. "The deck has always been stacked against our love. It killed me holding on to that secret. After my high school prom, Yolanda sent Andrea pictures of us demanding more money if she wanted me to stay away from you. I found this out after I caught you kissing Yasmine in college."

She chuckled then held her hands over her eyes.

"I am sorry for hurting you and lying to you."

She cut him short. "But you still allow your mother to abuse me, so you're not that sorry."

Aiden's heart broke into a million pieces. "I never knew Andrea did those things."

Aiden's head suddenly began to throb. Tamia's words were like bricks being tossed at his heart and head.

She nervously chuckled.

"You're so fucking clueless. Do you think that is all she did?"

He hunched his shoulders, but he knew his mother was capable of so much more.

He wanted to tell Tamia about his conversation with Yasmine, but he didn't want to hurt her more than she was already hurting.

"So you didn't know your mother sent Yolanda an envelope full of pictures of you and Yasmine with a letter. Detailing how much you loved Yasmine, noting I was something for you to indulge in while visiting your grandmother because rich boys don't marry hood girls."

"Tamia, I didn't know."

He approached her, and she shoved him in the chest. When he didn't budge, she shrieked, pushing him repeatedly until her thrust turned into lashes across his chest.

He didn't stop her because he felt as if he deserved every hit.

He pulled her into his strong arms. She tugged out of his embrace.

"After catching you kissing Yasmine, I wanted to hate you, but my heart fought against common sense. Then when Ma'Dear passed, you showed up in Atlanta, and I foolishly made love to you because I felt special. After all, Aiden Parkwood paused his traveling to check on me."

"Yolanda called my mother and passed the dreadful news about Ma'Dear. No matter how mad you were at me, I knew I had to be there for you. Plus, I told my mother I was still going to marry you once I was done abroad. She encouraged me to propose once I finished traveling."

Tamia scoffed.

"You are so blind to their treachery. After you left Atlanta, I was packing Ma'Dear's house, struggling to hold my tears at bay. The one ounce of joy inside of me was the lies you fed me the night before." She slammed her lids tightly, refusing to drop a tear.

Tamia wrenched the pain back down her throat.

"Those women who call themselves mothers must have sensed my tiny amount of joy because that's when Yolanda gave me the envelope Andrea sent her."

She paused, then waved her trembling hands in front of herself before ringing them together.

"Seeing you and Yasmine's life overlapping our years together and not having Ma'Dear broke me down to the studs. And you ask why I hate them both. Andrea paid Yolanda to hurt me. Shit, what Andrea didn't know is Yolanda would have done it for free."

Aiden pulled Tamia in her arms. The more she tugged, the tighter he held her. She slammed the palms of her hands against his back.

He continued to whisper how much he loves her. Her body shuddered the loosened as he freely sobbed on his shoulder.

Kissing the hollow behind her ear, he rubbed her back.

Exhausted by grief, her lungs cinched tight, extracting her breath, forcing her body to disintegrate and slip from his grasp.

Aiden caught her right before she hit the floor.

He swept her hair back, smothering her forehead with kisses before he spoke. "I will never let them hurt you again. I will protect you from them."

Letting out a whine, she swung her gaze upward until her teary eyes connected with his puffy red ones. "Who will protect me from you?"

Aiden was unable to summon words due to the shock of her question.

"I asked you to tell me the truth twice, and both times you lied to my face. I forgave Yolanda; I would have forgiven you."

He went to speak, but gibberish spilled from his mouth.

He knew Tamia was referring to him smashing Yasmine. He had only one excuse. He lied to protect her feelings, not harm them.

"You have loved me for fifteen years and kept Yasmine close for the same amount of time. But, hell, maybe you don't love either one of us."

Whispering harshly, Aiden bellowed, "I don't love her, but I love you with every inch of my heart. Do you know I paid Davis to spy on you while I was away to make sure no man stole you away from me?"

"It sounds more like crazy possessiveness than love. Always desiring what you don't deserve."

Aiden rocked his head back and forth in disbelief. His mind refused to believe this was happening.

Finally, he attempted to persuade himself that he had passed out on the sofa and had a nightmare.

Tamia went to pull herself off the floor. Aiden touched her arm, and her face twisted in disgust.

"Love is for suckers and the faint at heart. I will never allow another man to hurt me again. I will be a coldhearted bitch. Fuck everybody's feelings."

Aiden's temples pounded with each beat of his heart. "I will never give up on us."

Tamia's eyebrows knitted together as her jaw trembled in rage. "You did each time you fucked Yasmine, then smiled in my face."

Chapter 21

P op-pop was the first person to materialize from the deck. "That was a heavy, heavy mind thang," Pop-pop noted. Aiden wanted to run to his grandfather and show him his bleeding heart.

Aiden wished his dad was still alive more than he ever did before. Over the years, he caught himself crying when watching a father and son interaction or reading about a father and son duo. He came to understand that he would never stop missing his father.

Yet, he still didn't quite understand why God decided to take his dad. His grandmother gave him a speech about every creature having an expiration date.

Although the ideology made sense, he didn't grasp why his father's stamped expiration date arrived before his prime or before his grandparents, who had already lived longer than his dad.

A tightening pain surged Aiden's chest, and his Pop-pop swaddled him in his arms. "I need my dad," the wounded boy inside of him wailed.

His grandfather made circles on his back with the palm of his hands. "I know, grandson. I miss my son every day."

"It should have been her, not him."

Andrea's heart crumbled when she heard those words. She, too, wondered why God left her to raise a boy she barely knew.

Aiden was a meal ticket to her. She granted Steven a child, and he provided her with a lavish lifestyle.

Over the years, she grew to love her son dearly, but she never possessed the motherly gene.

"I am not fond of your mother either but don't say that, son."

Andrea stepped deeper into the darkness as Yolanda trotted into view.

Her voice cracked as she began to speak, "My daughter told not one lie. Your mother and I did everything she said."

Aiden lifted his head off his grandfather's shoulder.

Yolanda expelled a shaky breath as she turned to Pop-pop, unable to look at Aiden.

"Sir, I have five kids. As Tamia grew and her body developed, I became jealous of my child because she reminded me of everything I could have been if I never had children. I never congratulated her on all of her achievements; instead, I belittled her."

Yolanda wrapped her arms loosely around her body, darting her hands from her elbow to her wrist while rocking on her heels. She nodded her head up and down readily.

"When your grandson came along, Tamia beamed with joy. Again, she had something I wished I had--a man's unconditional love, not that kiddy puppy dog bullshit. Real love. Aiden took care of my daughter. But she is wrong about one thing. I didn't make her get an abortion because Andrea paid me. I did it because I didn't want her to end up like me."

Yolanda dropped her head, overwhelmed with emotions, as she cried. Aiden's heart ached for her. He loved her daughter. How could he not love her as well? He knew precisely who Yolanda was. Well, he thought he did until this moment.

Aiden stepped closer to Yolanda and wrapped her in his arms. She hid her face in Aiden's elbow.

"I didn't see my hatred for my child until your mother approached me to destroy my baby because you two had found each other again. Your mother felt Tamia was beneath the Parkwood name. She thought I detested my own child that much. Your mother's only goal was to obliterate Tamia."

Aiden nodded his head but remained silent.

Yolanda glanced up at Aiden. "I am sorry for all the pain I caused you two. Your mother advised me to keep Tamia away from your community event; therefore, I made sure Tamia was present. You promised to take her to Magic Mountain when you guys were kids. With busy school schedules, you guys never went. I know I was wrong for reading you guys' letters, but I am glad I did. I sent you two invitations and a car to take you there."

Yolanda chuckled, but Aiden didn't. He figured he must have missed the joke.

"I used your mother's bribery money to bring you and Tamia closer. When my baby walked in smiling from ear to ear, it warmed my heart. I could see the love wrapped around her aura. I wanted to make popcorn and hear about my baby's day. Instead of expressing those emotions, I picked a fight with her to drive her back to your arms. I tried to make it right the only way I knew how Aiden."

"We both did," was Aiden's only response.

"Do you know when I lost everything, none of my kids would allow me to stay with them? Tamia, the mistreated child, gave me an olive branch, and I was too stubborn to thank her. But I fixed your mother and that girl, Yasmine, and your mother enlisted to hurt my damn baby. I knew if I told Tamia not to be with you, she would."

She eased out of Aiden's arms and slapped his hand. "I didn't expect you to stick your hand in the damn cookie jar."

Aiden dropped his head in shame.

"We both fucked up. Please know I will never stop fighting to get your daughter back, and I swear I stopped seeing Yasmine once Tamia allowed me back into her life. I should have told her what I did when she gave me three chances to tell the truth."

Yolanda knew Aiden was telling the truth.

While at the salon, Yolanda overheard Stacy complaining about her boss and how she was doing all her work. When Stacy mentioned the Parkwood brand, Yolanda remembered where she heard that name before. That's when she recalled that was Aiden's last name.

Yolanda couldn't stop laughing when Stacy shared information with her because California was not as big as it seemed. They were all connected by one dot or another.

After asking Stacy a couple of questions, a plan unfolded in Yolanda's mind. It didn't take long or a ton of money to get Stacy to betray her boss.

You should never mistreat the person that manages your life better than you do. She told Yolanda everything about Yasmine and her schedule.

Yolanda kissed Aiden on the cheek.

"Son, if a woman asks you a direct question three times, she already knows the truth. If you own up to it, it was a mistake you will never repeat. If you lie, you are trying to make it a habit."

Aiden nervously hooted. "I wish you would have told me that before tonight."

"We are both still learning." Yolanda hugged Aiden tightly.

"I have to see about my baby. Understand before I can help you get your girlfriend back, I have to fight to get my daughter back first, and then I'll work on getting her to forgive us both."

Aiden kissed Yolanda on the cheek before she left.

Aiden scanned the room for his mother, but she was nowhere in sight. His side gate was locked, so Andrea was still there. He'd only invited his mother, grandparents, Yolanda, and Tamia's sister, Tasha, who did not show up.

"Aiden," his grandfather said to gain his attention. "I tell you. This night has been a heavy, heavy mind thang." Aiden nodded in agreement. "I didn't want you to get married, son."

"That's not why I proposed. I love Tamia, Pop-pop. I have loved her since I was a young boy." Aiden smiled as his years with Tamia flashed in his head.

"Then why didn't you bring her to meet the family? Were you hiding her from us or us from her?"

Aiden hunched his shoulders, although he knew the truth. His mother had convinced him his grandparents would never approve of Tamia.

"That is not an answer, young man. Use your damn words."

"Mom did not approve of her and made me believe you wouldn't either."

"Your mother cannot speak for grandma and me. All we ever wanted was your happiness."

"But, Mom…"

"It is time for you to set your mother free and be your own man. I grew up the day I fell in love with your grandmother. Cut the cord, Aiden. The pain I heard in that young lady's voice stemmed from disappointment because you permitted your mother to harm her more than you're cheating. And I am not saying that was right because you know better, son. You have never witnessed me or your father deceive our hearts. Pleasing one woman is hard enough, and you sought to satisfy two. You have always been an overachiever." Pop-pop chuckled.

His grandma cleared her throat.

"Believe me when I say, one woman will always suffer because no man can equally appease two females. Not if he's loving her the right way."

Everyone turned at the sound of Andrea smacking her lips.

"Of course, you would tell my son to forsake me. You never thought I was good enough for your family."

"You never loved my family. You loved our money," Aiden's grandmother said, stepping beside her husband.

Pop-pop nodded in agreement.

"We never cared about your lineage. Our only concern was how you treated our son and grandson. We allow you to stay in our home because Steven chose you and asked us to look after you and his son. Well, honey, Aiden is grown. So, I hope you have saved up your coins because we are cutting your purse strings."

Before Andrea could address her in-laws, Aiden spoke. "Mom, how could you? Yasmine tried to tell me you forced her to sleep with Brooklyn's husband because you and her mother wanted my grandfather's money. I refused to believe her."

"I did what was best for you."

His body shivered as a cold chill slithered up his spine.

"You did what was best for you. If Tamia can forgive Yolanda, I can forgive you, but I will not support you. I will no longer do your bidding. And once I get my future wife back, if you ever disrespect her, I will cut you out of my life forever."

"Over a common hoodrat?"

"Mother, the only one that is a common rat is you."

Chapter 22

Tamia sat at a table positioned in the dark shadows of the bar, spinning her empty shot glass, waiting for Ty and Tre. She couldn't believe she had thrown out her rule book for Aiden only to be deceived once again.

"You broke all your rules for the same man that forced you to create your rules in the first place," she muttered under her breath.

Ty planting a kiss on her cheek pulled her from her thoughts.

"Are you losing your mind, Babygirl?"

She tried to force a smile upon her face. Her honorary brothers and Aiden were the main reasons she would never trust men.

Since they were kids, she'd watched them gallop over women's hearts. She might have been a member of the trifling three, but she kept the men inline. She wasn't a creep like them. She could only imagine what type of men they would be without her pressing the pause button on some of their bullshit.

"What did Aiden do?" Tre asked as he approached the table.

"What you're not going to do to Miya. This shit hurts, and you better never hurt my girl this way. So, get your dick under control."

"Damn, why are you stepping on my fucking neck?" Tre questioned.

"If you can't get your shit together, then you need to leave my girl alone."

Tre rubbed his eyes because this was not Tamia sitting before him, he thought. "You knew the type of man I was before I started dating your girl. You even exploited that side of me."

Tamia dropped her head in shame. "I was wrong."

"Yes, you were, but I still fucked the shit out of Brooklyn's ass. It turns out Brooklyn and her husband are swingers, so your plan was a bust, but at least I got a chance to bust."

"You weren't supposed to fuck her. And it doesn't matter anymore. Aiden followed my directive and worked with Brooklyn instead of trying to destroy her."

"I still can't believe you allowed this fool to date your girl. You should have passed her off to me," Ty stated. "I would have treated that fresh cat right. Do you realize virgins are rare at her age?"

"I did not pass her off to anyone. Tre asked her to go out on a date, and her naive ass made this dawg her man. I tried to convince her to smash another man," she admitted.

Tamia didn't know if it was the alcohol or not, but she was tired of pretending she was okay with Tre's relationship with Miya.

"What the fuck, Mia Amour?"

"Don't call me that. Only Aiden can call me 'Mia Amour,'" she barked. "Break it off, Tre. I don't want Miya to feel the pain inside of me right now." He shook his head in protest.

She looked at Ty. "And no, you can't date her either."

Her phone rattled against the table. She glanced at the screen. "Speaking of my angel."

Tamia's mouth hung open as Miya accused her of trying to destroy her relationship with Tre. Demanding she stay out of her business and stop trying to control her and Tre.

"So, you're a big girl now, I see?" Tamia said to Miya. "I can't believe you called me a hater. From this point on, I will keep my hatin' ass out of your business, sis."

Before Miya could say another disparaging word, Tamia disconnected the call.

Tamia tossed back the shot the waitress placed on the table. She pointed at Tre, then Ty.

"You fuck for orgasms, and you fuck for cash. I'll fake it for orgasms and money. A man can't do anything but devour my lovely fold and pay me for the privilege."

A dumbfounded expression invaded Tre's face. "So, what are you faking?"

She chuckled. "That I am going to let those fools hit this, and when they can't hold out anymore, I'll move on."

"Let me get my ammunition ready," Ty retorted.

Tre chuckled.

"Damn, what did Aiden do?" Ty asked.

"Do you know this fool's other pussy lived in the same zip code as him? I wonder how many times she crept over to his house before I came home, or he crept to her house for a quick suck and fuck."

Tamia snatched her phone off the table and pulled up the picture of Yasmine, showing Ty and Tre. "Would you pick her over me?"

"No, I wouldn't pick Yasmine over you," Ty stated.

Tamia turned her entire body around to face Ty. "Did you know Aiden was fucking her?"

"Hell no," he rapidly responded. "Somebody hired Chocolate Ty to smash her."

Tamia's eyes rolled around her head. She hated when Ty referred to his escort name as if it was an entirely different person. "Was the pussy good?"

Ty twisted his face as if something smelled foul.

"No, the shit is juicy for two minutes, then it's the Sierra Desert." He extended his neck and gawked at Tre. He swung his head from left to right before speaking. "The head is A-1. I mean stellar like a motherfucker."

"Damn," Tre responded, extending the word into ten syllables, slapping palms with Ty.

"Good for her," Tamia scoffed.

"And Chocolate Ty," Ty replied, "I will be charging that bitch to suck Chocolate Ty's dick again."

Ty's eyes washed over Tamia, waiting for her speech.

Tamia shook her head and threw her hands in the air.

"Do you, man, do you."

"What about Aiden?" Tre asked. He didn't like this new nonchalant Tamia.

She ignored his question because she didn't know the answer. She only hoped that she would wake up one day and the love she had for Aiden would have vanished.

"Since I was a child, I fought to be the opposite of what people expected from an inner-city bred kid. Unfortunately, my mother and even one of my best friends have labeled me. From this point on, I'll become every label they have placed upon me. I hope the world is ready."

She scoffed.

"My new mantra is fuck everybody's feelings. I'm looking out for myself."

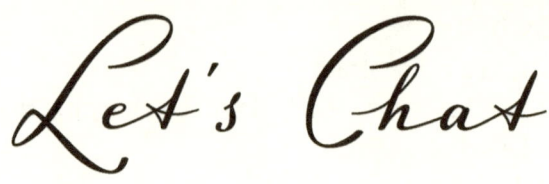

Let's Chat

I hope you enjoyed reading

BAE NOVELLA THE COLLECTION

Want to chat about this book? Join the conversation with other readers at iamchristat.com

You can also reach Christat
on Facebook (www. facebook.com/iamchristat**)**
on Twitter (www.twitter.com/iamchristat**)**
or Instagram (www.instagram.com/iamchristat**)**

You are just one click away from...
• Being the first to hear about author events
• Exclusive giveaways
• Free bonus content
• Sneak peeks at our newest titles

Happy reading! CLICK HERE TO SIGN UP

Continue reading for a snippet
of BAE Series book three
– Lyrics Between Us!

"Not Tonight" (Remix)
Lil Kim
Miya

HE MELODIC LYRICS OF "THE MISEDUCATION of Lauryn Hill" stimulated dopamine sparks in my brain's nucleus, activating joy in my soul and energizing my body as I decorated the tiny apartment.

A knock on the front door interrupted, "Doo Wop (That Thing)." A glance at my watch confirmed it was Imani; she's always an hour early for any BAE event. I spun on my heels and shuffled over to the front door.

Since I launched the Black and Educated social group in high school, my girls have granted me the honor of hosting our tenth anniversary. Tonight's theme is Pajama Jammy Jam, and I expect us to party until the cops come knocking.

I hugged Imani before going into the kitchen to finish cooking. I danced all around the postage-sized kitchen while Imani twerked in her seat. Our voices coordinated as we started singing on cue to Gwen Stefani's "Hollaback Girl."

"Did you create a scorching playlist for us tonight?" Imani questioned, flinging her arms above her head while tapping her feet in celebration before dancing towards me.

Imani waved her hand in my face, cutting me off before I could answer, singing, "The BAEs are bananas. B-A-N-A-N-A-S!" I joined in on the excitement, dancing around the living room with my BAE until the song ended.

"Bring Em Out" by T.I. started blasting from the subwoofers as I headed towards the kitchen. Imani paused, pumping her fist at the song choice before she spoke.

"Okay, heffa, you're trying to kill us tonight."

I pumped my fist in the air, giving Imani her response as Imani fanned me, hyping me up more.

"Tonight is going to be hot because you are on fire!"

I plopped onto the barstool next to a panting Imani. She gazed at her watch. "I thought this event started at 6:30 pm?"

I frowned before sliding a bowl of chips in her direction, watching as she poured herself a glass of sweet Argentinian wine. "Can a BAE event ever start on time? Where is Naja?" she asked as she took her first sip. I frowned.

"How can you live where the party is hosted and still be late?"

Pausing the song, I rapidly chewed the Doritos in my mouth before I swallowed, then answered. "Imani, Naja is still getting dressed, and I know she can hear us because this apartment is a mere 725 square feet. Shit, I can hear the bugs at night creeping across the floors. Tamia is fifteen minutes out, and Lexi has to make her grand entrance."

"You will require a wider apartment if you keep eating all those chips."

We both snickered at her joke.

Imani headed towards the back bedroom. "Naja moved to the front. We switched rooms since her late-night booty calls with Dakari disturbed me." Imani paused and turned around. I whispered sneakily. "And girl, he always waits until he's at the front door to hold a full conversation; these pre-med students are long-winded."

Clapping her palms together, Imani probed excitedly, "Dakari or Naja?"

"Both of them!" I said, laughing at her reaction.

"Hey, BAEs!" Naja hummed. Her ebony presence dominated the space. "Did I hear someone call my name?" Turning at the sound of her voice in the narrow passageway, I took in the cheeky, black, long sleeve romper hugging Naja's curves as she danced into the living room.

Smiling joyfully, I leered at my two ebony queens, forever classy with a hint of seduction. I stroked my gear's comfortable fluffy fabric and wondered if my outfit was acceptable for tonight before swiftly waving the doubt away.

"Y'all in here jamming and talking shit!" Naja smirked, hugging Imani before making her spin around so she could comment on her attire. "I see you killing this sexy pink and black spaghetti strap cami. Sexy and elegant as usual. Are those lace pajama shorts made of chiffon or satin?"

Before Imani could answer, I did. "Those sexy shorts are silk."

Naja gave a crisp nod as her feet tapped the floor incessantly while gazing at the clock's green glow on the kitchen microwave. "How long before Tamia and Lexi arrive, Miya?"

I rolled my eyes. It always astounds me when someone who comes late becomes impatient after arriving. They tend to forget people felt the same annoyance waiting on them.

"Tamia is ten minutes away, and Lexi has not called," Imani informed Naja. "She's probably fighting Paxton off so she can walk out the door. Every time she tries to leave, Paxton goes through separation anxiety."

Imani was forever defending Lexi in some way or another. Since I was eight and she was ten, I had been rolling my eyes at Imani's comments. We were best friends first, but like always, Lexi stole her away.

Glancing back as I headed to the front door, I caught Naja smiling ear to ear as I walked by, and I felt a bit disappointed hearing Imani compliment her on her sexy ensemble and mention nothing about mine.

My cousin Lexi stood there as I opened the door, dropping the white dress shirt she wore to the middle of her torso. She placed her hands on her hips and greeted me, revealing a lace bralette set featuring a multi-strap neckline with spaghetti straps and gold O-ring accents. The backside was hardly conservative as she twirled, flaunting the far from modest attire, displaying more flesh than material.

"Oh, shit, Diva," Tamia shouted, walking up to us. "Sexy Lexi!"

Running her hands over the high-waisted garter belt with the same accents as her bralette, Lexi caressed the material around her thigh as she modeled the matching panties with cutout panels.

"I know I live in the Trojan apartments, but did you have to walk in here looking like you're ready to get fucked?"

I rolled my eyes as Lexi twirled once more, smirking at me.

"Girl, I need to take pictures of you against this red door. You look like a sexy dominatrix!" Tamia continued.

"You want some red-light action?" Lexi joked, posing before the door. "Girl, I need to take some pictures of you too!"

These heifers were acting like my apartment door was the champagne room, and those satin pink and gray capris Tamia wore with that gray lace bra and matching robe could not contend with Lexi's sexy attire. I had no more words for Lexi and Tamia.

Stepping aside and allowing them to sashay into the apartment, I watched Imani and Naja's reactions to Lexi's outfit, their jaws dropping briefly before praising her attire.

Silently, I stood there, watching them pass around compliments. When Lexi cast her eyes upon me, tingling warmth filled my limbs. I stared down at my empty hands when she addressed me. I smoothed out my leopard onesie, my lower lip sticking out in a giant pout. The circle had already declared me the crybaby, and I battled with pride, struggling to suck my lip back in.

"Lexi, I cannot believe Paxton let you out of the house!" Imani shouted, forcing me to lower the volume.

Lexi snickered. "Girl, Paxton was not at home."

"Explains the outfit," I replied rapidly.

"No, it does not, smartass," Lexi snarled before fixating on Imani. "Do you remember the outfit I bought last week for tonight?"

Imani snapped her fingers in agreement.

"Girl, Paxton found the satin gown and demanded I model the outfit. I tried to protest. I even told him it was for my BAE event tonight, but no matter what I said, he insisted he wanted me in that gown," Lexi stated, running her hands over her body, carrying on with her tale. "I showed him this outfit; he tossed it on the floor. Sick of arguing with him, I conceded and slid my phat ass into the damn baby doll gown. I was going to buy another outfit today, but work swamped me." Lexi's arms waved in mock exasperation as she said, "Paxton had three tests today, which meant I was his last-minute study buddy."

"Girl, Paxton is your hubby, and you would do anything for that man just like I would do the same for Winten," Imani stated.

I wanted to tell them that calling Paxton and Winten their husbands did not make them wives. But as always, Imani and Lexi dominated the entire conversation and turned it into the Sexy Lexi Show.

Blushing, Lexi cooed as she spoke. "On top of that, I had a report due by 3:00 pm. By the time I arrived at work, I was exhausted. I contemplated what to wear and spotted this outfit on our bedroom floor. Being rebellious, I jumped into the outfit, Paxton tossed out like trash."

"They say one man's trash is another man's treasure," Tamia interjected.

We all stared at her, shaking our heads and erupting into laughter.

Lashing out, I snidely quipped, "I don't think that statement is related to nipples covered with dental floss." Lexi fanned away my witty remark. Annoyed, I poured myself a glass of wine before giving the bottle to Naja. Once everyone had a full glass, we toasted to the BAEs.

"We have snacks, wine, and a massage therapist coming in an hour. I have food in the oven."

Tamia placed one hand on her hip with an attitude. "You mean five massage therapists."

I matched her condescension and reiterated, "One!"

"Good thing I brought two blunts. Bitch, we will be here until tomorrow if we all want a massage," Tamia asserted as the other girls nodded in agreement.

Sometimes I wonder why I was even friends with these ungrateful heifers. I walked to the counter and turned my playlist on, making Lexi jump up. Dropping her derriere low, she popped it as Snoop Dogg and Pharrell's "Drop It Like It's Hot" thumped from the speakers. Tamia lit a joint, passing it around while we danced to Destiny's Child's "Soldier" with Lexi. We were tipsy when 50 Cent's "Candy Shop" blazed from the speakers.

I whined my hips to the beat, making Tamia point and chuckle at me, and soon they were all laughing. Grumbling, I rolled and popped my hips harder.

"You don't have to be stiff," Tamia gibed.

"Heffa, leave my cousin alone! She will get a swerve in her hips once she starts having sex," Lexi countered.

"I know why she's still a virgin," Tamia proclaimed loudly.

Rolling my eyes, I remained silent because she would enlighten us with her distorted opinion, regardless of my reply. I stopped the music, plastering on the fakest smile I could muster.

Tamia pulled on my outfit. "A man cannot find the pussy under all this shit. Look at what the rest of us are wearing. Now glance at what you have on. What man will get hard? Miya, why are you running around dressed like a teenage little girl?" Naja and Imani agreed with Tamia while Lexi kept a straight face.

I examined my outfit again. It was toasty and comfortable, and I honestly didn't see the problem.

"I bet I'll be the first to get married," I fired back, wondering why those words popped into my head. "Men love a woman that hasn't been stepped in. Men marry women that keep their goodies on lock and only reveal them in the bedroom."

Tamia gawked at her fingertips, rubbing them together as she spoke. "The men I deal with don't expect a woman to be a virgin. Then again, I wouldn't expect you to know what a real man is."

Being a virgin used to be a badge of honor. Now it means you are a nerd or unfuckable, and I was neither. I surmise men have lowered their expectations, or promiscuous women have become the social norm.

Hell, men had hinted they wanted to taste me and sleep with me. However, I promised my mother and father I wouldn't have sex until I graduated from college to ease their hood statistic concerns. Most girls in the neighborhood were pregnant by the age of sixteen.

Lexi and I made a similar declaration at eleven years old, vowing not to have sex until marriage. The summer before high school, I went off to music camp, but Lexi stayed at home. When I returned, Lexi had transformed into Sexy Lexi, the girl engaging in sex. Imani followed shortly after.

"I will be the first to get married," Lexi remarked, leveling a confident gaze. "I've been with Paxton since middle school."

Lifting myself off the floor and onto my knees, I waved my hands in Lexi's face. "Newsflash. Invested time means nothing. How many stories have you read where athletes leave their childhood, high school, or college sweetheart to marry a white girl after signing their contract?"

We all high-fived in agreement except Lexi.

"That will not be Paxton and me," Lexi barked. "And heffa, I am half white; he can marry that side. Shit, we've invested time, unlike the rest of you!"

Surprisingly, Naja rolled her neck, snapping her fingers. "Dakari and I have more time invested than any of you youngsters. We have been bathing together since we were two years old in Jamaica. Our parents have been planning our wedding since puberty."

"Time means nothing," I stressed again before bringing my point home. "If it did, Imani could claim the third spot since she and Winten met in high school."

The memory of the day Winten Johnson walked into my classroom at Locke High School captivated me. I was mesmerized by his flawless, bright skin and pearly white teeth. I created a playlist for him full of love ballads and songs declaring I wanted to be his girl. I didn't recall adding Biz Markie, "Just A Friend," yet he referred to me as his little homie.

I invited him over to my house to ask him if he had a girlfriend, but when I walked into my room, I caught him and Imani kissing on my damn bed! It turns out they met while I was at music camp.

My crushes viewed me as their homegirl but never a girlfriend. The girlfriend title only applied to Lexi and Imani. Yet, the title wife will be mine. A sly grin graced my face.

My mind drifted to my wedding and courting playlist. My cheeks turned rosy as I blushed when I added Ginuwine's "Pony." The sides of my mouth curled upward, and I struggled to cover my excitement as I mentally jotted down Mariah Carey's "Emotions" and K-Ci & JoJo's "All My Life." This time, I won't demonstrate the same shyness towards my future husband as I did with Winten. I will pen daily love notes for my husband while rocking Aaliyah's "4 Page Letter." The idea of marriage and beating Lexi ignited my soul with passion.

Breaking out of my thoughts, I shook my head, holding firm to my original statement. "I will be married first!"

"Miya, I agree," Tamia proclaimed, catching the other BAEs off guard.

I smiled, stretching out my arm for Tamia to slap my palm. She pretended to hit it, then pulled back. "But! Your husband will cheat. You will not be able to satisfy him in bed."

"Tamia, show me the stats. What number of men cheat on their virgin wives?" Lexi demanded, sounding like statistical Naja.

And on cue, Naja interjected. "Forty percent of married couples are impacted by infidelity. Studies show that a partner who is sexually experienced knows what they enjoy and chooses someone with whom they mesh sexually. However, other statistics have revealed that sexually experienced partners prefer to teach inexperienced partners their erotic desires."

"Damn, Lexi. I am only playing with your cousin. And Naja, not everyone lives by facts and statistics like your analytical ass," Tamia countered, trying to drive her point home. "Seriously, the order of marriage will be Naja, Lexi, Imani, me, and then you, Miya."

Unanimously, we all rolled our eyes at her comment.

Damn. What a joke. Even Tamia believed she would marry before me. She should find a man who loves her first. Tamia always chooses men out of her league. Even worse than that, she mistreats the men who adore her.

Tamia advertises my virginity whenever we are out and jokes about me having a chastity lock to embarrass me. Naja once said that Tamia does it to protect me from the dogs out in these streets. A couple of times, Tamia had explicitly told men what she would do to them, and if the guy still showed interest, she would degrade him. Her goal was to make men crave her, not protect me. She is the only BAE that represents five personality types in our group. She's the "I know somebody" friend and the "flirty, funny, mother hen, and turn-up" friend. I used to be surprised each time a new personality trait appeared. Before realizing every group of friends has a Tamia.

I stepped back into the conversation when my girls agreed Lexi or Naja would be the first to marry or have a double ceremony. It was a tossup between Imani and Tamia, but I always… somehow always placed dead last.

I sulked, sitting cross-legged on the floor as the girls circled me, expressing why they believed I would be last… the first reason being my fear of having sex, then my fear of talking to men. The third was the fact that I expressed myself through music too much. They emphasized that most men did not have the time to listen to a playlist to see how I felt. I couldn't recall the fourth through tenth reasons because I zoned out.

My competitive nature got the best of me. I was ready to place a bet. "Okay, why don't you put your money against your hypothesis. We all have good jobs. We will drop a hundred dollars each month into an account for the next five years. The first two people to get married will get the money in the bank," I propose.

Naja huffed. "I am too old to be betting on my future."

"Heffa, please!" I taunted, "I have seen you bet on your parents' marriage. It's okay to admit you fear losing."

"My problem is the prize doesn't seem fair," Imani muttered. "I think the first person who gets married gets half of whatever is in the bank. The second and third person gets half of whatever is left in the bank each time they get married. The fourth person will bleed the account dry, and the fifth person gets nothing but congratulations."

"Don't you think this is childish?" Lexi exclaimed. "Besides, I do not want to take all of your hard-earned cash."

Scowls of various styles graced our faces, contemplating Lexi's words before declaring we were all in.

Hopping off the floor, I retrieved paper to write out the terms. The first guideline stated that we could not get married until 2007 because Tamia and I were a part of USC's Trojan class of 2006. *Go Trojans!* Naja will graduate from USC Keck School of Medicine, earning her third degree. Lexi and Imani graduated two years ago with dual degrees but were still validating their positions at work.

The second rule declared that engagements did not count. You must walk down the aisle to win the bet. And if you elope, you must present a marriage license and pictures. My mind implored me to add another clause. I omitted the clause since no BAE would dare marry without her sisters present.

"Are we done partying?" Tamia asked, signing the contract, making it official.

Resuming my playlist as the answer, we all danced, singing along with the music, marveling at how Naja sang the hook and performed Busta's part of "Touch It." The girl could flow. If she ever gave up on medicine, she could be the next Missy Elliot.

"Run This Town"
Jay-Z

Malik

IN JANUARY 2006, I WAIVED MY senior college season and declared myself eligible for the NFL Draft. My mother was livid. She is a firm believer in always having a backup plan; according to her, that's a college degree. Since childhood, football has been my sole plan. My sports manager—Kyle—incorporated an education clause into my contract to ease my mother's anxieties. He assured her we had the leverage to achieve this goal since various teams were scouting me.

Numerous commentators predicted San Francisco would draft me to achieve a formidable offensive team because I was the NCAA's top-ranked wingback for three years.

Two months later, at Radio City Music Hall, the Atlanta Falcons signed me as their new running back the evening before the draft.

After announcing my new team to the world, I stepped off the stage and dialed my mother. I was bouncing on the tip of my toes, listening as her words filled me with pride. Pops snatched the phone from my hand, saving me from my mother's charitable wish list. I made a mental note to bless her church and two charities because everyone knew I would run through the fiery pits of hell to make Mary Ann Walker proud.

A few commentators declared the 2006 NFL draft was the worst in NFL history. As a rookie, I was determined to prove I was worth every penny of my $52.5 million contract. Reebok reported receiving over ten thousand orders for my Atlanta jersey the following day. However, my number wasn't assigned yet. Thanks to my mother and Kyle, I secured over five million dollars in endorsements within a month, which allowed me to purchase my mother's dream estate in Temecula Wine Country.

During minicamp, I bonded with the Atlanta Dirty Birds. The team accepted me, but the city had doubts. During the first game, the fans showered me with love, cheering as I performed the Dirty Bird dance. I dedicated my first touchdown to the state, earning my team's respect and the city's love.

I thought life couldn't get any better until Sabrina Bollinger made me her target of affection. I tried to stay away from her and focus on my first season and senior college year. However, Sabrina was aggressive, and that intrigued me. Whenever I lost a game or struggled with school assignments, she would appear to alleviate my stress.

Some players have lucky socks, drawers, and undershirts. I had Sabrina. I stockpiled 140 yards against New York in the first game Sabrina attended, and the Falcons won. Every game she attended, I massed massive yards. Sabrina became my good luck charm.

Sitting on the jet, rehearsing my speech, I was headed to my parents' twelve-bedroom horse ranch in Temecula, California, to get my grandmother's wedding ring and my mother's blessings. After dating Sabrina for over a year, she's confident she is the woman for me.

I approached the back entrance of my parent's home, and the aromatic scent of sauteed vegetables smothered the atmosphere. Placing my bag on the ground, I leaned against the stone wall as the melodic sounds of horns and trumpets wailed by the pool. My eyes devoured the horse stables, two villas, two guest houses, and the rock cavern. Last month, my parent's massive estate was featured in Temecula Wine Country's Modern Ranch homes edition.

I closed my eyes and swayed from side to side as the piano's bold, rich tones dominated the song. Music has been my therapist, lover, and closest friend. Musical notes connect my DNA strands. Music was always a building block for my father and me. A man of few words, he allowed music to express his moods for as long as I can remember, and I could always tell if my father had a beautiful or a horrible day at work by the songs he played.

His favorite thing to say to me was, "Son, embrace the musical language. Music can help us express emotions that are hard to verbalize."

I adore the way my pops love my mom through music and actions. I had vowed to love Sabrina the same way. First, I must get her to enjoy songs that speak to her heart, not her twerking skills.

As usual, the sliding French doors were wide open. I knew I could genuinely surprise my queen. I slowly crept into the dining room. My mother stood at the stove cooking, and Pops sat on a barstool singing to her. My father noticed me sneaking into the house and smiled.

I placed my index finger on my lips. I eased behind my mother and planted a kiss on her wavy black tresses. Pops smiled brightly.

"Mark, we will never eat if you keep getting fresh."

I could see how my mother could get me and my father confused. We're twins. He's about two inches taller than me.

"Oooh, Ma. You and Pops are undercover freaks!"

She spun around, waving the serving spoon at my father and me before squealing while jumping around the kitchen island. "I missed you, Queen." I kissed her on her olive cheeks. My mother wrapped her petite arms around my waist, squeezing tightly.

"Mark, did you know Malik was coming?"

My father hunched his shoulders. I called him a week prior and told him I was coming this weekend. My father promised to have my mother floating on cloud nine upon my arrival – a small task since my mother stays ecstatic.

Growing up, I recall my parents having eight quarrels. I asked my parents what kept them from arguing. They both shared similar advice. "I seek God's guidance before jumping to conclusions," Pops admitted. He continued to say, "The same time it takes to think of something negative to say, I could kiss my wife on the cheek and calm the both of us."

He advised me always to take my problems to God concerning my marriage and life. Then, he joked how he reminded God that Jesus gave him this woman, so they both needed to keep her in line.

My mother proudly acknowledged maintaining a peaceful home by being a snitch. I recall thinking, "Who was she telling?" It must be Granny and Papa, but Papa was too old to spank my dad's butt. I will never forget the sincerity in my mother's eyes when I asked her the same question.

"I tell God about my problems. He is the only being who can change hearts and minds. God directed your father to me. So, God needs to provide him with the knowledge and wisdom to lead this family and provide for us."

Faith and music have preserved the peace and love that fills my parents' home. The thing I admired most about my parents was their hearts. God directed their paths towards each other, and I think God did the same with Sabrina and me.

"Are you here for the entire weekend, Malik?" my mother questioned.

I smiled brightly, revealing my pearly white teeth. "No, ma'am. I leave tomorrow. I came here on a mission with a purpose."

"Oh no, I recognize this smile," my mother teased. "It yells, 'Mom, I hit the pole at school in your brand-new car. Please forgive me!'"

My father chuckled at my mother's theatrics, then walked into the living room and sat in his oversized recliner.

"Mark, why are you moving away? Malik Walker, I hope you're not here to upset me."

I raised my eyebrows and frantically shook my head. "Mary, love, can we eat?" my father asked.

I winked at him.

After I helped my mother set the table, I ran to the cellar and retrieved a sweet red wine. My mother looked at my father while I opened the wine bottle and allowed it to breathe.

"Mark and Malik Walker, are you two up to something?" My mother glared at Pops and me. "All week, my king has been singing to me nonstop. Now don't get me wrong, singing is regular for him, but it raised my suspicions when he sang me a bathroom teetee song."

My father's eyes ogled. He hunched his shoulders. My mother continued, "Now, you are overfilling my glass with wine while giving me those lost puppy dog eyes."

I smiled brightly at my mother and winked.

My father reached out his hand to my mother and me to say grace. After we prayed, my mother was even more skeptical of Pops and me. I gawked at my father's choice of words. Did he have to ask God to allow cooler heads to prevail and intercede between my mother and me?

"Malik, have you changed your mind concerning your college degree?" I attempted to answer, but my mother plowed on. "College tuition reimbursement is a part of your contract outside your twenty-million-dollar guarantee."

"Mom, I am still attending school. I came tonight…. Because. Well. God has sent my wife, and she will replace you as my queen, and I wanted Grandma's wedding ring so I can propose to her."

My mother placed her fork and knife on the plate. She finished chewing the grilled chicken in her mouth, taking a nip of water, then two sips of wine before tilting her head towards the ceiling. "What queen do you have in your life? The only person you have been dating is that little gold-digging white girl."

I ran my clammy hands over my jeans, then rested them on my lap under the table. "Mom, white women can be queens, too."

My mom's eyes rapidly fluttered. My father shook his head, leaving his seat to walk over and stand behind my mother. He kneaded her shoulders as she heaved with anger. My mother began caressing his hands as my father kissed her forehead before releasing her shoulders and strolling over to the bar.

He raised a cognac glass in the air. I held up two fingers, requesting a double.

My mother cleared her throat. "Her color has nothing to do with her not being a queen. Do you know the name of the most powerful chess piece on a chessboard that resides adjacent to the King? This piece can move in a straight line vertically, horizontally, or diagonally. She is not limited to one space. Furthermore, she can cover twenty-seven squares on the board, and she goes by the name of Queen!" My mother educated me.

My knees bounced up and down under the table. Getting this ring was not going to be easy.

My mother wagged her index finger in the air as she spoke. "Your grandmother's mother, my mother, and I are queens. Against all the odds, we continue to move vertically, horizontally, or diagonally no matter what life has thrown at us. We remain the most powerful players in our homes, school, and the boardroom. In a time where women had to fight for an education, the female rulers in your family tree independently fought so you could inherit wealth and a birthright."

"Mom, I understand—" My mother waved her index finger above her head and then balled her hand into a tight fist. Instantly, a knot formed in my throat, and I ceased talking.

My mother continued her speech despite my interruption. "Now, you have the nerve to attempt to destroy my mother's, mother's, mother's legacy by coming in here, asking for my mother's ring to give to a high school dropout."

I glanced over my mother's head and witnessed the sun dipping low. The night's blue hue elevated itself towards the sky, and so did my mother's mood and tone.

"For Pete's sake, Malik, the girl follows NFL players around like a job!"

My mother shoved her plate forward, and it collided with her centerpiece. My father stepped toward my mother, but she fanned him away with her index finger. Pops froze.

"Mom, she has a GED, and she works. She's a receptionist," I exclaimed.

My mother closed her eyes tightly, speaking through clenched lips. "Did you consult God, son?"

I lowered my head.

"We are Walker's. That means we never look down. You can never move forward, traveling backward," my father said.

My father was right. Slowly, I lifted my head. I was afraid to question God concerning Sabrina being my wife. What if God did not send Sabrina? I was not ready to be without her. I refused to ask the question. My eyes trailed upwards until my eyes met my mother's golden-brown ones. I contemplated telling her the truth but knew it would not bring me closer to getting my grandmother's ring. So, my response could only be what I hoped.

"Mom, God sent her to me," I whined.

"Son, sometimes people think God sent them a gift when it's a distraction from the enemy to obscure their view from their blessings."

"I did not have to ask God if he sent her. I feel it in my heart," I honestly admitted. "I have been praying you would too, Mom."

"God's acceptance is all you two need, not ours," my mother retorted, aiming a finger at my father, then at herself. "Malik, besides Denise, this is the only woman you have fornicated with, correct? I still do not know what happened between you and her to this day. She was a good Christian girl."

Getting over my first love rocked my belief in true love. After we separated, I called her house once a week, never speaking. I only played Brian McKnight's "Anytime." I didn't stop calling her home until her mother called my mother complaining about me blasting her ears with "I Miss You" by Aaron Hall. My mother was livid, but my father understood my anguish.

I glanced at my dad, shocked he didn't tell my mother about my college days. Women threw themselves at me every day in college, and I was a fat kid sampling their cake until my father busted me with a girl getting head. He gave me a speech about being a better role model for my baby brother.

Before I could tell my mother what had happened to Denise, she continued speaking. "Do you think it's lust or love? I am sure Susan is doing unimaginable sexual things to you, considering she has more experience than you. Do not allow sex to distract you from your blessings." My mother pointed a finger in the air as she paused after each word in this last statement.

I eyeballed my father. "Sorry, Son, I don't keep secrets from my wife. I hope you will not either," my father informed me as he looked at my mother. "Usually, your mother doesn't share what I confide in her."

"Sorry, my King, but this is my baby."

"Mom, I am not a baby anymore. I am a grown man. Can I get the ring or not?"

"Not!" The pitch of her voice made me and my father shudder.

"You raised me to make solid decisions, and my life indicates that," I shrieked. "Can't you trust me and stand behind this decision?"

My mother reached her hands across the table. I turned my palms upright, and she laid her hands in mine. I engulfed her hands and instantly felt a surge of love exuding. She peered past my exterior into my soul. The innocent little boy dwelling in me crumbled.

"I raised you to be a king so God could direct you to your strong queen. In this world, a black king needs someone to have his back. Life will get tough, but a strong queen can make it better with a simple hug or smile. Her light can brighten his darkest path, and when her king's compass breaks, she becomes his navigation. She is his bridge to God when he's spiritually wounded or churched out. She pulls her king back under the umbrella of protection after he wanders too far away from God's grace and mercy."

"Amen," my father shrilled, cutting my mother off.

Pops continued where my mother stopped. "They say a man changes after he finds the right woman. A man changes once he finds his queen. A king recognizes his queen because her light shines like a beam guiding his path."

I caressed my mother's hand, and Proverbs 18:22 invaded my thoughts. My heart sung. *"He who finds a wife finds what is good and receives favor from the Lord."*

I slumped in my chair as the words danced across my heart.

"Son, God does not send a woman to find her king. He directs you towards her. A man is drawn to her essence because it is familiar to him. In her presence, he feels solidarity. His missing half will reunify his body, mind, and soul. He is confident she will pour into him. He understands his job is to pour into her mentally, physically, emotionally, financially, sexually, and spiritually. He will safeguard her crown at all costs. Understand, a wife can only give the world what her king gives her. That means you will pour into each other daily, but you should always pour more into her. Is Sabrina strong enough to refill you after you have poured into her and the world?" My father paused, waiting on my response.

"I have only met her a few times; however, she comes off egotistical and destitute. A wife must restore and refill her family. One of her jobs is to be her husband's helpmate. Your mother and I have raised you to uplift, provide, protect, and pour into your queen. Can this girl refill you, Son?" Pops asked again, differently.

I bucked my eyes at my father. "Damn, Pops!" I mouthed.

My mother's superpowers kicked in. "Do you have something to add, Son?" I shook my head.

My mother can genuinely see and hear all, even when no words are swirling in the air.

When I attempted to ask my mother if Pops could return to being a man of minimal words, my tongue twisted in knots. He had tons to say tonight, and they were all directed to lash me. I did not have the bravery to voice my thoughts. Instead, I confessed. "I am not sure if she can refill my soul, but Sabrina is ready for us to be married."

My mother snatched her hands from my grip. "I will give you my mother's ring after Sabrina tells me what it means to be a Proverbs 31 Woman and a queen."

My mother stepped away from the farmhouse sustainable hardwood table before I could continue to plead my case.

"Malik, I love you," she voiced her back towards me. "However, boy, the next time you ask for my mother's ring, I pray you are ready to be a husband because God has presented you with your wife and not because a woman is demanding to become your mate."

www.ingramcontent.com/pod-product-compliance
Lightning Source LLC
Chambersburg PA
CBHW022035240626
47154CB00007B/2412